BLOOD AND SANGRIA

Detective Sergeant Judy Kane resigned from the Breckland Police and joined her husband Ben to run a harbour-front bar in Porto Viejo in Spain. Judy's crime fighting instincts are roused when a body is trawled up from the sea in the nets of a fishing boat, and she discovers that the victim was one of her old training friends. Someone is running a joint piracy and drug smuggling operation: yachts are disappearing; their owners murdered and thrown overboard. The two prime suspects are both named Harry — which one is it? . . . Judy and Ben's lives depend upon getting the answer right.

Books by Robert Charles
Published by The House of Ulverscroft:

A CLASH OF HAWKS
THE HOUR OF THE WOLF
THE FLIGHT OF THE RAVEN
THE SCREAM OF A DOVE
THE PREY OF THE FALCON
THE VENOM OF THE COBRA
THE ARMS OF THE MANTIS
THE SNARL OF THE LYNX
A LANCE FOR THE DEVIL
THE SUN VIRGIN
STAMBOUL INTRIGUE
THE FOURTH SHADOW
DARK VENDETTA
NOTHING TO LOSE
MISSION OF MURDER
ARCTIC ASSIGNMENT
STRIKEFAST
ASSASSINS FOR PEACE
THE FACELESS FUGITIVE
ONE MUST SURVIVE
DEAD BEFORE MIDNIGHT
THIS SIDE OF HELL
THREE DAYS TO LIVE
SEA VENGEANCE
THE BIG FISH
FALCON SAS — BLOOD RIVER
FALCON SAS — FIRESTRIKE
PERSONS REPORTED
ANCIENT SINS

ROBERT CHARLES

BLOOD AND SANGRIA

Complete and Unabridged

ULVERSCROFT
Leicester

First published in Great Britain in 2010

First Large Print Edition
published 2010

The moral right of the author has been asserted

Copyright © 2010 by Robert C. Smith
All rights reserved

British Library CIP Data

Charles, Robert, *1938* –
Blood and sangria.
1. English- -Spain- -Fiction. 2. Ex-police officers- -
Fiction. 3. Hijacking of yachts- -Fiction.
4. Drug traffic- -Fiction. 5. Murder- -Investigation- -
Fiction. 6. Detective and mystery stories.
7. Large type books.
I. Title
823.9′14–dc22

ISBN 978–1–44480–058–6

Published by
F. A. Thorpe (Publishing)
Anstey, Leicestershire

Set by Words & Graphics Ltd.
Anstey, Leicestershire
Printed and bound in Great Britain by
T. J. International Ltd., Padstow, Cornwall

PROLOGUE

Georgina Harrington knew she was going to die, but the really miserable aspect was that she had shamed herself. She could smell her own sweat and urine.

Anyone who had been left in her position would have smelled the same. She had been handcuffed to an iron bed-frame and left to struggle helplessly for the past twenty-four hours. The gag in her mouth had all but choked her and left her unable to cry out. At first she had thought that she was going to suffocate but slowly she had been able to regulate her breathing through her nose.

She had pulled and twisted her wrists against the unyielding steel bracelets until they bled and finally she had given up the futile struggle. It was ironic that from somewhere he had been able to produce a pair of standard Metropolitan police issue handcuffs. They were a wry joke on his part and she wondered dully where he had obtained them.

She wore only her underwear but in the dry Spanish mid-summer heat it was oppressively hot inside the villa. Even if she had not been

1

scared she would still have perspired heavily. The sheets of the bed on which she lay were soaked.

Normally he kept the air conditioning full on cold at this time of year. He must have switched it off deliberately to make her even more uncomfortable when he had left.

The blood had dried and the scabs had cracked on her lips and face where he had beaten her. Her stomach muscles still throbbed from the pain of his punches. Her mouth was parched and she wondered if he was simply going to leave her to die of thirst.

She had slept fitfully a few times, collapsing into something that was more like exhaustion than sleep and then becoming aware again. However, she was awake when at last she heard the sound of his car returning.

She heard the approaching roar of the engine and then the screech of the tyres as he braked and sprayed up gravel from the drive. He always drove the car with flamboyant gestures, fast accelerating and fast braking. There was no hope that it could be anyone else.

Fear stabbed into Georgina's heart. The waiting was over, but the worst was yet to come.

She heard his key in the lock, then the bang of the closing outer door. She heard his footsteps on the Spanish tiles, the slap of his sandals, and then the sudden hum of the air conditioning as he switched it back on. She stared at the heavy brass handle of the bedroom door, waiting for it to turn. The handle stayed immobile. Faintly she heard him go into the kitchen. She heard the click of the fridge door and the pop as a beer can was opened.

He was tormenting her. He knew she must be able to hear him.

Georgina felt tears forming in the corners of her eyes. She blinked and struggled to hold them back. It would be the last weakness and she told herself that she damned well wasn't going to cry.

Ten minutes passed in silence. She could only imagine what he might be doing. Perhaps he was sitting in the armchair, enjoying his beer, checking for emails or playing spider solitaire on his computer screen, or just standing by the wide French windows and looking down the beach and out to sea.

Finally she heard the fridge door click again, and another can popped. A moment later, startling her and making her heart pound, the door handle turned and the bedroom door opened. Georgina stared wide-eyed, wriggling herself backward on the bed.

Harry came into the room with the still frothing can of Budweiser in his hand. Good old affable Harry, fat jolly Harry, always ready for a laugh and a giggle. Happy Harry for whom it was never too early for a drink and never too late for anything because the night was always young, Harry who had wined her and dined her and loved her all too often. It was part of the job but she had enjoyed it. For a man of his size and weight he had proved a surprisingly able lover.

But somehow he had guessed or found out. She still didn't know what kind of mistake she had made but like a juicy, gasping little fish he had played her along.

And now she knew with gut-wrenching certainty he was planning to kill her.

Jolly Harry wasn't such an affable, easy going man after all. He was all ice and stone inside and the jollity was an act that was all on the surface.

She had played a game, but so had he. They had deceived each other, but now they both knew the truth. And now she was going to die for it.

He stared at her impassively, as though he was reading her thoughts. Then carefully he raised the beer can, tipped it to his mouth and swallowed deeply. Then he smiled and licked his lips.

It was a subtle form of torture. He knew that she had to be desperate for a drink. Georgina closed her eyes and refused to look at him. She concentrated on holding back her tears.

'I found Dave and Luis,' he said calmly. 'It took me a while to track down which bar they were drinking in. Still, they're on the way now, bringing the yacht round. They should be here in about an hour. It'll be dark by then, no chance of anyone seeing us go aboard.'

He came closer and took another swallow from the beer can. 'We'll take another little cruise, our last sail together. You always enjoyed sailing on my yacht, the luxury life, champagne and sunshine, sex and swimming. Well, I can offer you one last swim, but maybe this time we'll look for deeper water. No secluded little cove, no nice sandy beach within easy reach. No last screw. Sorry, Georgie, but you really blew it.'

He didn't even take the gag off. There was nothing more to discuss.

He took another pull at the beer can and then set it down gently on her chest, balanced just above the level of her breasts. The can was cold enough to burn her skin and there were beads of icy dew trickling down over the glistening Budweiser logo. With the gag in her mouth and her arms stretched and secured above and behind her there was no way she could reach it.

Harry grinned amiably. 'Such a shame, Georgie, you were a really good lay. Pity you had to turn out to be an undercover cop.'

He turned and walked away to wait for the yacht to arrive.

1

The bar was heaving with life and laughter and Judy Kane was elated. The deafening buzz of jokes and toasts, conversations shouted to be heard and the clink and rattle of beer bottles and glasses was sweet and merry music to her ears. She knew she was flushed and sweating despite the two large fans whirling at full speed against the red, blue and bottle-green tiles of the ceiling but she didn't care. She was rushed off her feet but this was opening night at *The Conquistador*, their Spanish dream come true.

After all the stress, grief and headaches of the past few months it had all been worth it. First the painful decision to sell their cosy little country cottage in Breckland. Then all the arguments and discussions with the Spanish estate agents and the *Gestor* over the complexities of Spanish property law and licensing laws, all the financial dealings with the banks and the transfers of their pensions and other funds. They had still ended up with an uncomfortably large mortgage but at least they had finally got the package together. All the problems of language and decoration and renovation had followed. But at last most of the major difficulties were behind them. She could speak passable Spanish now. The bar was legally theirs. She and Ben were the new owners of *The Conquistador*. The bar was open and running and it was busy.

If no one had turned up she would have wept. With a full house she was almost weeping anyway, but if she was to let them go these would be tears of joy. She had tasted nothing stronger than tea and coffee all day but she felt as intoxicated as the happy throng on the other side of the bar counter.

The Perez Xavier Trio were doing their utmost on the small raised platform of a stage that elevated them head and shoulders above the crowd. Perez and his brother Jaime were dressed in tight black trousers and heavily frilled gold silk shirts, Perez playing a massive red and silver accordion and Jaime strumming an elaborate Spanish guitar. They were a handsome pair with magnificent black moustaches and their sister Dolores was a classic raven-haired beauty. Dolores wore a gorgeous red satin gown, played maracas with gusto, sang like an angel, and vibrated her hips and swirled her skirts with sensuous elegance at every version of the flamenco. Their performance was a mixture of old Spain and modern pop that seemed to be pleasing both the tourists and the locals. At the moment they were doing *Viva Espana* with additional foot-stomping and hand clapping. The crowd was roaring.

Judy took another order and bumped into Ben at the beer pump where he was filling more glasses. His white shirt, fresh only an hour ago, was damp and sticking to his back between his broad shoulders. Strands of his unruly blonde hair had drifted down to stick across his forehead. His grin was wider than hers and she knew he too was happy. She gave him an impulsive kiss on the cheek and there were cheers from their supporters. She was aware of Isabella queuing up behind her with more empty glasses and smiling approval.

'This is fantastic,' she shouted into Ben's ear. 'Better than I ever expected.'

'I still think we should have renamed it the *Pina Colada*,' Ben teased her. 'We might have pulled in a few more.'

'It has always been *The Conquistador* and it stays *The Conquistador!*'

Judy pushed him away to serve, knowing that particular battle had been won. Ben had wanted to change the name but she had been adamant that it stayed the same. The wooden figure which gave the bar its name, with its flared pantaloons, harquebus and sword, which was meant to represent a Fifteenth Century Soldier of Fortune, stood larger than life in the open doorway. Someone had draped coloured party ribbons round its neck and a young couple who could barely stand were hanging on to its arms to have their photographs taken. However, the grim, brown teak visage of the old wooden soldier still looked just as fierce and commanding as it had when she had first seen and fallen in love with it. The conquistador was a definite asset and she had refused to have him moved or the bar name changed.

Beyond the bar she could see the palm-shaded promenade and the harbour. Starlight and moonlight reflected on the still waters and on the white and cream painted hulls of the sleek tourist yachts. The faint tang of salt and fish drifted in from the large fleet of local fishing trawlers tied up on the far dock, fighting a losing battle as it encountered the fug of cigarette smoke.

Porto Viejo was picture postcard Spain. The harbour was tucked neatly into the bay between the blue-domed, hill-top church of Santa Maria to the north and an ancient Moorish castle on an equally high cliff top on the south side. The church was the size of a small cathedral and the castle ruins against a red Mediterranean sunset were as romantic as anyone could wish for. Below the castle began a perfect and seemingly endless beach.

Judy knew they were lucky to have found the place, and twice blessed to find exactly the kind of bar they were looking for up for sale on the corner of the harbour.

Everything was happening exactly as they had dreamed that it would be. It was almost too good to be true. Suddenly she wondered if they would ever be able to maintain the pace. Perhaps they had bitten off more than they could chew.

Some of the elation left her for a moment as the pang of doubt intruded. She watched Ben moving along the bar and saw that he was limping slightly. The shattered leg had healed well but its legacy of aches and pains and limitations had forced his early retirement from the Breckland Fire Brigade. She had taken the decision to retire with him. In all the excitement of moving direct to the end-of-career dream, they had both failed to take into account the fact that running a bar would also be a busy lifestyle with long hours on their feet. Ben would say nothing, his cheery grin would stay constant, but he couldn't stop that stiffening left leg from dragging a little.

There was a lull in the madness. For a moment it seemed that everyone had a full glass and the Perez Xavier trio had them all captivated as Dolores spun into another pride-filled dance. Judy paused to catch her breath and Isabella stopped beside her.

Isabella was another asset. The slim, dark-haired Spanish beauty with the sparkling eyes and saucy smile had worked for the previous owners. She was local, she knew the bar and she knew the trade and she had been pleased to have her old job back. Her husband Antonio was the *tapas* chef and an equally valuable asset in the kitchen. His bowls of Andalusian snacks wafted up delicious aromas from the glass-fronted casing along the edge of the bar.

'Is very good, is going very well, *Si*,' Isabella said brightly.

'It's wonderful,' Judy laughed. 'But will it always be as busy as this? I don't know if I can keep going so fast.'

Isabella shrugged, twirling her long black hair over one bare shoulder. 'This is special night, opening night. And you have the trio. When Dolores dances you will always have the townspeople come in.'

'Thank you,' Judy said. Isabella had recommended the Perez Xavier trio and they were proving a huge attraction. 'We can't afford them every night but I think we should have them at least twice a week.' She looked around. 'All these people, half of them have told me their names and I can't remember any of them.'

'It is easy,' Isabella said. 'I will help you. Over there is Ricardo, he is a fisherman.' She made a firm thumb up sign with a wicked grin. 'Next to him the dark-haired boy is Luis. He is a bad boy, he does not work but tries it on with all the girls, but — ' Her little finger pointed downward and her lips pouted sadly.

'The one with the beard is Pedro,' Isabella continued. 'He is another fisherman on the trawlers. The one in the red shirt is Arturo, he is a *bombero*, a fireman. The good-looking one is Miguel, he is a policeman.' She rattled off more names, each one accompanied by a thumb up or the downward little finger and the sorry pout.

Judy found herself laughing. It seemed that Isabella's opinions of all men were summed up in the same way. Whether they were the result of guesswork, hearsay or personal experience Judy didn't want to ask. However, she had always sensed that Isabella was perfectly happy with her husband.

'What about the tourists?' she asked.

'Some of them are one-week visitors. The others are from the yachts. Roger, the tall man with the white hair, he has the *Blue*

Lady. The English couple are Peter and Jane, they have *Wave Dancer*. The Frenchman is very rich, he has the big one called *Dominique.* It is named after his first wife. The big fat man trying to impress the two girls is called Harry. He has the *Seagull Two.*'

The firm thumb and the drooped little finger were still alternating but now Judy knew it was mostly guesswork. 'You are not as wicked as you pretend,' she accused.

Isabella laughed.

'It's good to see so many people here,' Judy said. 'I was terrified no one would turn up.'

'I tell all the local men they must come,' Isabella admitted. 'I tell them all I will never smile at them again if they do not come here tonight.'

'You are a treasure,' Judy said, and meant it. 'But what about the women, you have only named the men.'

'The girl in the green top is Juanita, she is my friend. The one with the big dangly ear-rings, she is Maria, she is in love with Ricardo. The six English girls I do not know, I think they are what you call a hen party. The other Maria and Conchita, the two with the very short skirts, they are working girls.'

Judy frowned. The old instincts had kicked in and she had formed the suspicion when the two girls had first appeared at the bar.

14

The make-up had been too heavy, the eyes bored and speculative while they waited. Now Maria and Conchita were coming on to a pair of young English boys who were obviously on a girl-hunting holiday.

'What should I do?' she asked.

Isabella shrugged. 'You do not take any notice. You do nothing, unless they cause trouble. Miguel is a policeman. He knows what they are. It is his business if he decides to do something.'

Judy realized that Isabella was right. She was not Detective Sergeant Judy Kane anymore. She was a bar owner in Spain. How her customers earned their living was none of her business as long as somebody paid for their drinks.

On stage the dance and the music ended with a final swirl and a stamp from Dolores. She flung one arm high and the whole assembly joined her in a definitive 'Ole!' Then the faces were turning back to the bar, glasses were drained and pushed up for refilling.

They were off again, almost running, and only Isabella seemed unflustered. Judy was tiring and her arm was beginning to ache from pulling on the beer pump. Ben was grinning like a big blonde Cheshire cat, stolidly ignoring the nagging pain in his leg.

There was another blonde head in the

crowd. Another large fair-headed Englishman had pushed up to the bar where Isabella was serving. Somehow Judy knew from his manner and the red sunburn on his Anglo-Saxon nose that he had to be English. He looked almost a double for Ben, except that he was younger, his face was harder and his eyes colder. Despite the similarities she felt that Ben's impish grin would be totally alien on this man's face.

Isabella took the blonde man's order and joined Judy at the beer pump.

'Who is that one?' Judy asked. She was curious because physically the man was so like Ben.

'His name is Dave, they call him Blondie.' Isabella shrugged. 'New here, I think, but not a tourist.' She wriggled her fingers, uncommitted to thumb up or little finger down, which meant she did not know. 'He is friends with Luis, so perhaps he is another bad boy.'

Judy moved away with her filled glasses. She served them to the trawler fisherman Pedro and one of his shipmates, answered their smiles and took the money over to the cash register. There were mirror tiles on the back of the bar behind the spirit bottles and optics and in them she saw Antonio bustle in to replace his bowls of steaming fish and meat, the grilled shrimps, the squid rings and salads and tortillas. Behind Antonio she could also see Blondie Dave talking to dark-haired Luis. They were a poorly matched pair, total opposites in size and appearance, but they seemed close.

The big, jolly fat man named Harry left his female companions and pushed up beside them with three empty glasses. Judy saw a brief exchange of glances between Blondie Dave and Fat Harry, but then it seemed that both men had decided not to acknowledge each other. Harry looked away and shouted his order at Isabella. Blondie Dave and dark-haired Luis turned their backs to the fat man and eased away from the crowded bar.

Now what was that about, Judy wondered, and then told herself again that she wasn't a detective sergeant any more. Her police career was over. She had resigned to be with Ben. As with the working girls she had to live and let live. Her only business now was running the bar.

★   ★   ★

The Spanish postal service was slow, but setting up and running a new business was generating a lot of mail. Ben had become a regular visitor to the post office which was situated half way up the hill to the church behind the harbour. The *Correos* was a large glaringly white Moorish building with a columned portico, standing between a modern glass and steel bank building and the mellow cream ramparts of the *Comisaria*, the home of the Policia National. The whole street was a clash of old and new architectural styles that could only be developing Spain.

On the morning after their grand and glorious opening night Ben took his usual morning stroll with a handful of letters to drop into the yellow post box. He had forgotten his sunglasses and his eyes were squinted against the bright light. There was still a smile on his face. He was thinking a little about their new venture which was so far a triumphant success, but mostly about the ecstatic kisses and hugs with Judy when they had at last collapsed into bed in the early hours of the morning, almost but not quite too exhausted to make love.

His route passed the Porto Viejo Fire Station, the home of the *Bomberos*. Through wide open doors he could see that the truck bay was empty. The local fire engine was out somewhere on a shout. He wondered briefly what they might be dealing with, a house fire, an RTA, some version of persons trapped. He felt a pang of nostalgia for the old days as all the old fire service messages, all the possibilities, flitted through his mind.

He walked on to the *Correos* building, dropped his letters into the post box and began the return journey. When he passed the fire station the second time he could see that the fire crew had returned. The big red fire engine was parked in the centre of the drill yard which was visible through the open doors at the front and back of the parking bay. The locker shutters were all open and the *Bomberos* were busy cleaning, rolling and re-stowing coils of hose and preparing for the next job.

Two men stood on the pavement by the bay doors. One wore the *Bombero* uniform with silver officer rank bars on his shoulders. The other was a civilian. They were both familiar. Ben was sure he had served them with drinks the night before. They chatted amiably and then the civilian walked away. The *Bombero* turned to go back into the fire station. He recognized Ben and smiled. Ben recalled that Isabella had mentioned the man's name, it was Arturo.

'*Buenos Dias*,' Ben said cheerfully.

'*Buenos Dias*,' The response was equally cheerful with white teeth flashing in the lean, dark face. 'I think you are the new man at the *Conquistador*, the Englishman.' He was confident enough in his guess to speak in English.

'That's me, and you were drinking Stella last night. I served you at least twice.'

'It was a good night. You have picked a good bar and a good place to run your business. I think you will do well.'

'Thank you.' Ben offered his hand. 'I'm Ben Kane.'

'Arturo Marota.' The handshake was firm. 'I have noticed your interest. You look this way often when you pass our fire station. You like fire engines?'

'I used to ride them,' Ben admitted. 'Back in England I was the Station Commander at Granchester, in the Breckland Fire Brigade.'

Arturo showed surprise. 'You were a *Bombero?* You are young to be retired.'

'The leg,' Ben slapped his left thigh ruefully. 'I was in a car accident, on the way to a call. I got smashed up a bit. It took a long time before I could walk properly and it still plays me up. I couldn't pretend to be A One fit any more, so I took retirement. Judy and I had always said that one day we would come over here and run a bar in Spain.'

'But you still miss eating smoke,' Arturo nodded his understanding. He smiled again. 'Come inside and have a look round, see how we do things.' When Ben hesitated briefly he added. 'I am the Fire Chief. I am in charge here. I can invite who I like.'

They walked through the parking bay and into the drill yard. Most of the work there was finished. The lockers were re-stowed and closed, the fire truck had been washed down to get rid of the dust and grime from the morning outing and a few of the *Bomberos* were giving the paintwork a final polish with wash leather cloths. Arturo made introductions but his crew spoke only Spanish and responded with simple grins and salutes.

'What sort of fires did you fight in Breckland?' Arturo asked.

'Granchester was a town about the same size as Porto Viejo, but inland. We were surrounded with farmland and forest. So we got all the usual property fires, houses and factories. In the summer we dealt with forest fires, field fires. We attended more than enough road accidents.'

'It is much the same here. We have the main coast highway passing behind the town and much of the traffic drives too fast. We have no forest but plenty of scrub and grass fires in the hills. We are a big port so sometimes we can get called down to the harbour if there is a fire on board a yacht or a trawler.'

They exchanged fire-fighting stories and

experiences until one of the *Bomberos* drove the fire engine back into the bay. They were suddenly alone in the drill yard and Arturo glanced at his watch.

'It is time for a break. They have all disappeared into the mess room. Come and join us. There will be no English tea, but I can offer you coffee.' He led the way and then added. 'Come and meet Harry. He is English too. I think you will have much in common.'

Ben followed his new-found friend down a short corridor through the main building. They passed a room where fire-fighting kit hung ready to be swiftly grabbed and donned for the next shout, a watch-room, a small set of offices, and then into a wide rest room. Here the *Bomberos* sat in shirtsleeves around long bare tables, filling up with sandwiches and coffee. In Granchester the sandwiches would have been plates of bread, cheese and onion, but here they appeared to be bread and salami.

One man appeared out of place. He was sitting at a stool beside the bare metal counter where the food was served, chatting to the young Spanish woman in charge of the kitchen. He was a large, jovial-looking fat man wearing flowered shorts and a garish Hawaiian shirt that was all blue sea splashes and green palm trees. It was a small world here, Ben realized, for the fat man had also been in the bar the night before. He had spent most of the evening when he was not actually drinking with his arms around two very attractive young women.

'Hi, Harry,' Arturo said. 'Meet Ben Kane. He is another Englishman who loves fire engines.'

'Harry Avery,' the big man said, leaning forward to offer his hand but not bothering to get up. The hand was white with two large gold rings on the thick, pasty fingers, but his grip was hard. There was strength and confidence there behind the easy-going smile.

'Are you another ex-fireman?' Ben asked, although the bulk of the man made it hard to believe.

Harry laughed aloud and shook his head. 'No way, that would be too hot for me and too much like hard work. I always loved the idea of it though. When I was a kid there was a fire station right next door to where we lived in the East End. I was always watching the fire engines, always talking to the firemen. I guess it's a habit I never got out of. At home I've got every episode they ever made of London's Burning. I taped every show myself when they first appeared on TV.'

'Harry was like you,' Arturo spread his hands in an expressive shrug. 'Always looking into the fire station every time he passed, just like a little boy. So one day I take pity and invite him in. I haven't been able to get rid of him since.'

'But you have had a few free rides on my yacht,' Harry countered. 'Old Harry is not just a taker.'

'He is a good friend,' Arturo agreed. 'And perhaps I am flattered to have a fan. He also helps me speak my English.'

Ben accepted a cup of coffee and they settled into a comfortable three way chat about fires and fire engines.

2

Judy unlocked and opened the bar doors and then paused for a moment to unravel the last traces of red and yellow party tape from around the neck and sword hilt of the old wooden conquistador. The grainy teak face looked back at her impassively and she was tempted to give him a kiss. She was still feeling that good after all the heady excitement of the opening night.

Isabella smiled at her from behind the bar where she was giving the counter a final polish. Everything was spotless again, waiting for the next surge of customers. However, this morning Porto Viejo was quiet. There were only a few strollers along the harbour-front which basked in the sunshine. Most of the bars and restaurants that lined the palm-shaded promenade were only just opening up.

Judy settled for a thank-you pat on the old adventurer's wooden cheek and turned her attention to the yachts in the harbour. She decided that she would never tire of this view of masts and palm trees, white hulls and blue water.

Immediately across the road, tucked neatly

into the corner of the harbour, was a large white motor yacht with smartly varnished woodwork, neatly coiled ropes and a furled blue sail. The name *Wave Dancer* was painted in wavy blue letters above a wavy blue line on her sleek bow. A slim blonde woman wearing white shorts and a brief white top emerged on deck, stretched her arms and yawned at the sun. Then she caught Judy's eye across the promenade and smiles passed between them. Judy recognized one of her customers from last night.

After a minute a man appeared to join her, also dressed in white shorts and a white tee shirt. They conversed for a moment, reached mutual agreement and then came ashore. They crossed the road arm in arm and approached the bar. Judy saw that they were older than the fit, tanned bodies suggested at a distance. She guessed middle fifties.

'Hi there,' the man said cheerfully. He had a Suffolk accent and everything about him was English. 'You gave me this headache so I think I'll let you cure it. I need the hair of the dog.'

The woman laughed. 'He can have a beer and serve him right. I'll settle for a cup of coffee.'

'Come on in.' Judy smiled a welcome.

Behind the bar the ever efficient Isabella

was already holding up a pint glass with one hand on the Stella pump. When she received a nod of acknowledgement she began to fill the glass.

'I'm Judy Kane,' Judy introduced herself. 'My husband Ben should be around somewhere. We've just opened up. Last night was our first night, so you were among our first customers.'

'Jane Shepherd,' the woman said. 'And this is my husband Peter. Last night was a very good night. The best we've had yet in Porto Viejo. I think you may have found yourself a little goldmine.'

'Well thank you.'

They shook hands all round. Judy decided that she too could use a cup of coffee and sat down to join them.

'Let me guess,' she said looking at Peter Shepherd. 'You're from Ipswich.'

Peter grinned. 'Is it that obvious? Do I look like a farmer?'

'Not quite, that's why I'm guessing town, not country.'

'You're spot on,' Jane said. 'We lived in Woodbridge but Peter's company was based in Ipswich. You know your accents. You sound Suffolk yourself.'

'Breckland,' Judy said. 'We moved here from Granchester.'

'What made you move to Spain?'

'Ben had to leave his job, so we decided why wait for retirement age to do what we always wanted to do. We pooled our resources and here we are.'

'We took early retirement,' Jane said. 'Peter sold his company so we decided to sail the Med. We've had a smaller boat for years on the Deben. We did the usual thing, weekend sailings down the coast to the Orwell or the Blackwater, or across the channel to France or Holland when we had a little more time. When the chance came we decided to buy a bigger boat and sail the world.'

'*Wave Dancer* is a yacht,' Peter said, 'Not a boat. And we're not exactly aiming for the world. The Atlantic and the Pacific are for younger sailors who want to do the Chichester thing. Just wandering around the Med will do nicely for me.'

'It's alright,' Jane leaned toward him and patted his cheek. 'I won't make you sail the nasty big Atlantic if you don't want to.'

Judy sipped her coffee and decided she liked these two. They were easy and relaxed together, like her and Ben.

'What business were you in?' She asked.

'Advertising,' Peter said.

'He's the Beanie Man,' Jane added with a smile.

Judy wrinkled her brow, looking puzzled.

'Tasty Beans,' Jane prompted. 'You must remember all those ads with the gang of kids, the Beanie gang.'

'There were five of them,' Peter said with affection. 'Off screen they were lovely kids to work with. Onscreen we turned them into the most unruly gang of little horrors. They were a blend of the Perishers, Peanuts, and a sort of comprehensive St. Trinians.'

'They were always up to mischief,' Jane said just as fondly. 'Plain Jane was our grand-daughter Lucy. The others always ganged up on her.'

'I loved the red Indian sketch,' Peter reminisced. 'That was the first one. We had them all dressed up as red Indians, feathers and war-paint, tomahawks, the lot. The gang had Plain Jane tied to a totem pole, dancing around her, whooping and all that stuff. Then on comes Yummy Mummy and an older sister, both of them bearing great steaming plates of golden Tasty Beans. End of drama. They all tuck in.'

'Then they re-wrote the script with the kids as pirates and Lucy walking the plank. Then it was cannibals with Lucy in a cooking pot. Poor old Lucy was always tied up. Always the same ending, everything stopped for Tasty Beans.'

'It was a fantastic campaign,' Peter said, 'Our best ever. It went nation-wide on TV. That's pretty good going for a provincial agency.' He looked Judy up and down. 'Yummy Mummy was Suzy Champion. She looked a bit like you, beautiful blonde, thirtyish, lovely fit body. With a brood like that she'd have looked a lot more harassed in real life but we took poetic licence. Suzy did well too, she's gone on to film a new drama series for ITV, starring role.'

'Watch him,' Jane warned. 'I know he had a secret fancy for Suzy.'

'I was her producer and director and that was all. You're only jealous because I wouldn't let you play Yummy Mummy. I told you, it had to be Yummy Mummy, not Yummy Granny.' He neatly ducked the automatic slap of his wife's hand and Judy knew it was a well rehearsed tease.

'We did other campaigns as well,' Peter went on. 'We got to the point where I had to take on a creative director and an art director. The Agency was expanding, taking on a lot of London based clients. I reached fifty, the upper age limit for the advertising world. It was all getting too fast and furious so I struck a deal and let my directors buy me out. It was time to relax and enjoy.'

'So we sold our little boat and bought

Wave Dancer and here we are.' Jane pulled a wry face and added. 'Can you imagine, he actually wanted to rename *Wave Dancer* and call her *The Beanie*. I had to put my foot down there.'

Judy laughed. 'I can believe it. Ben wanted to rename the *Conquistador* and call it the *Pina Colada*.'

While Jane and Judy shared a chuckle Peter pretended to look affronted.

'How long are you planning to stay in Porto Viejo?' Judy asked when they resumed talking.

'We're not sure.' Jane finished her coffee and sprawled back in her chair. 'We had intended just a couple of weeks and then move down the coast but Peter has pulled a muscle in his shoulder. The weather got a little bit rough as we came down through the Bay of Biscay. The yacht rolled and Peter had to grab for a handrail. It happened quick and caught him off balance.'

'We sailed her through the Straights and past Gib,' Peter continued the story. 'The weather eased once we were in the Med and this was our first planned stop. The problem is that once we stopped and I rested, the shoulder stiffened and I woke up with this bloody muscle pain.'

'We might just stay here until he's fit

31

again,' Jane shrugged. 'Or, if we get bored, we might hire someone to help sail *Wave Dancer* on the next leg.'

'Stay,' Judy urged them. 'You can always spend a few more nights drinking at the *Conquistador*.'

★ ★ ★

After finishing his beer Peter decided that what he really needed to clear off his hangover was a swim. He and Jane returned to their yacht and a few minutes later Judy gave them a final wave as they reappeared and strolled along the harbour-front with rolled towels under their arms. They were headed for where the long sand beach began below the overhang of the south cliff with its ramparts of ruined castle. Judy found herself wishing that she could go with them as she turned to clear the table.

There were more holiday-makers appearing around the harbour, admiring the moored pleasure yachts and fishing boats. The visitors were in no hurry and had no particular place to go. They browsed the small shops, the women turning over the clothes rails while their men studied postcards and souvenirs. A few couples studied the menus outside the restaurants. The bar was getting busier now as people wandered in for a beer or coffee, but it was nothing that Isabella could not handle without help.

After half an hour Ben returned but he was not alone. Judy remembered the large fat man with whom Ben was chatting amiably as another face from the happy crowd who had filled the bar last night.

'Hi, Jude,' Ben said cheerfully. 'Meet Harry Avery. We bumped into each other at the fire station. Harry is a big fan of fire engines.'

'I might have known,' Judy pretended to scold him. 'I send you to the post office and you end up at the fire station. You know they won't let you drive one any more.'

Ben grinned. 'They just might. The *Bomberos* seem a pretty easy going lot. Their captain is a real nice guy.'

Harry shook his head. 'One thing Arturo won't let me do is drive the fire engine, not even just around the yard. And I do let him steer my yacht.'

Harry extended a hand and Judy gripped it briefly. Harry smiled happily but Judy was not impressed. She noticed that although Harry was heavily overweight he was not exactly flabby. He was friendly and flashy, the Hawaiian beach shirt was garish, but it was almost as though the image he presented was a deliberate camouflage. She sensed that the

33

surface was all for show and found herself instinctively wary of the man.

It was just a feeling and she knew her instincts could be wrong. It was something that had caused frequent arguments with DI Ron Harding, her old boss and usual partner with Breckland CID. She had been proved wrong in the past, but not often. Usually her first reading of a suspect was dead right.

She had to remind herself that all of that was over. She was no longer a cop. Harry Avery wasn't even a suspect in anything.

'Harry's from London,' Ben said, 'The East End.'

'One of my aunts lived in the East End,' Judy recalled. 'We used to go there and visit when I was a kid. Which part did you live in?'

'Well, it was not exactly the East End,' Harry smiled. 'But it was near enough. I'm an ex-pat now, of course. I moved out here a few years ago. I've got a nice little villa way down beyond the end of the south beach, plus a yacht in the harbour. Mine is the *Seabird Two*. She's tied up at one of the pontoons on the far side of the harbour, just before you get to the commercial dock and the trawlers.'

It was an easy answer. Harry was casual and relaxed but Judy knew that he had neatly evaded her question. She obligingly looked to the far corner of the harbour but from this distance she couldn't read the names on the tight lines of bows and sterns.

'A villa and a boat,' she said brightly. 'You are doing well. What did you do before you retired?'

'This and that,' Harry shrugged his shoulders, 'A bit of used car dealing, nothing exciting.'

Judy nodded and decided that she should let it go. Old habits could easily become bad habits and it was none of her business.

'How about a beer,' Ben offered. 'This one is on the house.'

Just when she was about to give Harry Avery the benefit of the doubt resentment kicked in. They had a heavy mortgage to pay and this was a business they were supposed to be running together. They couldn't afford to give away too many free beers.

She made a mental note to say something firmly but tactfully later when they were alone. Two boys at heart, both in love with fire engines was not a recipe for a free ride. Then Harry said cheerfully.

'Okay, I'll have a Stella. But sometime you and Judy have to come out with me on the *Seabird*. We can take a little cruise down the coast. There are some lovely little coves where we can swim and party. I'm a pretty fair cook with a barbecue.' He patted his ample stomach. 'And I know a couple of goodtime girls who will make up the crew.'

Judy reconsidered. Maybe Harry Avery wasn't such a bad guy to know after all.

⋆ ⋆ ⋆

It was dusk when the trawler fleet sailed out from Porto Viejo harbour. There were twelve of them, slipping their mooring lines and one by one sliding out past the harbour wall into a rose and golden sunset. The sun lingered for a moment, silhouetting the dark ruins of the old Moorish castle on the frowning hill top and then it was gone. The streaks of rose and gold began to fade as the last boat left the harbour and the first boat grew small and distant on the horizon.

The tourists who had come to line the harbour wall lowered their cameras and began to drift away, returning to the bars and the restaurants.

The *Serrano* was the fifth boat in line. Once clear of the harbour the fleet began to disperse and the *Serrano* turned her bows south and followed the coast. After an hour of sailing she turned east, heading further out into the Mediterranean. Her captain was a brawny, bearded and weather-beaten man named Pedro who liked to sing Spanish love songs when there was nothing else to do. His crew joked that his wife was always glad to see him sail.

Pedro began to pay close attention to his echo sounder, noting the larger fish shoals and the direction in which they were swimming. He based his decision on the information the modern technology provided together with his own wealth of experience and finally ordered the casting of the nets. They rumbled over the steel roller and trailed behind the fishing vessel as she moved slowly at half engine speed.

By midnight the nets were out. The *Serrano* rolled gently on the soft heave of the waves, drifting under a black sky filled with sparkling stars. It was one of those clear, still nights when all was at peace. On a rough night the five man crew would have gone below to the cramped cabin and eating saloon, or crowded into the wheelhouse with the captain, but tonight they sat around the deck hatch. The old sailor who doubled as the cook produced plates of rice, grilled fish and bread. They smoked cigarettes and drank mugs of hot black coffee, gossiping, yawning and teasing the boy who was only on his second voyage.

At three o'clock in the morning the order was given to haul in the nets. The engine started and the winch erupted into clattering life. The vessel began to move slowly back along the long line of net, reeling it back in over the high stern gantry. Pedro leaned out of the open window of the wheelhouse, watching but still smoking the last of his cigarette. Three of the four men below had done this job so often there was no need for him to issue any further commands. The crew worked swiftly and efficiently at shaking out the nets and stowing the silvery harvest into the open hatchway or partially sorting the different species into plastic trays and buckets. The final sorting would be done later, for now the major task was to get the fish on board.

They were halfway down the line when the winch began to whine under a sudden strain. A Spanish curse was growled from the wheelhouse but it was muted and resigned. The winch was slowed until it was only just revolving, easing the dripping net on board inch by inch. Snarling the net or dragging up something large was not an unusual disruption and the work paused as the crew watched and waited.

They shared the hope that they had not caught a large shark, or something writhing and powerful enough to do too much damage to the net.

Their catch began to surface but there was no wriggling movement except from the smaller fish that still squirmed and fought against the mesh pulled tight into their gills. Something large and grey white broke the surface and streamed water as it was lifted clear.

They saw empty eye sockets in the fish-nibbled caricature of a human face. A body hung upright in the close folds of the net, a woman's body that was naked but for the torn shreds of her underclothes. One breast was bare but the nipple had been eaten away. The woman's hands were tied behind her back and a length of chain that had been tied around her legs still dangled through a torn hole in the net into the black sea.

The skipper's jaw dropped and his cigarette fell limply away from his lower lip. Two of his Catholic crew quickly made the sign of the cross and muttered a prayer. The boy choked, lunged for the ship's rail and vomited up his supper.

3

Judy awoke with the sunlight streaming through the cracks in the window blind in the large bedroom in their living quarters above the bar. Ben was still sound asleep behind her as she swung her legs out of the bed and walked over to the window. She pulled on the draw string to open the gaps wider and looked through the slats at the view over the harbour. The sun was already high. Some of the fishing boats were visible on the horizon, making their slow way home. One boat was already tied up beside the long fishermen's wharf and there seemed to be an unusual amount of activity around her. Judy narrowed her eyes against the glare and saw that there was a police car and an ambulance amongst the knot of vehicles and moving figures.

Some sort of accident, she thought, a bad start to somebody's day.

She turned away from the window, pulled off her short nightdress of pale blue silk and threw it on to a chair. She stood for a moment looking down at Ben. He slept naked and had pushed down the single sheet that had been enough for both of them through the warm night. His broad chest still rose and fell slowly and peacefully.

Judy frowned briefly. Last night had been another good night in the bar but somehow they had fallen into an argument as they prepared for bed. She shook her head and went into the en-suite shower and turned on the water. It stung cold for a moment, causing her to gasp, and shocking her fully awake. Then the water flowed warm and she reached for the shower gel and began to lather her neck and shoulders.

It felt good, she relaxed and her mind went back to Ben.

The argument had surprised her. Just for the record and the principle she had decided to mention the subject of free beer. Ben usually acknowledged things when she was right and that would be the end of it but perhaps last night had been the wrong time. They had both been working hard and they were tired. Ben had snapped back at her and suddenly it had become a full scale row. They had ended up sleeping back to back.

There had been several arguments lately she realized. Probably all due to the sub-conscious pulls of stress and worry. They had both changed jobs and they had re-located their home. Ben's accident had turned their world upside down. It had all been forced upon them too quickly and there had been endless hard and heavy decisions to be made.

She soaped the rest of her body, looking down at her own firm breasts and flat stomach. Ben was getting heavier, she had noticed, putting on weight around his waist, but she was still as trim and slim as ever. With the beach and the sea close at hand they had both taken to swimming at every opportunity but most of their time had been consumed with the business. She had also taken to running most days for an hour along the beach. Ben's damaged leg kept him from running with her, so there he was slipping behind.

She realized that she hadn't run since they had opened the bar. She would have to find the time or she too would be putting on some flab around the middle.

She let the hot water sluice away the rest of the soap bubbles and turned off the shower. Stepping out she towelled herself dry before going back into the bedroom. Ben was awake his eyes wide open, watching her appreciatively.

'Playing Peeking Ben again,' she accused. But the boyish grin was back on his face and she couldn't be cross with him. He was her big, blonde teddy bear again. She found clean underwear, put it on and sat down on the bed beside him. She stared at him for a moment, sighed and leaned down to kiss him.

'I'm sorry about last night.'

'Me too, I guess we're both on an emotional roundabout, too many highs, too many lows, too much worry. You had a point, but one beer for Harry was no big deal.'

'I guess if you had bought him a beer in any other bar I wouldn't have noticed. It's what boys do.'

Ben lifted her hand and kissed it. 'I wanted this,' he said. 'But for later. I didn't want to leave the Fire Service until my time was up. One drunken kid joy-riding in a stolen car and BANG, it was all over. If I hadn't been out that night on a shout, if he hadn't been on the wrong side of the road on a blind bend at the top of the hill. Damn it all it wasn't even my call. I was standing in that night because Reg Watson was on holiday in the bloody Seychelles.'

He stopped, drew a deep breath and looked up at her sadly. 'Sorry, Jude, I know it was the end of your career too. And you loved being a cop just as much as I loved being a fireman. You and Ron Harding were soft cop and hard cop. Your superintendent Grant said it on your retirement night. You were the best double act Breckland CID ever had.'

Judy smiled. 'We're still a double act. And the bar's going well.'

Ben smiled too, and after a moment began to tentatively stroke the inside of her thigh.

'You blew your chance last night,' she told him and pushed his hand away. She stood and went to find a fresh pair of shorts and a tee shirt, which was virtually the new day uniform for the new job. 'Right now we've got work to do.'

★ ★ ★

By the time they had made coffee and eaten breakfast Isabella had arrived. Antonio would appear later to start cooking up his *tapas* specialities and Isabella's friend Juanita would come in for two evenings in mid week to give them a break but Isabella was employed full time. Most of the time one or two of them could run the bar and they had a rest and duty rota to ensure that they all had some time free.

Isabella usually brought in the latest port gossip and today she had plenty to talk about.

'The *Serrano* has trawled up a body,' she told them with a horrified thrill in her voice. 'That is Pedro's boat. He is the big fisherman who was in here on the first night. They say it is the body of a woman. The police are all over the dockside. They are questioning Pedro and all of his crew, taking statements and photographs. They are taking away his nets in case there are any more clues caught up in the mesh. Pedro is angry. He cannot fish without nets. It is all a terrible business.'

'There are plenty of nets laid out along the fishermen's wharf,' Ben said. 'The old boys always seem to be sitting there in the sun mending nets. They must have some to spare.'

'Perhaps,' Isabella shrugged. 'But Pedro wants his own nets, not some old borrowed nets that will be worn and weak.'

'The body,' Judy said, 'Was it someone who drowned while swimming?'

'I don't think so,' Isabella was positive. 'Nobody thinks that. They say the poor woman had some big chain tied around her legs. And her hands were tied behind her back. Nobody goes swimming with chain around their legs and their hands tied.'

'Definitely suspicious,' Judy said wryly. 'Is there anyone missing locally?'

'I do not think so.' Isabella had confidence in the gossip grapevine. 'If any woman was missing from Porto Viejo there would be talk.'

'How long had the body been in the water?'

'This I do not know. Nobody has said. But

one of the fishermen said that the fish had begun to eat her. Oh, it is so horrible.'

'Was she fished up close to the port?'

Isabella had to think. 'A few miles out to sea, just a few miles down the coast. Everybody is talking and some are saying different things to others. Some are making guesses. They say she was nearly naked, just in her panties and brassiere.' She shuddered, as though being found naked was somehow as awful as being drowned.

'Was she drowned?' Judy asked. 'Or was she dead before she went into the water?'

'Whoa there,' Ben interrupted. 'You've given all this up, remember?'

'Sorry,' Judy said. 'But I can't help missing the job, just as you can't stop yourself from wandering into fire stations to look at the fire engines. I'm only curious.'

'Perhaps Pedro will come in later. I think he will want a drink when the police have finished with him. Then I will learn more.' Isabella wrinkled her pretty face. 'Poor Ramon, he is the boy on the crew. They say he will never go to sea again. It will be too terrible for him to watch the nets coming out of the sea. All the time he will be thinking of that poor woman's body being hauled up to the surface of the waves. He is saying that he wants never, never to go back to the fishing.'

* ★ ★

Throughout the day the rumours and the gossip continued to fly around Porto Viejo. Pedro did not come into the *Conquistador* for a drink but whenever a local man appeared Isabella would pump him for the latest information. However, at this stage there was little to be known beyond the basic facts. The area of the fishermen's wharf where the *Serrano* was tied up alongside had been isolated with official barrier tape and the police had yet to issue any statements.

A bar was still the best place to argue and exchange speculations and so most of the harbour-front bars were busy, including the *Conquistador*. Judy and Ben found themselves constantly explaining what had happend to the tourists and visitors who had picked up on the prevailing buzz of excitement. When dusk finally came the fishing fleet sailed again on their regular nocturnal pursuit of a fresh catch. A larger crowd than usual watched them disappear into the sunset but the *Serrano* remained tied up at her berth. All the police activity around her had ceased and the vessel lay silent and alone.

For Ben and Judy and Isabella it became another busy night. The tasty smells from Antonio's *tapas* dishes floated up around the

47

bar. The cigarette smoke grew thicker and the tasks of filling food plates and re-filling glasses became faster. The noise volume of talk and laughter became louder.

Judy was well pleased with the way things were going. Like everywhere else along the Spanish coast there were several large ex-pat developments of villas and apartments just outside the town, all with their own golf courses and swimming pools. Also there were large numbers of foreign visitors filling the hotels and bringing their boats into the large harbour. She and Ben had debated over whether they should aim exclusively for this trade or try to include the locals. So far keeping the bar much as it was and employing Isabella and Antonio seemed to be giving them the best of both worlds.

Early in the evening Peter and Jane Shepherd came in but stayed for only one drink. Jane was wearing an elegant blue gown with white diamonds at her ears and throat. She was high in spirits and clinging close to her husband's arm. 'It's our wedding anniversary,' she confided as he led her away. 'We're dining at the *Casa Paco*. They do the best *paella Valencia* in town. You must try it. Get Ben to take you on your night off.'

'I'll twist his arm,' Judy promised. She watched them walk off arm-in-arm along the harbour-front and then they were out of sight and there was another customer waiting to be served.

The succession of faces coming up to the bar and then melting back into the crowd was a pleasurable mix. A lot of new faces, which was to be expected in a holiday resort, but she also recognized many of the local faces that Isabella had identified on the first night. Most of those wanted to chat to Isabella as much as possible. Judy had the good feeling that with Isabella she was going to hold the local trade as well as pulling in the tourists.

She saw Arturo come in with Harry Avery. Ben served them and lingered to talk over the bar. She guessed they were talking fire engines again but decided to be charitable. Ben gave them a few minutes but then reluctantly moved away to serve. Arturo and Harry took their drinks to one of the outside tables.

The working girls came in. Maria and Conchita, Judy remembered their names. They wore the same too-short skirts revealing too much bare thigh, but their shirts, knotted at the waist, looked fresh and clean. Maria wore salacious red, Conchita wore wicked black. Judy smiled inwardly at the mental associations she was making.

She moved to serve them, letting the smile

show on her face, reflecting wryly that both their trades demanded fixed smiles. Maria asked for two small glasses of beer and paid for them from her shoulder bag. Judy noted that the shoulder bags that both girls carried were not over large, they were careless of who looked inside and the clothing they wore allowed practically no hiding places. They looked a little bit rough but their faces were bright and alert and the pupils of their eyes were normal.

Most of the working girls with whom Judy had come into contact in the course of her old job had been on drugs, working to feed the habit, which meant that quite often they could be dealing as well as soliciting. Judy decided that these two were probably just on the game. If they didn't pull any trade here they would move on to tour the other bars along the waterfront.

However, she made a mental note to watch that they didn't spend too much time in the toilets. That was where anything illicit usually changed hands. She would tolerate them passing through, but there would be no drug dealing at the *Conquistador*.

Isabella seemed to read her mind. 'They are just lazy girls,' she murmured in passing as the two girls moved away. 'They don't like to work and they have no pride so they think theirs is the easy way to make a living.'

'Are they local?' Judy asked.

'No, I think they come from Madrid, or Barcelona, some big city.'

They were called to different ends of the bar and the conversation finished.

★ ★ ★

Sometime later Judy noticed that the blonde haired Englishman who looked like a younger but sour-faced version of Ben had again appeared in the crowd. He had a beer in his hand so Isabella or Ben must have served him while she was busy with another customer. Blondie Dave was with the swarthy, dark haired Spanish boy who Isabella had called Luis. The two of them were grinning and exchanging some kind of banter with Maria and Conchita.

The two girls were well practised at this sort of gambit but tonight they were holding back. Both of them had their arms folded over their chests as they sipped their drinks. Also they were standing, not sitting which would have shown even more of their legs, so they were not exactly displaying their wares. Judy guessed they would prefer punters flushed with a year's hard earned holiday money. Dave and Luis gave the impression of a couple of beach bums who looked as though they wouldn't have a spare euro between them.

There was a sudden rush of customers and she lost track of the foursome until a few gaps cleared again along the bar. They were closer to the doorway now and Judy noticed that it was the girls who were edging away. They obviously wanted to move on to another bar but Blondie Dave was partially blocking their exit. All four of them appeared to be arguing, probably about a price.

Finally some agreement was reached and the four went out together. The last Judy saw of them Blondie Dave had his arm around Maria's waist, while the smaller Luis was waving his hands expressively and chattering rapidly to Conchita.

Judy was not sorry to see them go. The nature of their new business meant that she must be impartial and friendly to everybody, but there were always going to be some customers she would rather not have on the premises.

She got on with serving the next wave of customers. Arturo and Harry were back at the bar with empty glasses. The lean-faced Arturo had the relaxed and confident manner plus the easy grin which she had come to associate with firemen. Although she had to admit that having married one she was biased. She decided she liked Arturo. Fat Harry Avery she was still not sure about.

★ ★ ★

The next morning Isabella appeared with the local newspaper in her hand. She laid it on the bar counter while she hung up her handbag and short jacket and called out her usual, cheerful, '*Beunos dias*,' to Ben and Judy who were polishing glasses and re-stocking the shelves. She returned to the paper and unfolded it to display the front page.

'The *Serrano* is in the news,' she told them. 'The story is here, all about the poor woman who was fished up in their nets.'

Judy moved closer to look, while Ben finished rubbing at a stubborn smear on another glass. The story was rare drama for sleepy Porto Viejo and the paper had given it the entire front page. There were pictures of the trawler moored at the Fishermen's Wharf, pictures of Captain Pedro, with and without his crew, and a black and white photo-fit sketch of the dead woman's face.

Judy stared at the crude line drawn image and suddenly the rest of the pictures and the text seemed to dissolve into a blur. She was looking at a snub nose, a square face with a square jaw, and hair cut in a short white fringe over the forehead. She guessed that the hair colour was meant to be blonde. Suddenly her skin began to crawl, as though someone had slipped something horrible like a handful of wet maggots down the back of her tee shirt.

'Jude?' Ben was beside her, his hand on her arm. The concern in his face and voice told her that her sense of shock was reflected on her face.

'She looks,' Judy said slowly, 'like someone I know. Someone I used to know. Someone I worked with.'

They both stared at her. Judy let her gaze go back to the photo-fit image, then to the columns of hazy text. She usually made an effort to read some of the news in Spanish, struggling to translate the words inside her head and calling on Isabella's help when some of them were wholly unfamiliar. It was all part of her effort to teach herself Spanish. Today she didn't even try. She just looked straight to Isabella for help.

'Tell me what it says about the dead woman, please.'

Isabella hesitated. She too looked puzzled and concerned. Then she obliged.

'The paper says she was pulled out of the sea by the *Serrano*. It says about the chain around her legs and the way her hands were tied.'

'Her description,' Judy said firmly. 'There must be a description of what they think she looked like.'

Isabella pursed her lips, read silently for a moment and then found what was wanted.

'It says she was white, female, about late twenties or early thirties years old. She was 170 centimetres tall. She weighed 200 kilo. She had fair hair.'

'170 centimetres,' Judy repeated, trying to think.

'About five foot six or seven,' Ben said helpfully.

Judy felt as though the maggots were wriggling again.

'It could be her,' she said slowly. 'I don't know how but it could be Georgie.'

'Georgie who?' Ben looked blank.

'Before your time,' She was thinking back. 'Her name was Georgina Harrington. We trained together. We were on the same initial training course at the police school in Hendon. I've lost touch since we were married, but she was the same age as me. We were only twenty then, now she'll be thirty.'

'Ten years ago,' Ben said. 'She could have changed.'

'Maybe, but it looks like her.'

She looked at Ben and then at Isabella. Both their faces were sceptical.

'I know it's only a crude sketch,' she said defensively. 'But it does look like Georgie.'

4

Judy moved purposefully up the steep path that led to the high perched ruins of the old castle. There was virtually no shadow from the rocks for the noon sun was almost directly overhead. She could feel the heat on her bare shoulders and a trickle of sweat stung her eyes. She had not stopped to apply sun-cream, or find a hat, or even to tie a sweatband around her temples and she knew that was foolish. She was pushing herself too hard in an effort to override her temper and she knew it.

She had tried to explain her feeling to Ben but for once he had showed not even a glimmer of understanding.

'It's only a sketch,' he insisted, shrugging his shoulders as he handed back the newspaper. 'It's just an artist's impression, probably nothing like the real woman anyway, whoever she was.'

'Police artists are highly trained,' she had snapped back. 'And this one is not based on the vague memories of a confused witness. It's not an identi-fit picture. They have the body and they work from the bone structure of a victim. And it does look like Georgie.'

'A woman you knew ten years ago. She could have changed in a dozen ways.'

'Yes, she could have changed her hair colour or hair style. She could have got fatter or slimmer. She could have changed any number of details of her make-up and personality, but there's no way she could change the basic bone structure of her face.'

'Alright, so it's the shape of her face, and she's about the right age. But there must be hundreds of women of that age with that shape of face, probably thousands. Why should it be someone you knew?'

'I don't know. I just have this feeling. I went cold when I saw this.' She almost shook the newspaper in his face.

Ben backed off. 'All I'm saying is that it's highly unlikely. You knew your friend Georgie ten years ago in London so what are the odds on her proving to be this poor creature who has just been dredged out of the sea here in Spain. It must be pretty much of a long shot. Even you must admit to that.'

'I'm not saying I'm certain it's Georgie. Just that it looks like her.'

'Perhaps it does. But that's all it is. It just looks like her.'

Judy frowned. The feeling that it could be Georgie was very strong. It was an instinctive gut reaction she couldn't really explain. She could claim a woman's intuition but that was something men usually scoffed at. Ben had learned better, or so she believed, and even her old boss, the hard-nosed and aptly named Ron Harding had been forced to grudgingly admit that sometimes it worked. This time she found herself reluctant to put it into words.

'It's just a feeling,' she repeated lamely.

Ben grinned. 'You're missing your old job. There's a murder mystery and you want to get involved. You want to be Detective Sergeant Kane again. Once a cop always a cop.'

'Like you can't stay away from fire engines.' She bit her lip and immediately wished she hadn't said that.

'Alright,' he raised his hands in surrender. 'But at least I'm not expecting Arturo to let me drive the pump on the next shout.'

'I'm not expecting anything either. I don't want to get involved. But it does look like Georgie.'

'How could it be?' Ben asked. 'You knew her in London. Ten years later you're here in Spain. She pops up out of the sea. How long and unlikely a coincidence is that?'

Isabella had diplomatically drifted away and made herself busy on the other side of the bar. Some customers had come in and Ben moved away to serve them coffee. Judy let it go and went outside to straighten the tables. Suddenly she wanted to get away and give herself time to think. She announced her intention of taking a walk, just to give herself some exercise. Ben had looked slightly startled, as though he had not fully realized how much he had annoyed her, and then he acknowledged that he and Isabella could, 'Hold the fort.'

Judy left them and walked briskly along the harbour. She headed for the south beach, intending to run, but at this time of day the sand was littered with too many sun-shades and sun-beds, and sprawling, half-naked bodies topping up their tan. She decided on the equally strenuous challenge of climbing up to the castle instead. At least she was unlikely to trip over any sun-bathers.

Half way up she realized that she had pushed herself enough. She stopped to rest, pausing to catch her breath and admire the view. She was already high enough to see over the harbour where the massed yachts lay at the long rows of pontoons. Behind the harbour the densely packed white houses and narrow lanes of old Porto Viejo climbed up to the next hill that was crowned with the blue and gold dome of the church. Splashes of colour showed here and there where the blue and red of bougainvillea filled tiny courtyards or trailed over ancient walls. The new town lay back from the harbour between the old town and the castle hill, a neater pattern of broad, tree-lined avenues and busy plazas.

When she was ready to move on she turned and looked down for a moment on the long south beach that was immediately below her. The beach was crowded but one figure had recognized her as she made her ascent and was now waving a carefree arm in acknowledgement. Judy noted the blonde hair and blue two piece swimsuit and waved back. Blue seemed to be Jane Shepherd's favourite colour.

Jane spread a blue towel on the sand and sat down and began to oil her upper arms. Judy could now see Peter standing beside his wife. He too waved briefly and then turned and began to pick his way through the maze of sun-beds and bodies to the sea. He wore red bathing shorts and when he reached the sea he waded straight out and plunged in. Judy watched him swim with strong over-arm strokes.

When she looked back Jane had stretched out on one elbow to read a book. Peter was obviously the athletic one of the two. Judy could see no one else she recognized on the beach and after a moment she turned away and resumed her climb.

When she reached the top she decided it was worth it. The views were stupendous and from the first day she had seen Porto Viejo this had been her favourite spot to meditate. There was enough of the old castle left to throw patches of cool shade and even a couple of old black cannons still pointing their snub noses out to sea. The roof and towers were long gone but some of the broken walls reached above her head, and a couple of bench seats had been strategically placed to enjoy both the shade patches and the views.

Judy sat down on one of the seats and closed her eyes against the glare that came off the sea. She felt hot and sweaty but at least the mid-day heat meant that she was alone, which was what she had wanted. The original castle had been built by the Moors in the Eighth Century, this being one of the furthest points north that they had reached. Its power had waxed and waned until it was taken by the Christians some three hundred years later. Some of the stories said that it had been conquered by the great El Cid, but there was no accurate documentation. Later parts of the castle had been restored to some extent as a defence against pirates and sea raiders from the Mediterranean, and then allowed to crumble again.

Judy had been fascinated by its history when they had first arrived and was looking forward to the next round of festivals celebrating the ancient battles of Moors and Christians that would parade through the main avenues of Porto Viejo. Today, however, she was not thinking about past history. Her thoughts went back to Georgie and Ben.

She had to concede that Ben had a point. The idea that Georgie could suddenly turn up here as a drowned body hauled up in a fishermen's net did seem a bit far fetched. But the pencil line face in the newspaper haunted her. The snub nose and the square jaw were so much like Georgie. There had always been something slightly pugnacious about Georgie's face in an attractive sort of way. One of the male trainee constables had once called her 'Bulldog,' a nickname which might have stuck if Georgie hadn't threatened to punch him on the nose if he ever used it again.

Judy sighed and her thoughts shifted to Ben. Was this the fourth or the fifth argument they had had in as many weeks. She couldn't remember. Could this one be rated as an argument or was it just a disagreement. Ben couldn't really be expected to understand her deeper feelings, even though he usually tried. She wasn't even sure that she understood this one herself. It was only a crude, pen sketch drawing. What hurt was that this time Ben had not even tried to understand her.

All through their marriage she had always been able to talk to Ben about any investigation she had worked on. He had always shown an interest and had often been able to see a new insight or a new angle for looking at some of her criminal puzzles. Quite often bouncing ideas and theories off Ben had proved more fruitful than the same exchanges with her police colleagues on the job or down at the station. Finding him dismissive and unresponsive was a new experience.

Perhaps the problem lay in the fact that she was no longer a police officer. Even if the body was Georgie it was no longer her business. Except that she would make it her business because Georgie had been a friend. Perhaps Ben sensed that and knew they already had enough to do in running the *Conquistador*.

She remembered her own irritation with Ben for allowing himself to be drawn to the nearest fire station. They were both supposed to be finished with the old way of life, putting their previous careers behind them. Making a go of the *Conquistador* was going to take all of their time and energies and they had already put everything they had into their new venture. If one of them strayed from that purpose it would be letting down the other.

Judy swore at her own frustration. She stood up and began to pace around the top of the castle hill, moving aimlessly through the remnants of old walls, staring moodily at the old cannon. She just wanted to be doing something. She had to agree with Ben that they could do without this new complication butting into their new lifestyle.

But she couldn't ignore it. The drawing had looked like Georgie. Her gut feeling wouldn't go away.

She sat down again on the bench seat and fished her cell phone out of the pocket of her shorts. She opened up her telephone directory and scanned through the names and numbers. Almost at the bottom of the list was the name Sally Russell.

Judy Kane, Georgina Harrington and Sally Russell, they had all been on the same training course at Hendon. All three of them had started out on their police careers together. They had gone their different ways but kept in touch for a long time afterwards. Sally was now a Detective Sergeant in Hull. They still exchanged cards at Christmas. The last time she had seen Sally was when she and Ben had been guests at Sally's wedding three years ago. Georgie hadn't been there, for some reason she couldn't remember. Somewhere in the upheaval of moving she had lost Georgie's telephone number, but she still had Sally's number.

She looked at it for a moment and then made the call.

The connection took a few moments but then she heard the familiar voice, crisp and clear.

'Hello, D.S. Russell.'

Judy guessed from the business like tone that Sally was working, probably at her desk in the CID room.

'Hello, Sal, its Judy.'

'Judy? Judy Kane. Hi, Jude, what are you up to?'

'Well, at the moment I'm sitting in the ruins of an old castle, looking out over the Med. It's all blue sky and blue sea, as far as the eye can see.'

'Some people have all the luck. Here its grey and raining outside the window and inside I'm suffocating under a pile of bloody paperwork. What can I do for you?'

'Have you heard from Georgie lately?'

'Georgie Harrington? No, not since Christmas anyway.'

66

'Do you know what she's doing these days?'

'As far as I know she's still a DS with the Met. I thought we were all racing each other to be the first DI until you opted out. I take it you are now in Sunny Spain, running the dream bar with that gorgeous hunk of a husband you've picked up.'

'You didn't do so badly yourself,' Judy returned the compliment. 'And yes I am now in Spain. I just needed to check up on Georgie.'

'Well the last I heard she was in Spain too. That's where her Christmas card came from. She sent an email too with a picture of herself sitting on some Spanish beach. I suppose she was on holiday. She's probably back at the daily grind, looking for flashers, pimps and dealers somewhere in the back streets of London. Aren't you lucky to be out of all that?'

Judy had the cold, sinking feeling in the pit of her stomach again. She said slowly. 'I guess so. Are you certain that Georgie was on holiday and that now she's home again?'

'Well, I assume that's what happened. Why, what's up?'

'I'm not sure. Do you know where in Spain she was staying?'

'Not exactly, the Christmas card came with

a Spanish stamp. The email picture was just a beach somewhere. What is the problem?'

Judy didn't want to explain, not yet. She said slowly.

'I just need to speak to Georgie. I've lost her number.'

'It probably wouldn't do you any good. The last time I tried to call her I just got that silly voice message, 'the number you have dialed has not been recognized.' I'm guessing that Georgie has changed her phone and hasn't got round to telling us yet.'

'Damn,' Judy said.

Sally Russell was sharp. She picked up on the undertone of irritation. 'What is wrong, Jude? What is this all about?'

'I'm not sure yet. I'll call you back when I've worked it out. Is there anything else you can tell me? I haven't talked to Georgie in ages. What's the latest?'

'Well, there might be a new man on the scene. Someone took the photograph she sent me, and she had that soppy look on her face that you only give a new boyfriend. Oh, and sometime back she did say that she'd moved within the Met. To the Drug Squad, I think.'

Judy had that ominous feeling again. She said slowly. 'Sal, I have to go. There's something I have to check out. I will call you back.'

Sally Russell started to protest but Judy shut down the phone. She knew she was being unforgivably rude but she would apologize later. Right now she needed to think.

Georgie had last been heard of in Spain. And she was now with the Metropolitan Police Drug Squad. The two facts fitted uncomfortably together.

Reluctantly Judy realized that there was now only one move she could make. Georgina Harrington had one distinguishing mark, and there was only one way to find out.

* * *

Judy descended the rugged slope of the hill at a brisk walk. She was in a hurry now, but to move any faster would have risked a slip and a fall on the steep sand and gravel path. Twice she almost lost her footing and had to slow her pace.

She reached level ground and quickened her step, heading back to the harbour. However, she was not heading back to the *Conquistador* and turned away from the promenade at the first avenue junction on her left. Leaving the palm trees and the small forest of masts and boats behind her she headed for the *Plaza Mayor*, the town's central square. There, on the left hand side facing the central fountain was the yellow-washed three storey building that housed the *Policia Nationale*.

Judy paused for a second then climbed the broad flight of four steps that led up to the large plate glass double doors. Inside she was in a large lobby with what looked like three separate reception desks with long queues of people at each one. More people seemed to be just waiting or idly moving around. The whole building seemed much more busy and confused than any of the orderly police stations in the UK. Judy stood uncertain for a moment, but there was order in the chaos and almost immediately a uniformed officer walked over and asked her business.

The question was politely asked in Spanish. Judy answered in the same language and was suddenly aware of how clumsy and limited her own Spanish still sounded. The man frowned, gave her a doubtful look and then called over a female colleague.

'*Este Englese?*' The woman asked.

'Yes,' Judy said, irritated because her Spanish was inadequate.

'You have some information for us,' the woman continued in perfect English, 'About the dead woman whose picture was in the paper?'

Judy nodded.

The two police officers conferred quickly in their own language. Then the woman turned back to Judy.

'*Per favor*, you will come with me please.'

Judy followed her through double doors on the far side of the room, leaving the noise and bustle behind them. She was led through a series of corridors past closed and open offices. Finally her guide knocked on one of the closed doors which bore a nameplate reading Inspector M. Garcia.

A voice answered. Her guide partly opened the door and put her head inside, blocking Judy out while she conferred in rapid Spanish with the man within. After a minute of what sounded like mild argument the woman officer opened the door fully and stood aside so that Judy could enter. 'Inspector Garcia will speak with you,' she said in English.

Judy thanked her. The woman shrugged and began her return journey along the empty corridors. Judy looked at the man behind the large desk that filled the centre of the room. She recognized the dark, lean face with its strong jaw, slightly sharp nose and intense brown eyes. It was mutual and his smile suddenly flashed very white and warm.

'I think I know you.' His English was also perfect. 'You are the English lady who now

71

runs the *Conquistador*.'

'Judy nodded. My name is Judy Kane. I think you were one of my customers on our first night.' Isabella had mentioned his name and she tried to remember.

He stood up from his desk and said politely. 'I am Miguel Garcia. How can I help you?'

Miguel, Judy remembered now. She also had a clear memory of Isabella grinning wickedly as she named every local man in the room, giving each of them a cheerful thumb up or a sad little finger down. Miguel had generated a very positive thumb up and Judy had a horrible feeling that she was suddenly blushing.

'You have some information for me?' Miguel asked, giving her a curious look.

'Yes,' Judy tried to make her face look normal. 'It's hot,' she said lamely. It was actually cool in the air-conditioned office and she had to add an explanation. 'I've just climbed up and down from the castle and then hurried here in the heat.'

'Perhaps you should sit.' Miguel smiled as though he understood and moved round his desk to pull back the facing visitor's chair. Judy sat down, feeling vaguely embarrassed and damning Isabella for being a saucy little minx. Miguel Garcia was a handsome man and despite herself she wondered if Isabella was right. Miguel returned to his own seat, leaned his elbows on the desk and made a steeple of his fingers as he watched her with enquiring eyes.

'It was something about the woman who was drowned,' he reminded her.

Judy drew a deep breath. 'I think I might know who she is.'

Miguel reached for a notepad and a pen, 'Her name?'

'If it is the woman I think it might be, then her name is Georgina Harrington.'

He pushed the pad and pen toward her. 'Will you write it down, please, in capital letters?'

Judy did as he asked.

'And her address in Porto Viejo.'

'Ahh,' Judy said awkwardly. 'That I don't know.'

'Did she have a house here? Which *urbanization*? Or perhaps she stayed in a hotel?'

'I don't know.'

'How do you know her?'

Judy had known that this was going to be difficult and his doubtful appraisal was making her even more uncomfortable.

'I worked with her ten years ago in England. I last saw her about five years ago.'

73

It did sound weak and she saw from his tightening lips that he was deciding that she was wasting his time. She also realized that with so little to say Ben had been right to be skeptical. She added quickly. 'We were both police officers.'

'Police officers?' There was a hint of uncertainty in his tone, a grudging concession that perhaps he should listen further.

'Yes,' Judy said firmly. 'We trained together at the Police Training School at Hendon.' She leaned forward and went on seriously. 'I know it sounds unlikely, but your police picture is such an accurate likeness. It's the same nose, the same facial structure, the same jaw-line, and the general description of age and height is spot on. And there is one easy way to check.'

'How can we check?' Miguel was interested.

'On her right arm, just inside the wrist, there is a small scar. Georgie started as a beat constable with the Metropolitan Police in London. On one of her first jobs she and her partner were called to a house that had been burgled. A neighbour had heard the old woman inside screaming and raised the alarm. The door was locked. The intruder had slammed it behind him as he ran out and the yale had snapped shut. Georgie looked through a window and saw the old lady lying with her head in a pool of blood on her living room carpet. Georgie was a quick thinker. She wrapped her police cap around her fist and punched a hole through the window to make an entry. But she cut the inside of her wrist when she reached in through the broken glass to lift the window catch.'

Judy had been speaking fast. She paused for breath then finished. 'The gash just missed the vein, but it left a scar, a thin diagonal white scar, about two centimetres long.'

Miguel stared at her thoughtfully for a long minute and then made up his mind. 'Come,' he said simply. 'We will find out.'

He stood up and led her out of the office, moving through more corridors but away from the front lobby. They exited from the back of the building into a large car park where he led her over to a dark green saloon car. He unlocked its doors with a remote click of his key and politely opened the passenger door for her. Judy climbed inside the car, realizing that here was a man of action. When he decided to do something it was done quickly and efficiently.

They drove in silence through the busy streets of Porto Viejo with Miguel handling the car deftly and at speed. If the body wasn't

Georgie there was nothing more to be said, Judy realized. If it was there would be a lot more questions and she had no answers to any of them.

The town's general hospital was only ten minutes away, on the edge of the town close to the inland coast road by-pass. The municipal mortuary was housed in one of the adjoining blocks away from the main entrance. Judy had guessed their destination and felt her mouth go dry as they got out of the car and went inside. This was the one part of her old job which she had always hated.

There was a reception desk where Miguel checked them in. Then, joined by a sombre attendant in a white coat they moved down another corridor, past more closed offices, and then down a flight of steps to a cold basement. Judy felt a familiar chill as she saw the white tiles, the large stainless steel sinks and the long, stainless steel autopsy tables. She was led over to a far wall that was set with a dozen polished steel drawers, like some grotesque oversize filing cabinet. The drawers marked only by their name tags and handles.

'Are you ready for this?' Miguel asked, sounding both courteous and sympathetic.

Judy wasn't, but there was no way to go back now. She nodded.

The attendant pulled out one of the long

sliding drawers. The body inside was covered with a white sheet. The feet were visible and one grey ankle had another name tag attached. Judy couldn't read the scribble of Spanish, which she guessed was not a name but a general description of how and where found. She nodded to the attendant who rolled down the sheet from the white, ravaged face.

Judy looked once and then looked away. There was no way she could identify the half eaten mess where the fish had nibbled. She marveled that the police artist had been able to get any sort of picture from just the general specifications. Again she felt, hoped and prayed that she was wrong. She would put up with Miguel's weary dismissal and be glad to get away.

Miguel lifted up one side of the sheet, exposing a limp right hand. Judy couldn't bring herself to touch the cold grey flesh but Miguel turned the hand palm upward.

The tiny, diagonal streak of scar tissue was still there, almost invisible against the mottled grey colour of the dead skin of the inner wrist.

Judy shuddered and nodded.

She had to turn away quickly and bumped into Miguel, pressing her face inadvertently against his white shirtfront and his chest. The tall Spanish policeman folded his arms around her shoulders and held her for a moment. His embrace was gentle, comforting and strong.

He moved her away and the attendant slid the tray with Georgie's body back into its place.

5

David James Blondell, Blondie Dave, woke up with a sliver of sunlight penetrating his eyelids, causing a sharp stab of pain which shot straight through to the back of his skull. He groaned and rolled away from the light which came through a gap in the torn and dirty rag of curtain that hung over the small cabin porthole above his cramped bunk.

He tried to remember what had happened last night. The way his head ached meant that he had drunk a fair number of lager beers. The local Spanish stuff was as weak as cat's piss and you needed at least a dozen to get decently hung over. He tried to grin, a drunkard's bravado, but that only made his face hurt and brought back another memory.

The bitch had scratched him. The mad bitch had tried to claw his bloody eye out.

He sat up slowly. He had learned not to sit up too fast in the narrow bunk space. He had hit his head too many times on the cross beams of the low deck-head. He glanced around the small forward cabin and saw that the second bunk on the opposite side was empty. Luis had gone. The two whores they had brought back here last night had also disappeared.

Dave guessed that Luis had gone home to his mother. The despairing old woman who looked like a shrivelled, black-dressed female gnome would scold him hopelessly, but at least she would provide him with a decent breakfast and do his washing. Dave had to fend for himself.

He swung his legs over the edge of the bunk and eased himself carefully down onto the deck. Groaning again and afraid to even touch a hand to his throbbing head he stumbled to the miniscule toilet to relieve himself. One pain slowly drained away but the other remained.

The broken down old fishing boat had once belonged to Luis's father. The old man had chain-smoked cheap cigarettes until he died of lung cancer and Luis had inherited the boat and nothing else. It should have been an honourable way to make a living except that Luis had no inclination to do any more work than was absolutely necessary. Now the boat was just a place to bring girls and to accommodate a down and out friend.

The boat was still littered with old nets and dead fish scales, residues of the days when it had been an honest working boat. It still stank of ancient diesel oil even though the rusting engine had not been started for the past two years or more. It was just a crappy old hulk, rotting away slowly in a forgotten corner of Porto Viejo harbour.

The two whores had stopped and protested as soon as they saw where they were being led. If they had expected one of the classy yachts they had certainly been unlucky. It had taken more arguing and coaxing to get them on board and only then after they had doubled their price. Luis had taken Conchita into the wheelhouse and Dave had pulled Maria down into the cabin.

Maria had immediately rebelled again. The cabin was too small. It was impossible in the tiny bunk spaces. The place stank. She had her pride. She now wanted three times the original price.

The gabble of mixed Spanish and English began to fall on deaf ears. Dave had tried to haul her down onto the deck space and pulled open her blouse. Maria had screamed, slapped and clawed. When she had scratched his face the stinging pain had caused Dave to stagger back, stumble and slip on his tee shirt which he had already discarded onto the deck. Maria had grabbed her opportunity and fled up the short gangway. As she reached the top she had shouted to Conchita. The two of them had scrambled off the boat together and run back along the harbour holding hands.

Dave groaned again and gingerly touched the beads of hard black scabs that now ran down his cheek. 'You bitch,' he said aloud. 'Bitch, bitch, bitch, stinking dirty whore.'

He found his tee shirt and a pair of faded yellow shorts and pulled them on. There was no food on the boat so he would have to go up into the town to find a cheap breakfast and coffee. For the moment he felt too fragile and sat down on the edge of the bunk, staring through the rag of curtain and the dirt-streaked porthole. His eyes could barely focus and he envied Luis being able to go home to his mother.

His own mother had always given him something for breakfast, usually corn flakes and toast, leaving him to eat them alone as she hurried off to work. He remembered a succession of so-called 'uncles' but never a father. Mostly it was just him and Mum and then a small sister. His single mum never had any real time for either of them. He had grown up in a south London tower block where there was nothing to do except skip school and hang about with the gang in the nearby wasteland come rubbish pit that had once been designated as a park.

His mind drifted back to those early, aimless days of growing up, the fights, the scrapes, dodging the 'old Bill.' Education was a waste of time because no one was ever going to employ him anyway, but he had learned things to help him survive.

By the time he was twelve he was a member of the Diehards, one of the street gangs who ran wild and terrorized their own turf. They were all vandals with cans of spray paint. They were all petty thieves. Car stealing and joy-riding was their most popular pastime and they usually left the car in flames. Throwing stones at firemen and police officers earned them 'respect' and a hit made one of them a hero for the night.

Their rivals and sworn enemies were the Rambos. Both gangs had named themselves after a movie series and tried to live up to the hard, tough image that the films implied. Most of the Diehards wore torn and dirty once-white vests under their hoody jackets.

Most of the older gang-members had 'contacts.' They were men you could meet in the darkened corner of a pub car park, or talk to through the half open window of a parked car. Contacts were shadows, rarely met in daylight, favouring the night. They could shift stolen goods for you, or supply you with the hard stuff. And you could expect a broken arm or a good kicking if you got out of order. Most of the contacts dealt in drugs.

The Diehards had their own contacts. The Rambos had theirs. Or perhaps it was the same shadowy men in the background dealing with both gangs. Either way there was still aggro at street level between the two gangs. They jealously guarded their own patches of turf. Each gang tried to score points of the other.

At sixteen Blondie Dave was big, contemptuous and tough. He knew it all and he had the scars to prove it. His problem was that he wanted more 'respect.' He wanted to be thought of as smart, as someone with brains as well as balls. He had ambitions to be the gang leader, except that there was no way he was going to be able to take over from Jason Miller. Big Jase was a thick-necked eighteen-stone bully at twenty, as hard as nails and twice as sharp.

Dave knew he would have to settle for second best, at least until Jase made a mistake and ended up in Wormwood Scrubs with his father and older brother. Dave began to look for a way to prove himself, to impress Big Jase and rise up through the gang hierarchy.

He found his answer at The Saracen's Head. The pub was on the edge of Rambo turf. Its car park was a known meeting place for the Rambos and some of their contacts. Dave had paid it a couple of wary visits, keeping his eyes and ears open, hoping to glean something that would help him score off the Rambos. He found his opportunity in the Gents toilet. One of the cubicles there had a window that overlooked a corner of the pub car park. The window was usually open a few inches to let in some fresh air. No one could see in from outside, but from inside the cubicle it was possible to peer out.

Dave had peered out on one black, raining night and saw an unmistakeable silhouette bending close to the open window of a stationary car. The self-styled King William of the Rambos was a tall black youth who favoured Rastafarian dreadlocks. It was a classic exchange, a package passed out from the car, a wad of notes passed inside. King William straightened up and his height confirmed his identity. The car window slid smoothly upward and the black vehicle rolled smoothly away and vanished into the rain. King William turned and went back into the pub.

Scared but exhilarated Dave had slipped out of the toilet, out through a back door and made good his escape.

He took the risk twice more, at the same time on the same night on each of the two following weeks. He avoided the pub bars and just sneaked into the toilets. Each time through the toilet window he saw King William meet with the dark car and make the exchange. It was a regular meet.

He finally told Big Jase. King William always came alone. The two of them could take him. They could knock him down from behind and grab the stuff. Then leg it back to Diehard turf. It would be a good earner and a good score off the Rambos. King William probably wouldn't dare say a word. If he did he would lose face with his own gang and with his contacts.

Big Jase liked the idea. They worked out the details and a week later they made the hit.

First they stole a car, a nondescript black saloon that some stupid punter had left parked in a darkened street. Big Jase jemmied the door with a large screwdriver and then crossed the ignition wires to get it started. They drove early into the Saracen car park, stopped in a far corner and then simply slid down in their seats and used the car as a hiding place.

It was a long wait but eventually it all happened as before. The long black car slid into the car park and stopped. King William appeared from the shadows and approached the window. There was a mutter of talk and the furtive exchange took place. King William stepped back and stuffed a package inside his long black overcoat. He said something in parting and then his dreadlocks swirled in greasy rat's tails around his head as he turned away. The black car reversed, drove past the stolen car where Dave and Big Jase were cowering low in their seats, and then exited the car park.

Dave inched one eye above the level of the car windowsill. King William had not gone back into the pub. Instead he was walking toward them. Dave guessed he was going straight home. This was going to be easier than he had hoped. He snatched at Big Jase's arm to warn him.

They stayed low for another half minute, hearing the crunch of boots on gravel as the leader of the Rambos walked past. Then together they pushed open the car doors, leaped out and made their assault.

From somewhere in the darkness a whistle shrilled in warning. King William had turned with surprising speed. One second his back was toward them, the next his dreadlocks were spinning and they were looking into his fierce black face where his teeth flashed white in a wolfish grin. Suddenly there was a sharp metallic click and a knife blade seemed to spring out of his hand.

Dave faltered. Big Jase continued to charge forward, either he was too hyped up with his own ferocity or he had too much momentum to stop. Jase let out an intimidating roar that changed into a gasping splutter that was part scream and part groan as the knife thudded home. Jase collapsed with his arms flailing around King William in a desperate bear hug. Whether Jase was trying to restrain King William or just hold himself up Dave never knew. He was only aware now of the rush of feet and the whooping yells of the Rambos as they stormed in from both sides of the car park.

Dave was petrified. King William had back-up. He was smart enough to have had his gang members concealed in the shadows and Dave had missed them. In blind panic Dave turned and ran.

There was no way out of the car park. He had enough sense to realize that and ran the only way possible. The back entrance to the pub was twenty yards away and like a frightened rabbit he shot across the intervening space and dived into the open doorway. The Rambos were far enough back to have been out of sight and so he had a head start.

He looked back once to see that Big Jase was down, sprawling on his face in the dirt, writhing and groaning. Whether he was cursing or begging for his life Dave again could not tell. The kicking had started. King

William was already putting the boot in and several of the Rambos had joined him, adding their own kicks with savage delight.

The rest of the Rambos had targeted him and were aiming straight for the back door of the pub, screaming insults and waving fists and weapons. A thrown brick smashed into the door jamb beside Dave's head and bounced off his shoulder. Dave turned and continued his headlong flight through the pub, avoiding the bars as always and using the side passage that led to the front doors. He escaped into the street still with a head start and sheer terror gave him speed. He knew that if the Rambos could catch him they would kill him.

He ran on to Diehard turf where he knew the Rambos would hesitate to follow. However, he knew he would now be in deep trouble with his own gang and made twists and turns to avoid their usual meeting points. Apart from that he ran straight home. He was sweating hard and gasping for breath as he stumbled up the last flight of stairs to the small flat where he lived with his mum and little sister. There was a stabbing pain in his side, like the knife pain Jason must have felt, like the knife pain he would probably feel when the Rambos or the Diehards caught him. He stumbled into the flat, slammed the door behind him and locked it.

He stood there panting in the darkness. Slowly he realized that he was alone. This was his mum's night out at the pub where she played bingo. That meant that his sister Ginny would also have sneaked out to hang out with her mates, giggling and gossiping, or whatever it was that ten year old girls did.

He was almost in tears but gradually he got his wits together. He couldn't stay here, that much was certain. There was nowhere in London where he would be safe now, probably nowhere in England. He went into his bedroom. He was still too scared to switch on a light and so he had fumbled around in the dark. Once, a couple of years ago, his mother had made one of her rare efforts to do something right for him. She had found the money for him to go on a subsidised school trip to France. It was when he was supposed to have been learning French, although he hadn't mastered more than half a dozen words. But she had got him a backpack and a passport. The passport was for five years and was still valid.

Dave found them both. He put a few bits of clothing, his ipod and a few other personal bits and pieces into the rucksack. He stared at his gameboy console and computer screen and cried real tears as he realized that he could not carry everything. He compromised by packing a few of his favourite game discs. He put on his coat and stuffed the passport into the inside pocket. Slinging the backpack onto one shoulder he went back into the kitchen. His eyes were accustomed to the gloom and he stared at the biscuit tin on the shelf. It was where his mum kept her spare cash. He took it down, opened it and stuffed the handful of rolled up notes into his pocket. Then he heard a key rattle in the door.

He felt guilt and fear surge through him. He put the empty tin back quickly and stepped away. The door opened and the light switch clicked. Light flooded over him. Ginny stood in the doorway staring at him. For a moment her plain, freckled face was startled. Then she pushed her wave of blonde hair back from her eyes and grinned.

'You're in dead trouble. The Diehards are looking for you. You led Big Jase into a trap with the Rambos. Then you ran away and left him. You're a traitor and a coward. The Diehards are going to give you a good kicking.' She seemed more excited than perturbed.

'It wasn't a trap, and I didn't have any bloody choice,' Dave snarled at her.

'Don't matter,' Ginny shrugged. 'The Diehards are going to get you anyway.' She paused. Her eyes were shining. 'Big Jase is dead. They say the Rambos kicked him to death. The Diehards say you're going to pay.'

Dave groaned. He had figured that the Diehards would see it this way.

'Where are you going?' Ginny asked, looking at his backpack.

'Anywhere, away from here,' Dave remembered the course of action he had already planned. He moved forward and snatched at her wrist. With his other hand he quickly twisted the door key away from her fingers.

'Hey,' Ginny protested. 'Ouch, that hurt me. What are you doing?'

'I'm leaving,' Dave told her. 'And you're staying here. I'm locking you in so you can't run off and tell anyone.'

Ginny stared at him. Her eyes blinked and she bit her lip, as if suddenly realizing that this really was serious. 'I wouldn't tell,' she said slowly.

'Maybe not,' Dave leaned down and kissed her forehead, a tentative brush of his lips. She wasn't much but she was all he had ever had. 'Goodbye, sis, say goodbye to mum for me.'

He left her quickly then and locked the door behind him. He put her key and his own together on the floor outside the door for his mum to find. For ages afterward he could picture her staring after him in sudden shock with her eyes starting to fill with tears.

★ ★ ★

He had jog-trotted through two miles of back streets before he had dared to get on a bus. Two bus rides later he had reached Waterloo station and taken a train through the Channel Tunnel to France. The schoolboy passport had got him through. Behind him he knew that with Jason dead the police would be looking for him as well as the Rambos and the Diehards. The 'contacts' the drug dealers who had had their business disrupted would also be keen to find him and teach him a lesson. For Blondie Dave there was no going back.

He had hitched his way down to the south of France and generally drifted around, sometimes finding seasonal work, touting for bars, mugging the occasional drunk, but more often getting free drinks and food from female holiday-makers. He had the good looks and muscles that appealed to some women who were just looking for a two week holiday romance.

As the weather got colder he had moved south into Spain. He had found short term jobs crewing for some of the larger yachts.

One of them had deposited him in Porto Viejo, dumping him ashore after he had flirted too brazenly with the owner's daughter. There he had met Luis.

The Spanish boy seemed to like him and at first he had thought that Luis was queer. Soon he realized that Luis was sex mad but only for girls. Luis had a dark eyed sex appeal of his own, but together they pulled more girls. Dave had the clashing blonde looks that made the women drool and most girls holidayed in pairs. The old boat that Luis had inherited from his father was also a free place to sleep, saving him money so that he didn't need to work so often. The relationship worked because it served them both.

So Dave had stayed in Porto Viejo, sleeping on the old fishing boat, lazing on the beach, getting an all over deep brown tan, conning willing women and just occasionally crewing short hauls on some of the boats to top up his food and beer money. Sometimes he hired on alone. Sometimes Luis would join him if the boat was big enough and needed two extra hands.

That was how they had met Harry and their luck had changed. Meeting Harry had changed everything. They had regular work and more money than they needed. Dave could afford to move out of the boat but it

94

had become a habit. He could even afford to move on, because good old Harry had fixed him up with a new passport now that the old schoolboy passport had expired. There were too many opportunities with Harry.

He stayed for a long time staring out through the porthole of the old fishing boat, looking at the rich yachts that lined the other side of the harbour. He had sailed on smart yachts before and he would sail on smart yachts again. He had found that he actually liked sailing and being on the sea. It wasn't like work at all. One day perhaps he would even own his own yacht. It was all possible.

There was one thing he had always known and that knowledge had been reinforced by working with Harry. It was much smarter to deal in drugs than to take them.

6

When they left the mortuary Miguel Garcia drove Judy back to the *Policia Nationale*. The Spanish policeman was silent and thoughtful and Judy was grateful for the chance to compose her own thoughts and calm her emotions. It had been bad enough fearing it might be Georgie but realizing the awful truth, that the drowned body was definitely that of her former friend, had left her feeling weak and sick.

Miguel led her back to his office, indicated that she should sit and gave her a paper cup of water from the cooler in the corner. He looked suitably apologetic as he sat down to face her across his desk and said quietly. 'Now I must ask you please for a formal statement.'

Judy nodded. She had known this was coming but there was little she could do except confirm in writing what she had already told him. When she had signed it he leaned back in his chair and tapped the single sheet of paper ruefully with his pencil.

'I shall of course check this out with London, but if your friend was working on some drug-related enquiry here without our knowledge then it may be difficult to get your London Drug Squad to give us more than the minimum of information.'

'Why?' Judy was surprised. 'Why wouldn't they cooperate?'

Miguel shrugged and spread his hands in a helpless gesture. 'It is sometimes difficult. We do have a big drug problem in Spain.' His white teeth flashed in a wry smile. 'It is not unusual. Every country in Europe has a big drug problem. We all try to work together to cut off the supply lines but it is not easy. There is big money involved. Enough I am afraid to buy policemen, sometimes very senior policemen. So sometimes cooperation is sought, sometimes it is avoided. The fact that your colleague was unknown to us suggests that this may be one of those operations conducted in secrecy.'

Judy frowned. 'It is beginning to look like an undercover job. The sort of thing Georgie would be good at. But now she's been murdered that must change things.'

'We will hope so.' Miguel rose from his chair. 'Can I drive you back to the *Conquistador*?'

Judy hesitated. She liked his company but she needed time to think before returning to Ben.

'I need the walk,' she smiled to let him know she wasn't being unfriendly. 'But you will keep me informed. I'd like to know what is happening.'

Miguel nodded. 'Professional courtesy, we owe you that much even if you are no longer a serving police officer.'

He escorted her back to the main entrance and thanked her politely before she descended the steps to the street. Judy was again becoming aware that he was a very handsome man, very fit, muscular and lean, with a tantalizing glimpse of dark chest hair showing in the open neck V of his crisp white shirt. She had to make an effort not to look back as she walked away. She remembered how he had held her close for a moment when she had found the scar on Georgie's wrist. She saw the mental picture of Isabella holding up that erect, positive thumb and laughed at her own schoolgirl fantasies. Damn Isabella and damn the fantasies. She was over sixteen and she was happily married to Ben. Still she had to admit that Miguel Garcia was having an unsettling effect on her metabolism.

She was still lost in her own thoughts as she reached the harbour. She began walking absently past the moored yachts when a loud voice hailed her.

'Ahoy there, Judy Kane, come on board and have a drink.'

She stopped and turned. The boat beside her was a sleek white yacht bearing the name *Seagull Two*. Harry Avery stood on the foredeck with his folded arms leaning on the rail. He wore bright green shorts and another garish red sunset patterned shirt. His colour coordination was atrocious. In his hand he gripped a full glass which he raised cheerfully in invitation.

'The sun is over the yardarm as they say, so it's time for a gin and tonic.'

Judy forced a smile. 'I'm a working girl. It's too early in the day for me.'

'Come aboard anyway, have a look at the Seagull. If you and Ben are going to crew for me then you might as well see what she's like.'

Judy hesitated. She didn't really like the fat man but he was a friend of Ben's and she had no wish to offend him. She could plead that she was needed at the *Conquistador*, but a few minutes more wouldn't make much difference. Harry was already moving to the top of the short steel gangway, waving a ring-glittering hand to coax her aboard.

Judy succumbed and joined him. The yacht looked brand new. Everything that was brass or wood was polished and sparkling. Her furled sails and neatly coiled ropes were pristine white. On the raised aft deck behind the central cabin two almost naked girls were sprawled wearing dark sunglasses and mainly string bikinis. Both bronze bodies glistened with oil. They lay languidly on their backs, cocktail glasses within reach, like the ultimate status symbols.

'That's Helen and Jenny,' Harry said casually. 'They're from Peckham, out here on a three week holiday. They have to fly home on Friday, so next week I'll need a new crew.'

Judy made the mental note that there was probably no Mrs Avery and said hello. One of the girls raised a limp hand in part acknowledgement. The other was either asleep or too lazy to move.

Harry began pointing out the features of the yacht, the height of the mast, the spread of the sails, the speed and power of her auxiliary engine.

'It's all in the rigging,' he told her cheerfully. 'Did you know that for sailing you have to fine tune the stress on your ropes and stays much the same as on land you would tune the carburettor of a car. It makes all the difference between whether she sails like a dream or wallows like an old sow.'

Judy hadn't known but she accepted his word. His schoolboy enthusiasm was beginning to win her over and she could see why

Ben had taken to the man. If he was as keen and knowledgeable on fire engines as he was for his boat then Ben would be a natural soul mate. Harry led her below, descending the gangway with a nimble ease for a man of his bulk. He gave her the guided tour of the main and guest bedrooms, the cockpit and the galley.

'Have a coke,' he insisted after she had again refused alcohol. He poured her a coca cola and refreshed his own drink from a small but well stocked and efficient refrigerator. The drink was ice cold.

He led her back on to the deck and they sat on two small camp stools beside a small table. The sun was warm overhead and spangles of silver light danced across the harbour. Just being on board *Seagull Two* was both pleasant and idyllic and Judy could see why Helen and Jenny had decided to spend their holiday with Harry. She wondered if they were old friends or just casual pick-ups but she didn't like to ask.

'Old Harry does a mean beach barbecue,' he was still trying to tempt her, 'Fish, shrimps, steaks, sausages, the lot, all the sauces and all the trimmings. You'll find out when you and Ben come and cruise with me.'

'We've only just opened,' Judy reminded him. 'It may be a while before we can take the time off.'

'Just a short cruise?'

'Even for a short cruise.'

Harry shrugged philosophically, sipped his gin and tonic and changed the subject.

'Ben tells me you were a cop?'

'That's right, a Detective Sergeant.'

'So you were CID, exciting stuff.'

'Sometimes, mostly it was burglaries, vandalism,' she played it down. 'Breckland wasn't exactly a high crime area.'

'And Ben was a fire officer. That's two jobs that take a lot of commitment. Must have been difficult sometimes, being married I mean, with the jobs pulling you apart.'

'It worked for us. Ben loved his work with the Fire Service. I enjoyed my work with the Police. So we understood each other. We made allowances.'

Harry nodded. 'Good for you. I guess you must miss it. I've figured out that Ben does.'

'We're making our life here now. This was the dream we were aiming for anyway. We've just had to make the move a bit sooner than we expected.'

'Good luck to you,' Harry raised his glass and squinted at the sun. 'It's a good life out here, sure as hell beats the British weather.'

They talked about Spain for a while and then Judy made her excuses and left. After she had waved goodbye she was thoughtful again as she walked the last two hundred yards back to the *Conquistador*. This time she was certain that Harry had been checking her out and that he had more than a passing interest in the fact that she had once been a police officer.

★ ★ ★

By nine o'clock that evening the *Conquistador* was crowded again. The Perez Xavier trio were playing, Judy and Ben had decided to give them two nights each week, and like magnets they were pulling in both the floating tourist trade and the locals. Judy saw Arturo come in with a couple of fit, easy-laughing young men who might as well have had *Bombero* stamped on their foreheads. Firemen she could recognize anywhere. Automatically they aimed for Isabella to be served. The bearded fishermen Pedro was also drinking with a group of his friends. His nets were still being held by the police but he was now enjoying his brief notoriety and making the most of the story he was continually asked to re-tell. Judy didn't want to hear it anymore and avoided him.

She had been in a sombre mood since returning from the mortuary, but being kept busy was helping to push the details into the

103

back of her mind. Ben had been suitably chastened when she had described the events of her morning and then he had commented that the whole business was probably now best left to the police. Judy couldn't yet see what other options she might have and had decided for the moment not to argue.

She saw the two working girls come in. Tonight they were both wearing tight black hipster jeans, blatantly displaying their navels with four inches of bare waist below knotted white shirts. Conchita had tied back her dark hair in a glossy Spanish bun. Maria had pinned her hair back on one side with a large sparkling clip of paste diamonds above her left ear. Judy guessed that they must have sensed her disapproval for they moved up to the far end of the bar where Ben was serving.

She kept watch on them anyway, as well as she could through the shifting patterns of the other customers. The two girls moved back toward the open doors and stood patiently sipping their drinks. For the moment there seemed to be no unattached men who might be interested. Their behaviour pattern was familiar and Judy knew that once they had finished slow-sipping their two small beers they would move on, presumably to try elsewhere.

She had a complicated order of eight

drinks to serve and then a chatty group of five young German lads who were trying to flirt in broken English while she filled their beer glasses. She was still learning the delicate juggling act of staying bright and friendly without giving a definite come-on which Isabella seemed to have developed as a classic art. It all distracted her for five minutes and she lost track of things. She didn't see Blondie Dave and his Spanish friend Luis come into the bar but when she again looked for Conchita and Maria, Dave and Luis had joined them.

The four were arguing again but on the small stage the trio were in full swing with Dolores swirling her skirts in a fast flamenco. Judy could only see the argument because the four participants were on the edge of the crowd and she couldn't hear above the shouts and the music. Then the dance ended. The music stopped as Perez rested his accordion and Jaime gave a last flourish with his guitar. All three of them bowed to hand-clapping applause and then there was a brief lull of near silence.

Judy heard Blondie Dave say angrily. 'You scratched my face you stupid bitch.' His normally handsome face was dark and ugly with rage and his hand was raised in a clenched fist.

Maria's face was pale in stark contrast to her black hair but she stood her ground.

'Go away,' she snapped back at him. 'Or I will scratch your stupid face again.'

Blondie Dave had obviously been drinking before he had arrived at the *Conquistador*. His face was flushed and his balance unsteady. His pride was still suffering and he had never been good at holding his temper.

'Bitch,' he repeated. And then he swung his fist and hit her hard and low in the stomach. Maria was knocked backward and collided with Conchita. Her friend struggled to hold her up and both their glasses went crashing to the floor. There was a sudden hush as all faces turned to stare. Dave was past the point of no return and lifted his arm for a back-handed blow that would have smashed the staggering girl in the mouth.

'HEY!'

While most of the crowd had been watching the dance Ben had taken the opportunity to move out from the bar and collect up the empty glasses from the tables around the perimeter of the room. He was only a few yards away from the sudden disturbance and moved quickly. He dropped his collecting tray with a rattle of glasses on to the nearest table. With one stride he closed the gap and caught Dave's upraised arm by the wrist, pulling the man round to face him.

'That's enough of that, sunshine.' Ben's voice was hard and positive. 'You're right out of order.'

They glared at each other, like two blonde bulls Judy thought. They were both broad-shouldered, powerful men, Ben older and sober, Dave drunk and dangerous.

'Let go of me,' Dave snarled.

'I'll let go of you,' Ben agreed, although he still held fast to Dave's wrist. 'But you're leaving now, is that understood?'

'Are you going try and throw me out?'

'If I have to,' Ben warned him.

Dave scowled. Suddenly he twisted his wrist, jerking it free. He pushed at Ben's chest with his other hand and then tried to swing a punch. Ben hit him in the same way that he had hit Maria, a straight punch low in the belly. Blondie Dave was pushed backwards by the blow, hit a table and fell on top of a chair. The wooden chair cracked and splintered and collapsed under his weight.

The two girls had backed away, holding on to each other with frightened faces. Maria was still gasping for breath with tears streaming down her cheeks. As if by magic a clear space had evolved around the two big blonde men. All the other customers within reach scrambled back.

Dave pushed himself to his knees and Luis moved to help him stand. Both of them faced up to Ben.

'Out,' Ben ordered. 'And don't come back.'

Dave clenched his fists in answer.

Ben balled his own fists but stepped back to give his opponent time to reconsider. 'Just go,' he said. 'You're not fit to fight.'

Dave was still getting his breath back and kept it verbal.

'Just try it,' he grated. 'Just try and throw me out.'

Luis looked alarmed. He moved sideways to give them more room and his foot kicked against the splintered chair. He looked down and saw a useful weapon. The chair had been virtually flattened and one of the legs was snapped off. Luis stooped and picked up the broken leg, tearing the rest of the chair away from it with his free hand. He grabbed for his friend's right arm and when Dave looked round he pushed the chair leg into Dave's hand.

Dave grinned and seemed undecided on whether he wanted to use the chair leg as a club or a dagger. The broken end was an ugly array of sharp splinters and he jabbed it toward Ben's eyes before changing his grip. Ben ducked back but still stood ready.

By this time Judy had hurried round the

bar and she caught Ben by the shoulder and tried to pull him away.

'Leave it,' she told him. She knew that even at this stage it didn't have to come to a fight. 'Let me deal with this. I've had the training.'

Ben resisted her pulling and used the same arm to hold her back. 'Maybe,' he said grimly. 'But you're not in uniform now. There's no backup coming with a truncheon and you're not wearing a bloody flak jacket.'

'Ben, leave it,' she snapped in his ear. 'I can talk him out of here.'

While they argued others were on their feet, shouting and remonstrating. Arturo was standing up at his table and it looked as though his fellow fire-fighters were ready to follow his lead. The big fishermen, Pedro, was also waving his hand and gesturing angrily at Luis. The Spanish youth seemed to be the target of all the waving and shouting and now he looked uncertain.

Judy realized that they had made good friends here. Arturo and his *Bomberos* were ready to pitch in and help Ben. Pedro and a few of the other fishermen were clearly telling Luis to behave himself. The Spanish dialogue was flying thick and fast but she grasped that the fishermen were well known to Luis and his family. Most of them had been friends of his father and were now speaking up in his father's name. They were telling him that he should behave himself and that he should be ashamed.

With Judy hanging on to his arm Ben was handicapped. While he tried to shake her off Blondie Dave was ready to take advantage. However, Luis had heard enough. He knew they were in a minority here. Ben was as big as Blondie Dave and Luis could see that the *Bomberos* were ready to move in. Now Luis simply wanted to get out. He was regretting his first course of action and snatched at Dave's arm again and tried to take the chair leg away from him.

Baffled by everything that was happening Blondie Dave was reduced to wrestling with his companion and cursing.

'We leave,' Luis shouted to the room in general. 'It is okay, we are going.' And to Dave he repeated desperately, 'Another time. There will be a better time.'

Blondie Dave also had the sense to realize that he was out-numbered and that the whole room was hostile toward him. The good sense surfaced slowly but then he threw down the chair leg and allowed Luis to drag him towards the door.

'Another time,' he shouted over his shoulder. 'You and me are going to settle this some other time.'

'Anytime,' Ben growled after him.

'Shut up,' Judy hissed in his ear. 'Just leave it.'

★ ★ ★

When the two trouble-makers had departed Judy thanked Pedro and the others who had intervened and then gave the Xavier brothers the nod to carry on quickly with their next number. The tune they chose was everyone's favourite, *Viva Espana*, and the atmosphere in the room soon returned to normal. Judy then whisked the still shaken Maria and Conchita into the kitchen behind the bar for a few words of comfort and advice. After checking that Maria was not seriously hurt she sent them to the ladies where Maria could repair her damaged make-up, and suggested that they leave discreetly by the back door and go home for the evening. It would be best if they could avoid their usual haunts and Blondie Dave for the next couple of nights. The girls were still frightened and nodded in grateful agreement.

For the rest of the night she was kept busy serving and it was not until the bar was closed and Isabella and Antonio had left at two o'clock in the morning that she was again able to speak privately to Ben.

'I could have handled that better,' she told him. 'I've done half a dozen training and refresher courses on how to handle volatile situations. The one thing you do not do is offer to fight. It's all a matter of keeping it cool and talking it out, and nine times out of ten it works. I could have calmed him down and disarmed him without any violence.'

'Maybe,' Ben said shortly. 'Or maybe you would have got that broken chair leg in your face or across your head. I wasn't taking that chance.'

'Ben, I love you for saying that. But we've got to establish some rules here. This is the first time we've had trouble with a drunk but it probably won't be the last. The next time something like this happens it will be best if you leave it to me.'

Ben's face showed his stubborn streak. His birth sign was Taurus and there were times when he stood his ground and refused to move, even with her. 'No way,' he said flatly. 'There's no way I'm just going to hide behind your skirts every time some drunken young yob is spoiling for a fight.'

'Ben, we own this place. The *Conquistador* is ours. We don't want the place smashed up just to prove that you are as macho as anyone else.'

They argued until they went to bed, both

112

of them tired and still irritable and without any clear agreement. Judy felt that she had got her point across and that in future Ben probably would hang back and give her a chance to pacify any potential trouble. But she knew he would be close with a ready fist if things even threatened to get out of hand. She didn't know whether to be glad about that or frustrated. She just had the feeling that he would probably still barge in too soon.

At least they kissed goodnight, although it was only briefly.

7

When Blondie Dave and Luis left the *Conquistador* Dave was still swearing about the big bastard who ran the pub, the rotten whore who had scratched his face and everybody else in general. He even began to berate Luis who was talking rapidly to try and calm him down.

'The local men all know my family,' Luis pleaded. 'They will tell my mother. They will tell my uncles. My mother and my uncles will say I should not be friends with you. It will make too much trouble.'

'For God's sake grow up,' Dave snarled at him. 'You can't cling to your mother for ever.'

'They were too many for you. You could not fight them all. It was best for you that we leave.'

'I could have beaten that big bastard.'

'It would have caused too much trouble. Perhaps made the police interested in us. Harry would not like it.'

'Fuck Harry.' Dave resented the fact that it always came back to Harry and keeping Harry happy.

They argued until Luis steered him into

another bar and bought two more beers. Their loud voices slowly sank in volume as Dave's hot anger gradually seeped into a sour muttering about vengeance and vague plans to catch Ben or the whore alone in an alley. Luis moved them on when other customers began to glance in their direction and by the time they reached the third bar Dave was quiet enough for them to be barely noticed. He drank for the rest of the night with a stony face, letting Luis chatter on while he continued to brood over his need for revenge.

By the time the night ended they were both helplessly drunk. Dave had tired of guzzling beer and switched to brandy and cokes. The fierce local *fundador* had gone to his head and his senses were reeling as they parted and said goodnight. Luis had decided to go home to his mother but now Dave was beyond caring or taunting him any further.

Luis disappeared unsteadily into the narrow streets leading up to the old town. Dave turned back along the harbour and made his equally befuddled way toward the far corner where the old fishing boat was moored. Twice he bumped into the palm trees along the promenade and then he staggered over to the water's edge to avoid them. He felt as though at any moment he was going to vomit and if he did that he was going to throw up into the water.

By this time his head was swimming and his vision was blurred. He knew he was going to have a real stinker of a hangover in the morning. He turned a corner of the harbour, managed to orientate himself in a straight line again and stumbled on. Then he fell over an iron bollard and a mooring line and crashed face down on the cold stones.

He sprawled there helpless with the wind knocked out of him. He had no idea of how long he lay there but gradually the slow click of high heels penetrated his senses. He opened one eye and through his alcoholic haze saw a pair of black, high-heeled shoes. He looked up past long shapely legs to a short black skirt with red lace knickers underneath. With an effort he twisted his neck a little further until he could see the face of Maria staring down at him.

She drew back her right foot and kicked him hard in the ribs.

The force of the kick shifted his whole body over. He hung helplessly on the edge of the harbour wall, his right arm slipping over and dangling down over the dark greasy water that lapped between the hulls of the moored boats.

'That is for the punch you gave me,' Maria told him viciously.

Dave groaned and tried to get up. His body slipped again and he suddenly realized the danger he was in. If he dropped into the water he would be incapable of swimming in his present condition. He would not be able to get himself out. He felt panic and tried to squirm his way to safety but only succeeded in slithering even further over the edge. He would have rolled off completely if Maria had not suddenly stooped and grabbed hold of his arm.

'Leave him,' another voice said. 'He is a pig.' And Dave realized that Conchita was also there. She was behind Maria, pulling at her friend's shoulder and trying to drag her away.

'No,' Maria said. 'I know he is a pig. I wanted to hurt him but I do not want to be responsible if he falls into the harbour and drowns.'

She continued to pull at Dave's arm, hauling him away from the edge. Dave struggled to get a hold of her elbow with his free hand and pull himself up. 'Help me,' he begged.

Maria hesitated. She had pulled him back from the edge and that was enough. But his face was pleading and he was no longer a threat. She glanced round and saw that the old boat hulk in which he lived was only a few yards away.

'We will put him on his boat,' she said to Conchita.

Dave was big and heavy, almost a dead weight, but between them the two girls got him up and dragged him along the harbour. They bundled him on to the old fishing boat and dumped him unceremoniously on the deck.

Dave sprawled on his back and blinked up at them, trying to focus his gaze on Maria.

'You kicked me,' he said petulantly

'You punched me,' she retorted coldly.

'You scratched me.'

'So perhaps we are even.'

He was staring up her skirt again, at that dancing vision of red lace underwear. All his plotting for revenge vanished from his mind, replaced by the basic lust which surged up within him. 'I still fancy you,' he blurted drunkenly, and was strangely surprised at his own feelings.

Maria laughed. In her trade she had taken punches and slaps before and had learned not to hold grudges after she had leveled the score. 'It will still cost you double,' she told him. 'But not on this stinking boat. Give me a call when you are washed and sober.'

She took a card from her handbag and dropped it on to his chest. Dave clutched it close and tried to read the telephone number as he passed out.

★ ★ ★

It was two days later when Jane Shepherd called in to chat. It was Isabella's day off, her friend Juanita would come in later, and Ben was out in the back yard checking in a delivery of wines and beer. Judy was alone at the bar but it was early morning, they had only just opened and there were no other customers. Judy joined Jane with a coffee and they sat at one of the outside tables close to the door. The sun shone in bright streamers through the gaps in the flowering red sun shades. As they sipped coffee they watched Peter moving about purposefully around the deck of *Wave Dancer* on the other side of the palm lined promenade.

'He's getting ready to sail,' Jane explained. 'I've just popped over to say goodbye.'

'You're leaving,' Judy was surprised.

'Only for a few days, four or five at the most, we're going down to Malaga to meet up with a friend of Peter's. His name is Jack Tolliver. He has a boat called the *Rosie B*. They're old drinking buddies from the yacht club back home. Jack's only putting in for a couple of days and then he's off on a three week tour of the Greek Islands. Jack isn't retired yet so his time is limited. So it's just a quick social call really. A day's cruise down to

119

Malaga to sink a few gins with good old Jack, then back here again.'

'Lucky you,' Judy said. 'I take it Peter's shoulder is better?'

'No, not really, he still complains it's giving him pain. He's hired a couple of deckhands just for this trip.' She paused to drink her coffee and then added. 'You probably know them. I've seen them drinking in here a few times.'

'Oh yes?' Judy made the non-committal murmur into an invitation to go on.

'David, the big blonde English boy, I think they call him Blondie Dave. He looks a bit like a younger version of your Ben. He's got a friend called Luis, a Spanish boy.'

Judy set her cup down and frowned. 'I know them,' she admitted. 'But I wouldn't recommend them.'

It was Jane's turn to furrow her brows and look uncertain. 'Why is that?'

Judy told her about the incident with Maria and Conchita and how Ben and Dave had almost come to blows.

'What were they fighting about?' Jane asked, 'David and these two girls?'

Judy shrugged. 'I don't really know. They all went off together the night before, so they must have had an earlier fight then. I did hear Blondie Dave shouting to Maria that she had scratched his face. Perhaps they had a fight over the price, or the service.'

'I noticed he had a scratch on his face, but he seemed polite and reasonable when he was talking to Peter. They came aboard *Wave Dancer* last night. They had heard somehow that Peter was looking for some help. We only really wanted one hand but they came together. The Spanish boy was very quiet. He just smiled a lot. I thought he probably didn't speak much English.'

She paused there, suddenly aware of the implication of what Judy had said. 'They argued over the price?'

Judy nodded. 'My best guess.'

'You mean the two Spanish girls are — ' she hesitated.

'Ladies of the night,' Judy nodded again.

'Well, that revises my first impression of David. But I suppose we have to live and let live. If he hasn't got a wife or girl friend then — ' her words trailed off, she was not sure how to finish.

'I'm finding that I have to change some of my values,' Judy agreed wryly. 'In my old job it was arrest them or move them on. Now I have to welcome everybody and turn a blind eye unless they are blatantly misbehaving themselves. As you say, live and let live, but I won't be serving Blondie

121

Dave in here anymore.'

'Is that because you don't want any more trouble between him and Ben?'

'That's one reason. But I did see the way he punched Maria. It was low in the stomach without any real warning. He has a nasty temper when he's drunk.'

'Perhaps it was just the drink. There was a really livid scratch on his face. If she did that to him then perhaps he had some cause.'

Judy shrugged. She didn't really want to pursue it.

Jane finished her coffee and stared doubtfully into the empty cup. 'I'll tell Peter,' she said at last. 'Maybe he'll change his mind about hiring them. It's short notice though. We're almost ready to leave.'

'Couldn't you crew for him, just for a one day sail?'

'I did offer, but he seems to think that I'm pretty hopeless around the boat. I don't know why because I'm not that bad a sailor. I get the ropes mixed up sometimes but I'm getting better.'

Judy nodded her understanding. 'It's a man thing I suppose, like the love affair they have with their cars. They don't like anyone else to drive.'

Jane laughed. 'You couldn't imagine, with boats they're ten times more possessive. I sometimes think the damn thing is more like a mistress.'

They talked for another five minutes, exchanging views on men and married life in general. Then a party of three came in and sat at one of the tables. Judy had to get up and take their order and return behind the bar. Jane waved goodbye, promised to be back in a few days to tell her about Malaga and then walked across the promenade to return to *Wave Dancer*.

Judy was kept occupied for the next hour as more customers drifted in. At this time of day she was serving more coffee and coca colas than alcohol. When *Wave Dancer* caught her attention again the yacht was moving. The engine had started and the sleek bow was already swinging away from the pontoon below the harbour wall.

She saw Luis throw a mooring rope to Blondie Dave and then jump on to the boat. Dave, who was wearing yellow shorts and a yellow baseball cap, steadied his friend and then coiled the rope neatly as *Wave Dancer* began to ease her way toward the harbour exit. Judy could see Peter at the wheel but he had his back toward her. Jane was on the foredeck waving. Judy waved briefly back before she turned to serve the tray of drinks she had just carried out from the bar.

She guessed that even if Jane had found the opportunity to warn Peter about their new deckhands there had probably been no time for him to change his plans. Now they were under way and it was too late. Judy felt strangely uneasy, the old instinct was kicking in again, but she told herself it was only a short voyage. And even if Blondie Dave were to get drunk again in Malaga there was no reason to suppose that he would automatically get violent.

She took another order and went back to the bar where Ben was now stationed at the beer pump. The day pattern was different, with people sitting at the outside tables and waiting to be served, while at night the much larger crowd simply mobbed the bar. When she returned to serve the drinks she saw that *Wave Dancer* was now moving out through the gap in the harbour wall. Her sail was hoisted and she was beginning to roll true to her name as she sliced into the twinkling blue of the Mediterranean Sea.

Moments later the yacht turned past the harbour wall and only the top of her sail and masthead were visible. Judy wrote down one beer and two coffees and when she looked up again *Wave Dancer* had passed from her line of sight.

* ★ ★

Juanita came in at noon. She was another dark-haired Spanish girl, almost as bright and bubbly as Isabella. She had a three year old daughter who was her pride and joy and her main topic of conversation. Her arrival gave Judy the chance to take another coffee break.

Usually she tried to get a full break from the noise and chatter of the bar. There was a patio corner of the back yard which they had filled with hanging baskets and flower pots full of geraniums. Sometimes Ben could join her there if the bar was not too busy and they could take a break together.

Today she had another visitor. Miguel Garcia strolled in just as she was about to leave the bar and she took him out into the patio. There was a table and three chairs there and they both sat. Miguel had declined a beer, claiming that he was on duty, and so they both sat with coffee again. Miguel wore dark trousers, polished black shoes and another crisp white shirt that was open at the neck. He pushed his sunglasses up on to the top of his head and smiled at her.

'This is the courtesy call I promised. I have been in contact with London about your poor friend Georgina.'

'What did they say?' Judy leaned forward,

unable to conceal her sudden surge of interest. She had tried to forget Georgie but it wasn't possible.

'They say that Sergeant Harrington was on leave and probably here on holiday. We sent them a DNA sample so they have been able to confirm that the body is definitely that of your friend. In return they have sent us a recent photograph and a full description to help us with our enquiries. I have arranged for this picture to appear in tomorrow's newspaper with an appeal to anyone who might be able to come forward with any information.'

He paused, reached across the table and gently touched her hand. 'I did not want you to have another distressing surprise, so I came to warn you before you see the picture.'

Judy was impressed by his concern. The light pressure of his fingers lingered for a moment on the back of her hand and then withdrew. His touch was brief, gallant and unintrusive and the memory remained.

'Is that all?' Judy couldn't quite believe that the Met were showing so little interest in one of their own.

'They are conducting an enquiry in London, speaking to her friends and colleagues to try and learn more about her possible movements, and they have promised to keep us informed. For the time being it seems that they are prepared to leave all enquiries in Spain to the *Policia Nationale*. It is all very flattering, of course, very professional, but my suspicions remain.'

'You still think that Georgie was engaged on some sort of undercover work?'

Miguel nodded. 'Some sort of on-going undercover operation,' he clarified. 'If it is still on-going they will not want it compromised and so they will not want too much interference from my department here in Porto Viejo.'

Judy frowned and then said slowly. 'Wait here a moment. I have something that might help.'

She made a quick trip to her computer desk in the living quarters she shared with Ben above the bar. She came back with two print-outs. One was a picture of Georgina Harrington sitting cross-legged on a sandy beach with a cream and yellow Spanish villa behind her. The other was a copy of Georgie's last e-mail to Sally Russell. Judy spread them on the table to show them to Miguel.

'These were on my computer last night. I was going to bring them round to you as soon as I could get away from the bar. It's Isabella's day off so I was waiting for Juanita to arrive to help Ben. You have just saved me a trip.'

The e-mail read simply:

'Hi Sal, here I am in Sunny Spain, a much better place to spend the winter than grey old England. We'll probably celebrate Christmas with a barbecue. You can keep all the Dickensian snow and stuff but have a Happy One. Love from Georgie.'

'The three of us did part of our training together,' Judy explained. 'I called Sally Russell before I came to you. I had to call her again afterwards to tell her what had happened. This was the last news she had from Georgie so she e-mailed it on.'

Miguel read the e-mail, studied the picture and then read the e-mail again. 'So she was here in Spain for Christmas,' he said. 'Which means a much longer stay than the normal two or three week package holiday.'

Judy nodded. 'So she was probably not in a hotel.' She tapped the photograph. 'Perhaps she stayed in this villa.'

'It is close to the beach,' Miguel observed, 'but other than that it could be anywhere along the coast. We have hundreds of *urbanizations*, and many thousands of such villas.'

He looked up and smiled. 'What I can do is to get one of my officers to show a copy of this picture to all the estate agencies in Porto Viejo. If the villa is local and has changed hands recently then perhaps someone will recognize it.'

Judy stared at the photograph and wished that there was more that they could do. She had already studied every detail and could see nothing that might help them to identify its location. Georgie was sitting cross-legged facing and smiling warmly at whoever had been holding the camera. Judy remembered what Sally had said: 'she was wearing that soppy look that you only give a new boyfriend.' The description fitted. The way Georgina's head was tilted to one side and her dreamy expression did suggest a hopeful new relationship. Judy desperately wanted to talk to the man behind the camera. Already she had convinced herself that it must have been a man who had taken the photograph.

'You can take these,' she told Miguel. 'I can print you up as many more as you need.'

'Thank you,' Miguel said. He hesitated, as if wondering whether he should share his next piece of information. Then he said slowly, 'The autopsy reports have been returned to us. They confirm that your friend drowned. She was alive when she was put into the water. There was nothing else. She was not pregnant. There were no wounds or injuries except for some marks on her wrists. They were not rope burns, it was something else. She had not eaten anything for at least twenty-four hours, so perhaps she was held prisoner somewhere for that length of time.'

Judy tightened her lips and stared down at the table. Miguel touched her hand again and then quickly withdrew. A shadow fell across the table. Judy looked up and saw that Ben had appeared carrying another cup of coffee.

'It's quietened down,' Ben informed her, nodding his head toward the bar. 'Juanita is holding the fort.' He set his coffee down on the table. 'I came to join you, if this isn't a private conversation?'

'Of course not,' Judy made the introductions and Miguel stood up to shake hands. When they had all re-seated themselves Judy explained what they had been talking about. Ben studied the picture of Georgina but had nothing to offer. Finally Miguel stood up, pleading the call of duty and promising to keep in touch before he departed.

Judy sat with Ben for a few more minutes before they both went back to the bar. She had not been able to stop herself from comparing the two men as they had faced each other to shake hands. Miguel was an inch taller than Ben, very fit and slim at the hips. Ben by contrast was definitely putting on weight. She felt angry with herself for making the comparison, and irritated with Ben for interrupting her few moments with the handsome Spaniard. However, she tried to keep her thoughts and feelings to herself as she went back to work.

★ ★ ★

Wave Dancer was making good time, cruising steadily under sail with a light breeze behind her. She was heading south and keeping the rugged Spanish coastline in sight off her starboard bow. She rolled gently through the swell, a soothing, relaxing movement. Jane lay on the foredeck in her blue bikini, soaking up the sun and feeling sleepy. Her head rested on a rolled up towel and her book lay discarded beside her. Her eyes were closed behind her sunglasses as she listened to the rippling purr of the sea brushing the yacht's hull, the creak of the rigging and the occasional murmur of the men's voices.

Peter had handed the wheel over to Blondie Dave but was still standing with him in the cockpit. Luis might not have existed but Jane guessed that he was sun-bathing or dozing at the stern of the boat. There was not really too much for two hired hands to do on a cruise this brief in fine weather, but Peter had pointed out that weather anywhere was always unpredictable. Still, she felt a little annoyed that he had not been able to trust her to give him any help he might need. She had passed on Judy's warning but Peter had argued that it was too late to find anyone to replace them.

She felt the yacht slow and roll more heavily as the bows turned and the sail lost wind. She opened her eyes and sat up as Peter joined her on the foredeck. Looking back she saw that Luis was lowering the sail. Blondie Dave still had the wheel and had started the engine. Under power again the yacht was headed into the mouth of a small cove that had opened up along the coastline.

'David knows this cove,' Peter told her as he sat down beside her. 'He says it's the perfect place to anchor up for a quick swim. He's stopped here before with other yachts. Apparently it's a popular picnic and overnight spot. It's got a perfect and private little sandy beach.'

'But I thought we were aiming for Malaga by nightfall?'

'We are, but we've got plenty of time and I fancy a dip.'

Jane said no more but stood up at the rail to watch as *Wave Dancer* eased into the cove. She had to agree that it was a lovely little spot, almost a lagoon of pure blue, encircled on three sides by pale yellow sand and then rising hill slopes and rugged jumbles of rock. As far as she could see there was no path descending from the cliff tops and the cove was deserted.

Peter stood beside her and seemed happy to leave the handling of the boat to Blondie Dave. They stopped in the middle of the cove, brought to a standstill by a short reverse brake of the propeller. Dave switched off the engine and *Wave Dancer* lay motionless, as if becalmed in the centre of the small bay. There was no need for an anchor.

'Didn't I tell you it was perfect,' Dave called up from the cockpit.

'You did,' Peter answered. 'We'll take a half hour break. I'm in for a swim.' He stripped off his white shorts. Underneath he wore his red swimming trunks. He dropped the shorts on the deck and placed his yachting cap on top. 'Are you coming?' he asked Jane.

Jane shook her head. 'I'll watch. It looks a bit too deep for me, and a bit too far to the shore.'

Peter laughed and headed for the stern of the boat. As he passed the cockpit he called out cheerfully. 'You have the bridge, Mister Blondell.'

'Ay, aye, sir.' Blondie Dave returned his

grin with a salute.

Peter stepped onto the short access ladder at the stern, posed for a few seconds on the top step, and then dived gracefully into the sea. For a few moments he swam alongside the boat. Dave and Luis watched him from the cockpit. Jane watched from the foredeck.

'Come on in,' he shouted up. 'The water's fine.'

'Swimming is not my thing,' Dave responded.

Peter shrugged his shoulders in the water and then turned and began a lazy over arm stroke to the shore. He waded out of the waves and began to explore the small beach. Soon he was scrambling up over the rocks at the far end of the cove. He was fifty three and still acting like a schoolboy.

Jane watched him fondly. She knew that when he returned to the yacht he would be ready for a drink. She was thirsty too and she headed down to the small open plan saloon and galley to mix something up. She smiled briefly at the two deckhands as she passed them in the cockpit. She was still a little bit wary of them, remembering what Judy had told her, but so far they had both been perfectly polite and respectful.

She decided on a jug of sangria. It was her favourite and if she had to make it then that was what it would be. She busied herself mixing the wine and lemonade, stirring in fresh orange juice and a generous measure of *Fundador* brandy. Through the starboard porthole she could see the beach but Peter had disappeared somewhere amongst the rocks. Then she chanced to glance to port and saw another yacht entering the cove.

The new arrival was similar in style and build to *Wave Dancer*, but she was coming in bow first and Jane could not read her name. The second yacht came closer and turned to lie alongside. Jane turned to look through the starboard porthole, searching for Peter, and missed the name of the new arrival as it slid past.

'I know this boat,' she heard Dave say to Luis. 'That's Harry,' and then, raising his voice in a cheerful shout, 'Ahoy there, Harry.'

Jane hesitated, wishing that Peter were here. She had been a little bit uncertain of wearing nothing but her bikini with the two new deckhands on board, but had then decided that she was not prepared to spend the whole cruise covered up. Now, with Peter ashore and more visitors appearing she felt even more uncomfortable. She could hear Blondie Dave exchanging greetings with the man he called Harry up on deck and so she knew that Harry had come on board. She felt that David was being lax, perhaps a bit cheeky, welcoming another yachtsman while Peter was absent, but it did sound as though they were old friends. She had to remember that the yachting fraternity were an easy going crowd who rarely stood on ceremony. She hunted for her shorts and tee shirt and began to put them on.

She emerged from the forward double bedroom still struggling into the tee shirt. As her head popped through she saw to her surprise that a large, fat man in a flowered shirt and baggy shorts was already descending the gangway from the cockpit. His back was toward her but the heavy bulk belonged to nobody she knew. This was going too far. The man had not even bothered to wait for an invitation. Jane felt a surge of indignation which came even before the sudden onset of fear. She opened her mouth to protest but was never given the opportunity.

The fat man had reached the deck. He turned and smiled at her, the beaming, jolly smile of a very happy man. It was a clown's smile but his eyes were not the eyes of a clown. His eyes were hard and cold.

In his right hand he held a heavy, blunt-nosed black automatic, something she recognized from a hundred old movies but had never expected to see in real life. Her throat froze and she stared in disbelief as he pointed the gun at her and calmly squeezed the trigger.

She felt the jack-hammer blow in the centre of her chest and her body was thrown backwards. Her hip hit the saloon table and her flailing arm knocked over the jug she had just prepared. She lost her balance and slipped down on her bottom. Then her upper body flopped backwards and she lay with glazed eyes staring up at the deck head.

The dark red, wine-based liquid from the over-turned jug pooled on the table and then began to drip into the bright pool of blood that was forming on the deck.

Harry moved closer, looking down without any signs of compassion. He dipped a finger in the spilled drink on the table and casually tasted it.

'Sangria,' he said aloud, nodding knowledgeably. 'They've no imagination, these Brits, it's always bloody sangria.'

8

It was the morning after *Wave Dancer* had sailed and Judy was opening up the sunshades over the outside tables. Like almost every morning in Spain it was already a gloriously sunny day. She was about to return inside where Ben was dealing out fresh beer mats and clean ash trays when she saw a yacht entering the harbour. For a moment she thought it was *Wave Dancer* returning for the boat was aiming for the still vacant berth at the pontoon directly opposite the *Conquistador*. The yacht was the same length and build with a similar sleek white hull. Then she saw the name on the bows, the one word *Apache* painted in vivid red. There was a large fat man at the wheel, sun-tanned and bare to the waist. The shape and bulk of the man reminded her of Harry Avery and she wondered what he was doing on board another yacht. Then the man half turned and she saw that his short beard and thick chest hair were white where Harry was almost hairless. The stranger wore a red baseball cap emblazoned with the words *New York Yankees*.

Judy watched as the *Apache* eased slowly into *Wave Dancer's* old berth. The big man jumped ashore with a mooring rope, twirled it expertly around a bollard and made it fast. As he stooped his large paunch heavily overhung the waistband of his shorts. A beer drinker, Judy thought. He was a potential customer and she gave him a wave as he straightened up. The big fat man grinned happily and waved back.

Judy went back inside the *Conquistador*. Isabella appeared five minutes later and brought in the local Spanish paper. Without waiting to take off her short jacket and her perky little red beret she called Judy over and opened the paper out on the bar counter. The whole of the third page had been given over to an up-date of the story of the body from the sea. There were two photographs, a head and shoulders portrait that must have been supplied from London and the picture of Georgie on the beach that Judy had received from Sally Russell.

Judy stood beside Isabella as she spread out the page and felt the now familiar sensations of anger and grief as they stuck abruptly in her throat. She was grateful that Miguel had warned her that this was coming. At the same time she felt a moment of approval for his efficiency. Miguel had obviously moved fast to get the second picture added to the report.

There were no customers in immediate need of service and so Ben moved closer to look over Isabella's other shoulder. Isabella read the report aloud for them, translating as well as she was able into English. The original story was re-stated and then the article was brought up to date with the small amount of new information that was now available. Georgie was now positively identified as Detective Sergeant Georgina Harrington, an English police officer. Judy saw her own name and that of the *Conquistador* in print and Isabella confirmed that she had been given the credit for naming the body.

There was a fresh appeal for information from the general public, either about the dead woman or the villa that was visible in the background of the second picture.

'Is that all?' Judy said at last. 'Isn't there any hint of who might have killed her, or why?'

'The *Policia Nationale* spokesman is still saying that this is an open-minded enquiry,' Isabella explained. She read intently for another minute and then offered. 'The paper is full of speculation. They think that this must all be something to do with drugs. Everybody knows that drug smuggling is a very big business in Spain. It is the Number

One crime for the really big criminals. The paper is saying that if your friend was involved in something secret then it must have to do with the drug traffic.'

'That makes sense,' Ben offered. 'To get her killed it had to be something big and the drugs trade would fit the bill. And you did say your friend Sally thought Georgie might have been transferred to the Drug Squad.'

'Miguel suggested that drugs were the most likely explanation,' Judy recalled. 'But so far there seems to be nothing to confirm the theory. Unless Miguel is keeping something from me the police haven't turned up anything on where she might have been staying or what she was really doing.'

'Well,' Ben said slowly, 'you are a civilian now. Miguel doesn't have to share any information with you or anybody outside the *Policia Nationale*.'

Judy felt a moment of irritation and tried to keep it from showing on her face. She knew that Ben was right. As a serving police officer she had never felt it necessary to share any information with any informant. Miguel had showed her some professional courtesy but it did not mean that he had told her everything of the progress of his investigations. She was shut out and rightly so, but she did not like to be reminded of the fact. She wanted to be involved. She wanted to take an active part in finding the answers and catching whoever had killed Georgie.

Rather than argue with Ben she moved away to where a middle-aged couple had just seated themselves at one of the outside tables. Taking their order for a beer and a coffee kept her busy for a few minutes. Isabella took the hint and put the paper away. Ben moved to his station by the beer pump. By the end of the day his leg would be aching and his limp would be noticeable and they had fallen into a routine where he usually served behind the bar while she and Isabella did the more mobile tasks of serving at the tables.

Judy tried to forget Georgie and the latest newspaper report but it was not possible. Ten minutes later Harry Avery walked in with Arturo the *Bombero* fire chief. Arturo was wearing grey shorts with a white tee shirt, a yachting cap and that easy smile she always associated with firemen. Harry was a garish contrast as usual. The shirt that topped his shorts was a flaming mixture of orange sunsets behind black palm trees. In his large ham-sized fist he carried another copy of the paper that Isabella had already shown her.

They gave her a hello and went straight up to the counter, seating themselves on bar stools. Ben had been idly polishing glasses, looking sombre. Probably he had sensed Judy's annoyance and was still wondering what he had said to upset her. However, he brightened up when he saw his two friends. He served them both a beer. There was no one needing Judy's attention and she did not want to seem aloof. She moved back behind the bar.

'It is my week off,' Arturo was saying cheerfully. 'Harry has invited me on to his boat so we are going for a short sail, after we are suitably refreshed, of course.'

'Jenny and Helen have left me,' Harry explained. 'I told them they were making a mistake. They could have stayed with me as permanent guests.' He shrugged wryly. 'They seemed to think their jobs back home were important. I guess I was just a holiday plaything.'

The three men shared a laugh. Judy smiled dutifully.

'So I need a crewman.' Harry punched Arturo lightly on the shoulder. 'It's a lovely day and it's time the *Seagull* felt the wind in her sails again.'

'I'll drink to that,' Arturo raised his glass. Harry did the same.

When Harry put the glass down he changed the subject, gesturing to his newspaper which now lay on the counter. 'I see you've got your name in the paper,' he said to Judy. 'It says here that you identified the body. She was a friend of yours.'

'We trained together,' Judy said. 'It was years ago but Georgie was one of those people you never forget.'

'A strange coincidence,' Harry said. His voice was casual and it seemed to Judy that all the traces of the recent laughter had vanished from behind his eyes. He was watching her face without blinking.

'Life's like that,' Judy shrugged. 'Faces from the past sometimes pop up in the most unexpected places. This one gave me quite a turn. One thing you do not expect is that they could turn up dead.'

'That's true,' Harry nodded and sipped thoughtfully at his beer. 'It must have been quite a shock.'

Judy refrained from answering. If he was trying to draw her out then he was going to have to work harder than this.

Harry looked down at the paper. 'It says here that she was still a police officer. She must have been working on something. What do you think?'

'She could have been on holiday.' Judy tried to be non-committal but then Ben chipped in.

'We've just been talking about that. The

most likely thing seems to be the drugs trade. There's plenty of it about.'

Harry nodded. 'They say that some of the main supply routes come up from North Africa into Spain. But the main ports of entry are probably the bigger ports like Alicante or Malaga. I've never heard any talk about Porto Viejo.'

'There are still a lot of boats in this harbour,' Ben gave his opinion. 'Not only the yachts and the pleasure boats, there's the fishing fleet, and lots of smaller fishing boats.'

Harry nodded. 'I guess that's right. This harbour's big enough, and there's a high turn over of tourist boats. The coastguard and the cops wouldn't be able to keep a close watch on all of them.' He looked to Judy again. 'Do you think your friend was working on something to do with drug trafficking?'

That was definitely a direct question, Judy thought. It felt strange to be on the receiving end of an interrogation, even one as polite and clumsy as this. 'I don't know,' she lied. 'It's a long time since I last saw her. I'm out of the force now and running a bar. It's not my job any more.'

Out of the corner of her eye she saw Ben give her a surprised look. She forestalled anything he might say by speaking to Arturo. 'You're a local man. You must know this town better than anyone. Could there be drug smugglers in Porto Viejo?'

'Is possible,' Arturo frowned. 'Twelve months ago my *bomberos* were called to a yacht fire in the harbour. The owner said that a propane gas tank had exploded. He claimed it was an accident. I had to do the fire report and could not prove otherwise. But I know the *policia* were suspicious. They had planned to board that yacht and search it because they had reasons to believe that there might have been drugs on board. It was very convenient that the yacht was destroyed by the fire before they arrived.'

Ben's professional interest was aroused. He had done his share of fire investigation work. 'A gas cylinder blowing up is easy to arrange,' he agreed. 'Just open the valve and throw a lighted match. A bit dodgy though, you could blow yourself up at the same time.'

'Dodgy?' Arturo's English obviously did not embrace slang.

'Risky,' Ben said. 'Dangerous.'

'Dangerous, ah, *si*.'

Judy leaned forward on the bar. 'What happened to the yacht owner?'

'He was a businessman from Madrid. He went back there. The insurance paid for his yacht but as far as I know he has not returned to Porto Viejo.'

146

'Did you know him?' She turned the question abruptly on Harry.

The fat man shrugged. 'It was before my time.'

Arturo nodded. 'How long you been here, Harry, about a year? It would have been a few weeks before you arrived.'

Harry nodded without speaking and picked up his glass. For a moment he concentrated on a long slow pull at his beer.

Arturo closed the subject with a shrug. 'Other than that I do not think there is any talk of drug smuggling in Porto Viejo. This is just a quiet little Spanish town.'

Harry put down his empty glass. 'One more and then we'll go,' he suggested.

Arturo nodded and drained his own glass. Ben pulled them two more pints. Harry paid and Judy took the money to the till. When she turned back a third man had entered the bar and was sliding on to the vacant seat next to Harry. She recognized the white-bearded man who had moored his yacht opposite the *Conquistador* as she had opened up. Side by side with Harry they could have been twins, both were large fat men with an almost identical physique. The white-bearded man looked to be about the same age, somewhere in his fifties. He had put on a beige short-sleeved shirt to go with his brown shorts so at least he had a more sober fashion taste.

'Hi there.' His voice had a definite American twang. 'I'll have a beer please.'

'Stella?' Ben queried. He already had his hand on the draught pump.

'Nope, I'll have a bottle of Budweiser if you have one?'

'On the cold shelf,' Ben said and turned to get it. He picked up a glass. Again the man shook his head.

'Just snap the top off, friend. I like to drink from the cold bottle. Why spoil it by putting it in a warm glass.'

Ben did as he was asked and pushed the bottle over the counter. The big man took a long pull from the neck of the bottle and then smacked his lips with satisfaction. He looked at Ben and Judy and then at the two men beside him.

'I'm Harry,' he introduced himself to all of them.

Harry in the Hawaiian shirt suddenly grinned. 'No,' he said. 'I'm Harry.'

The white-bearded man looked puzzled and then understood. 'Hey, so you're Harry too?'

'Harry Avery,' Harry Avery said.

'Harry Barlow.' The newcomer said and the two of them shook hands, both of them grinning as though having the same name was somehow the biggest joke in the world.

'Ben Kane,' Ben said. 'My wife Judy.'

They reached over the bar for more hand-shaking. Harry Barlow remembered to fish into his pocket for a ten euro note to pay for his beer. Harry Avery pushed his hand away.

'This one's on me. I can't let another Harry buy his own beer.'

'Well, cheers,' Harry Barlow raised his bottle and drank deeply.

Judy smiled. 'If you're all going to be pals I guess we'll have to tag you somehow to tell you apart.'

Ben grinned and recited: 'Tweedledum and Tweedledee, Harry A and Harry B.'

The two fat Harrys looked at each other. 'Hell,' Harry Barlow said, 'Do we really look like characters out of Alice in Wonderland?'

Harry Avery looked down ruefully at his stomach, then at Harry Barlow's identical paunch. 'I guess we do,' he said and laughed. They clinked beer glass and Budweiser bottle together, both said 'Cheers,' and drank to it.

'Just arrived?' Harry Avery asked.

Harry Barlow nodded and jerked a finger to point back over his shoulder. 'That's my boat opposite, the *Apache*. I always moor up as near as I can to a bar.'

Harry Avery turned to look and nodded approvingly. 'Nice boat. Where are you from?'

'Born and bred in good old Boston, Massachusetts, but I came up yesterday from Malaga and got in this morning. I made a late start so I laid up overnight in a little cove. Harbours can get noisy, so sometimes I like to sleep over where it's nice and peaceful.'

Harry Avery was still looking at the *Apache*. He said enviously, 'Did you sail her across the pond?'

'You mean the Atlantic? Sure. We had good weather and made good time, Boston to Cherbourg France in eight days.'

'Did you do that alone?'

'Hell, no, too much like hard work. My daughter and her boy-friend crewed for me. They stayed with me to bring the yacht round into the Mediterranean but then they left me at Malaga. They're students, doing the gap year thing. They're back-packing around Europe, and then planning to move on to India and South East Asia.'

'Sounds good,' Ben looked at Judy. 'Maybe we should have done that before we settled down and bought the Pina Colada.'

'The *Conquistador*,' she corrected him automatically. Then she added half seriously, 'Maybe we could do it later. We need another dream now for our next retirement.'

Ben glanced at her and smiled. The idea appealed to him too.

Harry Avery asked Harry Barlow, 'Are you staying long in Porto Viejo?'

'Haven't yet made up my mind,' the American answered. 'I've got a couple of months to play around this side of the Atlantic. I'll take a break then maybe move on. I need to take on a deckhand before I do too much.'

'I know a few people,' Harry Avery said. He looked at Ben and Judy, 'I'm planning to teach these two for a start.'

'I keep telling you,' Judy said firmly. 'We've only just opened. We can't take too much time off yet. Maybe later we'll take on some more staff.'

Harry Avery shrugged and then took another long look at the *Apache*. 'About thirty-five feet,' he guessed, 'Sixty square metres of sail or thereabouts and built for speed.'

'Thirty six feet,' Harry Barlow said proudly. 'Sixty eight square metres with all sail, and she loves the wind.'

'I've got the *Seagull Two*, on the other side of the harbour. We'd be a fair match. Maybe we could race sometime, just a short one down the coast.'

The American stared at the Englishman

and decided he was serious. He grinned. 'You're on, buddy. Give me a couple of days and I'll race you for a crate of Budweiser.'

'Make it two.'

'Done.'

They shook hands on it.

They spent the next ten minutes swapping the technical details for *Apache* and *Seagull Two*. Finally Harry Avery remembered that he had already planned a day sailing. He finished his beer and he and Arturo left. Harry Barlow tried to buy another round of drinks but was cheerfully refused.

'Next time, old buddy,' Harry Avery said as they parted. 'If I drink any more the cops could nail me for reckless sailing, cruising under the influence, or whatever they call it out here.'

The white-bearded American let them go and called for another Budweiser for himself. Ben served it. Judy had been called away by other customers at the tables but at the first opportunity she came back.

'You said you came up from Malaga,' she opened the conversation again. 'Did you see a boat down there named *Wave Dancer*? She's owned by an English couple, Jane and Peter Shepherd. They had your berth but they left yesterday.'

Harry Barlow thought for a minute and

then shook his head. 'I can't say that I did. But there are a lot of boats in Malaga harbour. If they only sailed yesterday then they could have arrived after I left, or I might have passed them on the way. You see quite a few sails along this coastline.'

He seemed to hold her gaze for longer than was necessary and the pause for thought had also been prolonged. It left Judy with the same uneasy feeling that she had first experienced with Harry Avery. One of her prime assets in her old job was being able to sense instinctively when someone was lying to her, or when they were not telling the whole truth. Now she again wondered if the man in front of her was putting on some kind of an act.

9

Six days after *Wave Dancer* had sailed Judy became concerned. Jane Shepherd had talked as though she expected to be back in Porto Viejo within four or five days. She was now up to forty-eight hours overdue. The two women had exchanged mobile telephone numbers before they parted and Judy tried giving her friend a call. There was no answer.

Judy tried twice more throughout the day. The following day she called again but still there was no response. *Wave Dancer* was now three days overdue.

Judy stared at her mobile phone and frowned. It was possible she had keyed in the wrong number, but her old job had taught her to be efficient and precise when taking notes and she did not usually make such mistakes. It was possible that Jane had given her the wrong number but again it was unlikely. Judy had a mental picture of *Wave Dancer* gliding serenely out of the harbour with Jane waving and Blondie Dave and Luis on board as short term deckhands. Judy knew that she might be worrying unnecessarily but she was worried.

She had walked into the patio corner of the yard to make her call and sat at the table where she and Ben usually took their coffee break. She fished into the pocket of her shorts and took out the card which Miguel had given her. He had asked her to call if she was able to think of anything more that might be helpful about Georgie. This had no connection but she wanted to believe that Miguel was a friend and that he might be able to help. She made up her mind and keyed in his number.

He answered immediately, his voice crisp and business-like. 'Hello, Inspector Garcia.'

Judy's heart sank a little, responding directly with name and rank meant that he was probably in his office, up to his ears in official paperwork and dealing with official calls only.

'Hello, Miguel, it's Judy Kane.'

'Hello, Judy,' his voice warmed which was encouraging. Then he went on directly, 'I am sorry, there is no news yet on your friend Georgie. That in itself tells us that she was not here on some innocent vacation. If she had been staying in a hotel, staying with friends, or even renting an apartment or a villa, then someone would have missed her. No matter how private she wanted to be someone should have noticed her. She would have to pay rent, buy groceries, pass neighbours, and yet no one has come forward.'

'It does all point toward some sort of clandestine operation,' Judy agreed. 'But this time I'm not calling about Georgie. I'm not even sure if I should be calling you at all, but I don't know anyone else who might be able to help me.'

'What is the problem?' His voice was curious and only a degree cooler.

'I'm worried about some friends of mine,' Judy took the plunge. 'Their names are Jane and Peter Shepherd. They have a boat named *Wave Dancer*. They sailed a week ago to visit some friends in Malaga. They should have been back three days ago but they haven't returned. I keep calling Jane's number but there is no answer.'

There was a moment of silence as though Miguel was thinking. Then he said slowly. 'It could be nothing. The tourist boats have no fixed itinerary. Their owners may decide to stay longer in one place than they first intended, or they may leave sooner. Sometimes they find a port to their liking, or with more attractions than they expected. Or they may meet new friends. They are usually free to come and go as they please.'

'So why isn't she answering her mobile phone?'

'Perhaps she has forgotten to charge up the batteries. Perhaps she has lost it or dropped it overboard. These things happen.'

'Of course, I'm sorry to have wasted your time.'

There was another thinking pause before Miguel said slowly, 'No, Judy, you were a professional police officer, I do not think you would waste my time. There must have been something more to cause your concern.'

Judy hesitated. 'There was something,' she admitted. 'They sailed with two deckhands, two men that I personally didn't like. One of them started a fight with Ben here at the *Conquistador*.'

'What were their names?'

'One was called Blondie Dave, he was English. He's the one who had the fight with Ben. The other was his friend, a Spanish boy called Luis.'

The pause was a little longer this time, indicating perhaps some more serious thinking. 'Judy,' Miguel said at last. 'I think we should meet to discuss this further. Can you give me an hour to make some phone calls to Malaga and then meet with me?'

'Yes, of course. Where do you want to meet?'

'I am busy this morning and I know you have your bar to run. Perhaps we could meet half way. At the other end of the harbour there is a small plaza, it is opposite the Fishermen's dock. There is a statue there of a fishermen and an anchor. Perhaps we could meet on one of the benches, in the shade of the palm trees.'

'I can make that, no problem.'

'I will see you in an hour. Perhaps I will have some news after I have telephoned Malaga.'

Miguel closed the call. Judy put her phone back into her pocket and returned to the bar. She had to serve a couple of customers to catch up and then found the opportunity to tell Ben that she would have to go out to meet Miguel. Inevitably he asked why. Judy explained. Ben continued to hold her gaze as if challenging her to look away first. Judy decided that this was a silly contest and turned her attention to polishing the beer pump.

'Miguel,' Ben said carefully. 'He's the good-looking guy, the Spanish caballero, a bit flash, looks as though he should have been a bullfighter?'

'He is not flash, what makes you say that?'

'The sunglasses perched on top of his head, the white shirt always with two buttons unfastened, just enough to show off the golden chain and his hairy chest.'

'Ben,' she stared at him and laughed, hoping it did not sound hollow. 'You can't be jealous?'

'I've noticed that it's Miguel, not Inspector Garcia. So why does he want to meet you in the plaza. Last time he came here.'

'Perhaps he just doesn't want anyone else to overhear whatever it is he might want to talk about. He's a police officer working on solving a crime. You don't do that by making public everything you think.'

'So, you could talk again in the yard.'

'He's busy. So are we. The fishermen's plaza is a half way point.'

Ben still looked doubtful but suddenly he smiled. 'Sorry, Jude,' he said ruefully. 'I guess I am getting jealous. Having to watch you being chatted up by all sorts of strange men is another new thing I have to learn to cope with.'

She kissed him briefly on the cheek. 'Don't think I haven't noticed that most of the young women prefer to be served by you. I guess its all part of running a bar, something we both have to get used to.'

Ben nodded although his smile looked a little forced. Nothing more was said and when she left to meet Miguel he gave her a wry wave. She blew him another kiss and went out.

It took only a few minutes to reach the far end of the harbour. There she found a stone bench shaded by palm trees on the edge of the small plaza and sat down to wait. The life-size bronze fisherman was holding his anchor upright and looking toward the empty berths along the fishermen's dock. The fishing fleet had sailed, including the *Serrano* now that Captain Pedro's nets had been returned.

Judy studied the pleasure boats that filled the rest of the harbour and then stared at the gap through the rough stone blocks of the harbour walls to the open blue sea. She was still looking for *Wave Dancer* to return but she looked in vain. She was still staring seaward when Miguel arrived and sat on the bench beside her.

He sat close, their thighs and shoulders touching, but she did not feel inclined to move away. She wasn't sure whether she welcomed the closeness or whether she was just being obstinate because Ben had been jealous. Miguel folded his arms but she was aware of the hardness of his biceps and thigh muscles, and those links of gold chain in the wisps of dark hair at his chest and throat. She wondered whether Ben had any cause to mistrust her, whether she could trust herself.

'I have spoken to the harbour master at Malaga,' Miguel said quietly. 'There is no record of a yacht named *Wave Dancer* taking up a berth there. I have also telephoned all the harbours between here and Malaga. Your friends and their vessel have not been seen anywhere.'

'What does that mean?' Judy suddenly forgot how close they were sitting as a new sense of alarm washed over her like a cold wave.

'It means they have vanished, the yacht has disappeared.'

'How can that happen? We have not had any storms.'

'The Mediterranean is usually a calm sea,' Miguel agreed. 'And certainly we have not seen any severe weather along this coastline over the past month. But yachts do disappear.'

He lowered his voice and said quietly, 'In the past twelve months four yachts have disappeared into the Mediterranean. A Spanish yacht, the *Catalan* sailed from Alicante, a British yacht named the *Oyster Catcher* sailed from Malaga, *Vagabond* sailed from here in Porto Viejo, the French yacht *Celeste* sailed from Marseilles in France, but she was believed to be heading down into

Spanish waters. None of these vessels have been seen again. This is why I took your concern seriously and made my enquiries.'

Judy stared at him. 'What do you think happened to them?'

'They were all large, expensive sea-going yachts, rich boy's toys you might say, none of them were worth less than one hundred thousand of your British pounds sterling.'

'So you are saying there is some kind of piracy racket, someone is stealing these boats and selling them on.'

'Piracy is what happens in the South China Seas,' Miguel said wryly. 'Here we have another name for it. We call it yacht-jacking. It happens here in the Mediterranean, and in the coastal waters around the United States. Yachts vanish at sea. We presume they have been hi-jacked. Somewhere they are re-fitted, repainted and given a new name, together with a new set of papers and a forged sales history, and then they are re-sold. It must be a very lucrative business.'

'What happens to the real owners and their crews?'

Miguel shrugged. 'The seas are wide and deep, they swallow up anything that goes overboard.'

Judy felt the cold chill settling in the pit of her stomach. 'You think this could have happened to *Wave Dancer*?'

Miguel nodded. '*Catalan* vanished twelve months ago. Three months later *Oyster Catcher* went missing. Six months ago it was *Celeste's* turn. Three months later *Vagabond* sailed and never returned. Now it seems that perhaps *Wave Dancer* has met the same fate. The disappearances seem to be regularly spaced. A yacht is lost somewhere in the Mediterranean at intervals of roughly every three months.'

Judy sat silent, finding it hard to believe as she stared out at the picture postcard view of the harbour. Everything looked so idyllic, a holiday world of lazy luxury where sun-bronzed people laughed and played and enjoyed themselves. She could see couples and small groups sunning themselves and sipping drinks as they lounged across the decks and cabin roofs of some of the nearest boats. On one deck two older men in shorts and sailor caps were patiently playing chess, on another a young couple cuddled and kissed and then moved out of sight into the cockpit and presumably down into the cabin for a more private display of affection.

It was difficult to believe that behind all of this there might be unseen shadows of cold-blooded piracy and brutal murder.

'We know the two English boats had taken

on extra crewmen before they sailed,' Miguel said quietly. 'Perhaps the others did the same but we have no definite information. We know that *Oyster Catcher* had taken on board two deckhands who were said to be working their way along the coast, but we have no descriptions. *Vagabond* took on board one short term deckhand, possibly English, or at least he spoke English very well. He was described as a young man, in his early twenties, well built with blonde hair.'

'Blondie Dave,' Judy said automatically. 'The description fits Blondie Dave.'

'He is one of the two men who sailed with your friends?'

Judy nodded. 'His friend is a dark haired Spanish boy named Luis.' She was thinking back to the night of the fight and remembered how several of her other customers had remonstrated with Luis. 'I think he's a local boy. When Dave had the fight with Ben, Pedro and some of the other fishermen started telling Luis off, I think they were friends of his father.'

'You speak of Pedro who is the captain of the *Serrano*?'

'Yes.'

'I will speak to him. Tell me exactly what happened on that night.'

Judy described the incident as well as she

could remember it. Miguel listened without interruption and finally said, 'I know these girls, Maria and Conchita, I will speak with them too.'

There seemed to be nothing more to say but now there was something else niggling at the back of Judy's mind.

'Can you give me another minute?' She asked. 'I need to make a phone call.'

Miguel nodded and leaned back on the bench to wait. Judy found her phone and called Sally Russell.

'Jude,' Sally said as soon as she recognized her voice. 'What's the latest on Georgie?'

'There isn't much to tell you,' Judy admitted. She was conscious of Miguel listening and tried to be tactful. 'The police enquiries at this end haven't received any response. Nobody has yet come forward with any real information. But I do have another question to ask.'

'Fire away, I'll do anything I can to help.'

'I seem to remember Georgie talking once about being invited to go sailing with some friends. Did she ever do that? Was she into yachts and sailing and stuff?'

'Yes,' the answer was positive. 'One of her pals in the Met had a small boat somewhere on the south coast, Littlehampton or somewhere like that. Georgie used to go down there quite a lot, most of her weekends I think. She got into yachting and sailing in a big way. You know Georgie, she was into anything healthy and active. She took to it like a duck to water. She could never afford a boat of her own but she crewed for several different people.'

'Thanks, Sal. I know I'm making a bad habit of this but I promise I'll ring back and talk later, right now I have to ring off.'

She closed the phone and turned back to Miguel. 'Georgina Harrington had taken up sailing,' she told him. 'She always played hard at anything that interested her. I wouldn't doubt that she made a good sailor.'

Miguel digested the information in thoughtful silence.

'She could have been mixed up in this yacht-jacking business,' Judy said impatiently. 'We've assumed that she must have been involved in some undercover drug-busting operation, but maybe we were on the wrong track.'

'Not necessarily. The drug-running and the yacht hi-jacking are not mutually exclusive. I do not think there could be two major criminal organizations operating out of Porto Viejo. If the centre is here then the same criminals could be involved in both crimes.'

They talked some more but now there was

little left to exchange. Miguel finally thanked her and promised to keep in touch. 'I have more to think about and new avenues of investigation to follow,' he told her as he left. 'I have much to do but this has been a useful talk.'

Judy watched him stride purposefully back up the avenue toward the *Policia Nationale* building and then sat for a while deep in thought.

In her mind's eye she could see Helen and Jenny in their skimpy bikinis, lazing and sun-bathing on the decks of *Seagull Two*. Harry Avery obviously made a habit of picking up lovely young women to act as his crewmates and now she knew that Georgie had been an accomplished yachtswoman.

★ ★ ★

Later that night, as darkness fell, *Wave Dancer* was holding a position close to the North African coast. The sunset lingered briefly over a spit of land that pointed now like an ominous black finger into the sea. The horizon blazed gold and red, softened into orange and purple and then the colours faded. The silhouette of the small peninsular merged into the night.

Blondie Dave stood at the wheel in the

small cockpit of the yacht with Luis waiting nervously beside him. The sails were furled and the auxiliary engine was running just enough to hold the yacht's position in the slow heaving sea. There was a light breeze carrying faint and distant sounds and smells from the shore. They heard a goat bleat and smelled wood smoke and burned meat. They were drifting too close and Dave turned the wheel and steered them away from the land. They had to stay close to the peninsula which was their rendezvous landmark and their nerves were on edge. They were in danger of running aground or of being discovered by the wrong people.

'Take the wheel,' Dave ordered Luis.

He handed over control of the boat and climbed up on to the roof of the fore cabin. He stood as high as he could with one hand on the mast. In the other he held a small flashlight. He waited, staring along the darkened coastline to the east. The lights of Algiers were too distant to be seen. There were hardly any lights to be seen at all, just a few pale winking glimmers among the low hills along the coast. At sea there was nothing.

The waiting was the worst part of the whole business. He was scared but he tried not to let it show, acting with his usual bravado. However, he didn't think Luis was fooled. Luis was scared silly and there was no way he could hide it. He was chain-smoking now to keep his jittery hands steady. Only the promise of big money kept him in place and he was probably praying for this stage of the job to be quickly over.

At last the expected light flashed out at sea, then a second light, one lantern held above another. Dave felt his heart beat faster, pointed his flashlight and turned it on and off three times. The lower of the two distant lights went out, the other returned three flashes. Dave counted up to ten seconds and then answered with two flashes. He counted again up to fifteen seconds and then saw the final flash.

They waited again until the Algerian fishing boat loomed up in the night beside them. The boat was sturdy and squat, constructed of wooden planks and timbers, there was a number painted on her bows but no name and a single box wheelhouse amidships. She wallowed clumsily beside the sleek, fibreglass shell of the yacht.

There were three men on her deck and a fourth in the wheelhouse. The brown-faced Arabs all looked tense and dangerous. The elaborate signal code had not fully reassured them. Two of them held black-nosed automatic handguns, just in case this was a trap, and all of them had ugly curved knives stuck into the rope belts at their waists. Two of them wore the loose-flowing Arab *burnouse*. The third wore shorts and a dirty grey vest.

'*Salaam*,' Blondie Dave said. His dry voice sounded like a croak and he held up both hands, one in the sign of peace, the other just to show that he was unarmed.

Luis managed a limp wave and a weak grin.

The crew of the fishing boat studied the yacht for a moment, staring hard into its corners and shadows until they were satisfied that the two men were alone. Then they answered the greetings and the grins. Two lines were quickly passed between the two boats, hauled close and made secure. The fishing boat had old bald car tyres slung as bumpers along her hull and *Wave Dancer* was temporarily held snug against them. Once a valuable package had been mishandled and dropped between the two boats. Now no chances were taken.

The exchange took place swiftly. A jute sack was passed from the fishing boat to the yacht. Dave opened the neck and counted the plastic wrapped white packages inside. Then he stabbed one with a small penknife, poked a finger inside the cut and tasted the white powder as he had been told. He was sweating because the three Arabs were watching with contemptuous disapproval. The taste was right and he nodded and smiled. If the taste had been wrong he would probably have nodded and smiled anyway. He would have been too scared to do anything else.

Luis passed over a black leather briefcase which was quickly taken into the wheelhouse. There it was opened and the thick bundles of notes inside were counted. The briefcase came back empty. There were smiles all round. Two more jute sacks were passed into the yacht and the transaction was satisfactorily completed. The lines were slipped and the two vessels drifted apart.

There were brief farewells and 'Salaams.' This was not a social event and both parties were now in a hurry. The fishing boat got under way and headed back the way it had come along the Algerian coastline. She left behind a stench of diesel fumes and the tang of rotting fish. She would now go on her lawful way and make an honest catch before returning to her home port.

Dave started up Wave Dancer's engine and headed out into the Mediterranean while Luis carried the three jute sacks down into the cabin and hid them below. He set a course north-north-west back towards Porto Viejo. The wind was behind him and as soon as Luis reappeared he ordered him to set the sails. He wanted to be safely out of Algerian territorial waters as quickly as possible.

After a while he allowed himself a sigh of relief. He knew these exchanges at sea were the most dangerous part of the whole operation. That was why Harry never took part and never used his own yacht. Harry was smart. Dave and Luis and a hi-jacked yacht were expendable. Dave guessed that if they were ever caught by the police then it was unlikely that he and Luis would ever live long enough to see a trial. Harry would find a way to reach them. Harry was that kind of man.

But Harry paid well and eventually Blondie Dave intended to cut and run to South America, as soon as he was rich enough for the money to last for the rest of his life.

So far it had all gone as planned.

Harry would be pleased.

10

After Miguel had left her Judy wandered over to the edge of the harbour. She was deep in thought and stared out at the packed ranks of moored boats tied up to the long pontoons. She read the bright, jaunty names on the rows of neat bows and heart-shaped sterns but they meant nothing to her. The names in her mind were *Catalan, Vagabond, Oyster Catcher* and *Celeste*, and now *Wave Dancer*. She wondered which proud name from this floating world of soft-living luxury would be the next.

Her gaze fell on one boat in particular and lingered. The yacht was *Seagull Two*. There was no sign of Harry Avery or of anyone else on board. The decks and cockpit were silent and deserted. She could not have said why, it was that inexplicable intuition kicking in again, but somehow she sensed that *Seagull Two* was the yacht least likely to go missing.

She needed more time to think, away from the distractions of serving up beers and coffees and mixing up the endless jugs of sangria. She turned away from the harbour and walked past the south beach. Without any

173

conscious decision her route led her up the steep path to the castle ruins on the cliff. There were tourists here, clicking cameras while their children played hide and seek around the broken walls. Judy moved further along the cliff to find a quiet spot and sat on a large rock looking out to sea.

She was frustrated with her inability to do anything. Georgie was dead. Peter and Jane Shepherd were possibly dead. She wanted to find out why. Miguel seemed glad of her help but she was sure he was not taking her fully into his confidence. She was excluded now that she was no longer a serving police officer. She had thought she could turn her back on her old world and make a new start here with a new way of life but with this mystery staring her in the face the escape to the sun just wasn't working.

She thought again about Harry Avery. She instinctively distrusted the fat man and she was sure he had something to hide. Harry used his yacht as a sex ticket and invited pretty young girls to act as his crew, and for someone like Georgina that would be the easy way into his world.

Judy thought long and hard and then she resorted again to her mobile phone. She put a call through to England, to Breckland CID. Her old boss, the man in command of the serious crimes team was Superintendent Charles Grant. She knew he thought highly of her, but he would also be too busy to hand out favours. Her usual investigating partner had been Detective Inspector Ron Harding, a tough no-nonsense copper who had initially resented being teamed with a woman. They had eventually learned to respect each other and she believed he had been genuinely sorry when she had decided to leave. When her call was answered she asked for Harding.

'Hello, Jude,' he seemed pleased to hear her voice. Then he threatened, 'If you've called to gloat about all that sex in the sunshine I'll hang up. It's bloody raining here again.'

'I promise not to gloat. How are you, Ron?'

'Over-worked and under-paid, situation normal.' She could picture him grinning and leaning back at his desk, his jacket off and a necktie as garish as one of Harry Avery's shirts hanging loose at his open neck. 'Why are you calling, Jude? Tell me you've called to say you love me. That fool Ben has run off with a younger woman and you want me to come out there and help you manage that nice little bar in Porto Viejo.'

'Not yet, but I do need some help.' With Harding it was always best to get straight to the point.

'What sort of help?'

She told him about Georgina Harrington's body being fished out of the sea and the disappearance of *Wave Dancer*. She kept it brief, only adding that the local police suspected some major drug smuggling involvement and that the yacht hi-jacking might be linked.

'Trust you to find yourself a murder enquiry,' Harding said. 'We haven't had a juicy murder here in Granchester since you left.' He paused and then added seriously, 'But it's not your job any more, Jude.'

'I know. That's what Ben keeps telling me. But Georgie was an old friend and she was one of us. Jane and Peter were new friends. Something nasty is happening here and I just can't ignore it.'

'So what do you want from me?'

'There's an ex-pat out here that I need to check out. He calls himself Harry Avery. He has a yacht called the *Seagull Two*. He's from the East End of London, but he's deliberately vague about exactly where and when. It's possible he was in the used car trade. He's a fat man but hard and fat, about fifty, a very flashy dresser. He has a fistful of rings and jewellery on each hand. He's about five feet eight inches tall, and he has a bald head.'

She could hear the faint scratch of a pen as

176

Harding scribbled it all down. She finished by saying, 'You were in the Met for a while before you came to Granchester. You must have some old contacts. Could you check this guy out and see if he has any background.'

'Will do,' Harding said. 'I'm in court this afternoon, witness in another petty thieving case, but I've just got time to make some computer checks and some phone calls before I go. If I get anything I'll come back to you.'

'Thanks, Ron. It's appreciated.'

'It's for old times' sake. Plus, of course, I'll expect free drinks all round when I bring the wife and kids to Porto Viejo for our holidays.'

'Make it soon.'

Harding laughed and rang off.

Judy put the phone back in her pocket. She felt better now that she had at least tried to do something and realized that it was unfair on Ben and Isabella to leave them doing all the work. She headed down the cliff path and back into Porto Viejo, aiming for the *Conquistador*.

She was half way along the harbour, walking on the opposite side of the promenade where the restaurants and cafes and their multi-coloured pavement umbrellas threw some shade, when she saw two men she recognized. They were standing with their backs toward her on the harbour's edge, looking over the boats. The promenade and two rows of palm trees were between her and the two men and they had not noticed her.

One of them was Arturo, the *Bombero* fire chief. He was obviously off duty again in shorts and a tee shirt. The second man was her *tapas* chef, Isabella's husband Antonio. They were talking together with the relaxed stance of old friends.

Judy hesitated for a moment and watched them. Isabella had always been the bright and chatty one with a good command of English. Antonio spoke only Spanish so Judy had never been able to talk with him directly. He was a thin unobtrusive man in his late twenties who was always in the background and seemed ill-matched with the voluble and bubbly Isabella. However, he was an excellent cook and a good worker, always willing to leave his kitchen and collect glasses when the bar was busy.

Judy hurried on but now there were more questions whirling around in her head. She was suspicious of Harry and that made her suspicious of his friend Arturo. Now there was a link between Arturo and Antonio.

She mentioned it casually to Isabella when she returned to the *Conquistador*. Isabella glanced at her wristwatch and answered calmly. 'Oh, he will be here in five minutes, he is not yet late.'

'I didn't know Antonio and Arturo were friends,' Judy remarked. 'Fire-fighting and cooking doesn't seem to give them much in common.'

'They were at school together, I think.' Isabella seemed unflustered and as always there was another customer waiting to be served.

The explanation was plausible enough. Porto Viejo was a small town and Judy guessed that most of the locals would have some sort of links, through extended family, schools or neighbours. She let it go but continued to ponder.

★ ★ ★

She waited twenty four hours for Harding to call back but then it was Miguel who called first. Again he wanted to see her and this time he asked her to come to the *Policia Nationale*. Ben was dubious when she told him. She could see the doubt in his face and the way his lips tightened briefly, but a visit to the police station was less threatening than a meeting outside so he made no direct comment. She waited for Isabella to arrive and once more left the two of them to run the bar.

The big cream coloured office block was a hive of activity as usual, but the young male police officer directing the human traffic in the wide entrance hall made a quick phone call and within a minute Miguel arrived to escort her back to his office. Judy was intrigued but kept the conversation to the normal pleasantries until the door was closed behind them.

'What is it?' she demanded at last. 'Have you made some sort of breakthrough?'

'Not exactly,' Miguel smiled wryly. 'But I have some film I want you to see.'

He placed his visitor's chair so that it faced the small portable television in the corner and gestured for her to sit down. Judy did so and tried to be patient as he brought his own chair from behind the desk and placed it beside her. He drew the curtains at the window to shut out as much light as possible and then sat down. They were touching again at thigh and elbow. A brief memory flashed in Judy's mind, of Isabella grinning and lewdly holding up a positive thumb. She felt that she ought to move her chair away a few inches but she didn't.

Miguel used a remote control to switch on the TV and she realized that it was already primed with a video. The film that began to show was of an open expanse of sea that had obviously been filmed from the air. The camera work seemed amateur and jerky and the camera was being panned widely from side to side. At first there was nothing to see except blue sea, blue sky and an empty horizon. The film had obviously not been edited in any way.

'This was taken yesterday by one of our coastguard planes,' Miguel confirmed her first guess. 'They can be called out to search for lost ships, or to investigate any vessel that has given us any cause for suspicion. They also make regular patrols, usually flying as close as they can to the North African coast to search for any unusual traffic patterns.'

'They're looking for drug smugglers,' Judy surmised.

'Or illegal immigrants, that is another sad trade which we are obliged to try and stop.'

Judy nodded and they watched in silence for a moment. A small triangle of white sail finally appeared in the top left hand corner of the screen. The camera turned towards it. The sail grew larger and became part of a white-hulled yacht. Miguel said nothing. Judy leaned forward, suddenly tense with anticipation. She knew what was coming. Without realizing she had placed her hand on Miguel's knee, pressing down hard.

The camera zoomed in, seeking identification. The angle was wrong to see the name on the stern but the camera operator panned along the length of the hull. The yacht flashed by swiftly but for a second she saw the name clear on the bows, wavy blue letters over a wavy blue line to represent the sea, *Wave Dancer*.

'That's it,' Judy breathed softly, 'Jane and Peter Shepherd's boat, *Wave Dancer*.'

'Keep watching,' Miguel told her. His shoulder pressed hard against hers as he too leaned forward.

The plane flew on, the camera twisting to stay on the yacht until she was lost from sight. The aircraft banked and turned. Sunlight flashed into the camera lens as the nose lifted, dazzling the two observers and causing them both to blink. Then the glare was gone and the camera picked up the yacht again. Now it was bows on, sailing toward them. As it hurtled closer Judy saw two heads in the cockpit. The camera's powerful zoom lens pulled in to close up once more and it seemed as though they passed within yards of two stiff-set and horrified faces.

One was Luis, his jaw sagging and his mouth hanging open. The other was Blondie Dave, tight-lipped but looking equally scared. Dave was at the wheel, holding the boat into the wind, letting it fill her sails and push her along at a fair rate of knots.

Within seconds the faces and the yacht were gone and there was only empty sea as the plane sped on its way. Miguel clicked the remote to stop the film, rewound it and played it again.

'Did you recognize the two men?' he asked when the screen went blank again.

Judy nodded, turning her face to look at him in the half darkness. 'One of them is called Luis, he's a local boy. The other they call Blondie Dave. They are the two I told you about. They caused the trouble in the *Conquistador*. Then they sailed with *Wave Dancer* as deckhands. Their jobs were supposed to be short term, just down to Malaga and back because Peter Shepherd had pulled a shoulder muscle.'

'Luis we know something about. His full name is Luis Alonso Lorca. His father was a small boat fisherman who died about two years ago. His widowed mother lives in a small house in the old town. He is an only child, spoiled and lazy. He lives with his mother but sometimes uses his father's old boat which is still moored in the harbour. We think the man you call Blondie Dave is his guest who sleeps rough on the boat. I learned all this from Pedro, the trawler captain who

183

was a friend of his father. It was confirmed by Maria, the prostitute who works the harbour front.'

He paused and then finished. 'It seems that Luis always has enough money to spend, although he does no work. Blondie Dave also seems to have enough for his needs although he chooses to sleep on the old boat. I suspect that he continues to give the appearance of a down and out bum so that he does not arouse suspicion.'

'So we are getting somewhere,' Judy said. She looked back at the blank screen of the television. 'Where was the film taken?'

'The film was shot late yesterday afternoon, in the middle of the Mediterranean, about halfway between here and Algiers. It is hard to tell with sailboats which have to tack with the wind, but my guess is that she has sailed down to North Africa and is now returning to Spain, possibly back to Porto Viejo.'

'So she did not go to Malaga.'

'No, my guess is that she has been used to pick up a consignment of illegal drugs, or possibly human immigrants. If it is people they would be kept in hiding down in the cabin.'

'And Jane and Peter?'

Judy knew the answer but she had to ask.

Her voice trembled a little and she suddenly shivered.

Miguel put his arm around her shoulders. It was a comfort gesture, something she had often done in her early days as a traffic patrol officer. She had dealt with trapped casualties in a variety of road accidents and the human touch was always the best form of reassurance. She thought nothing of it now and did not pull away.

'Jane and Peter could be alive, perhaps tied up down in the cabin. But I very much doubt it. There would be no point. The owners always disappear completely and there could be no reason to delay.'

Judy shivered again and Miguel squeezed her gently.

'What happens now?' she asked.

'When they reappear in Spain's territorial waters we can board the yacht and arrest them. The patrol plane made one pass and then had to return to re-fuel so we have lost them overnight. However, their heading looked to be Porto Viejo. We will find them again.'

'It's a big sea. They saw the plane. They could have changed their heading for anywhere along the coast, or turned back. You were lucky to find them the first time.'

'Not just luck perhaps. Our Coastguard

does keep a regular watch on the sea traffic between here and North Africa. Thanks to you we knew that *Wave Dancer* had gone missing.'

Miguel's arm was still around her shoulders, lingering far too long for a purely professional act of reassurance. Judy knew that she should pull away but she didn't want to. His voice had become slightly husky and she knew that he too found her attractive. She felt just a little bit weak and giddy, feelings she had not felt since her teens and her first dates with Ben. There was a chemical magnetism working that she could not resist. She looked into his face and tried to read his eyes.

For a moment she thought that he was going to kiss her. The air in the room seemed to vibrate with the undercurrent of sexual tension. She realized that she had pressed her hand on his thigh and she had not moved away when he had leaned close beside her. She had encouraged him and she held her breath in anticipation.

Miguel drew a deep breath and then stood up and moved to the window. He pulled back the curtains to let daylight flood into the room. He stood with his back to her and she knew the moment was past and she was not sure whether she was glad or sorry.

11

Blondie Dave felt a huge sense of relief when the daylight finally faded and darkness covered the Mediterranean Sea. The late afternoon and evening had been cloud covered and so tonight there was no spectacular sunset and for that he was glad. Now the clouds hid the moon and stars and the night was as dark as he could hope for. He showed no lights and hardly dared to take his gaze off the compass setting as *Wave Dancer* sailed blind, taking full advantage of the wind.

He and Luis had both been in a panic sweat since the Spanish coastguard plane had flown by them. As far as they knew the pilot could have had no real reason for suspicion but the fact that he had shown an interest had unnerved both of them. Luis had wanted to turn the yacht around and head anywhere out into the Mediterranean but Dave knew that Harry would not easily give up on his consignment of heroin. If they screwed up on Harry he would find them, somewhere, somehow, and if he thought that they had cheated him they would both end up with their throats cut in some dark alley or at the bottom of the sea. The bottom line was that they were more afraid of Harry than they were of the police.

So they held *Wave Dancer* on to her course, scanning the horizons and the sky. They were fearful that the plane would return and dreading at any moment to see a Spanish warship or coastguard cutter racing up to intercept them.

When nightfall mercifully cloaked them and they were still alone both men relaxed a little. They were safer now but they were still tense.

'If they are after us they will wait for us to enter Spanish territorial waters,' Luis said. 'That is when they will board us and arrest us. We dare not go back to Porto Viejo.'

'We were not putting into Porto Viejo anyway,' Dave growled, 'But you're right, we can't go into the twelve mile limit either.'

He frowned and chewed at his lower lip. 'We'll have to call Harry.'

Luis nodded but still looked unhappy.

Dave hunted in his pocket for his mobile phone. A radio signal might be overheard so he did not dare to use the yacht's radio. Instead he said a silent prayer for the man who had invented mobile phones. The prayer turned into a muttered curse of frustration when the call went unanswered. He let it ring for a full minute before Harry spoke and said hello.

Dave explained what had happened and finished with a note of desperation. 'We can't come in too close to shore. You'll have to tell the trawler to come well outside the twelve mile limit.'

There was a cold silence while Harry thought about it. Harry definitely did not like any threat or changes to his plans. He said at last, 'You're sure the plane was taking a good look at you? It was not just a chance fly past?'

'Damn it he came back again for a second look. He flew close enough to see our faces.'

'Okay,' Harry said. 'Make it the same time, same signals, but the trawler will be fifteen miles due east of Porto Viejo. I'll call the *Benissa* and tell them. And Dave, find something heavy to weigh down each of those jute sacks and keep them with you in the cockpit. At the first sign of the law the heroin goes straight over the side and straight down to the bottom.'

'Got it,' Dave said. 'We'll do that.'

Harry closed the call.

Dave passed on their instructions to Luis and the Spanish youth set about searching the close confines of the yacht for suitable weights. Eventually he found some full paint and varnish cans and some lengths of anchor chain in one of the storage lockers. The three jute sacks were brought up from the cabin and the weights added. If they ran foul of the authorities the drug trafficking evidence could be quickly abandoned, but Dave was aware that there would still be equally difficult questions to answer. They had no satisfactory explanation for the disappearance of the boat's owners. The knowledge kept him anxious and fretful as they sailed directly toward the Spanish coast.

With every nautical mile the tension grew. The wind stayed brisk and favourable, meaning that they could make good time without having to tack and constantly shift course. The moving pattern of the clouds sometimes left gaps when the starlight brightened the swelling black waves around them and then they both strained their eyes as they tried to probe out to the invisible horizons. There was always a sense of imminent danger when they had to search for a rendezvous but this was the worst they had ever experienced. Not only was the threat of being caught heightened by their earlier sighting of the coastguard plane, there was also the possibility that they would fail to find the *Benissa* now that she had forced to move further out from their shoreline landmarks.

The old castle ruins above Porto Viejo were floodlit at night and normally provided a guide. Now they were too far offshore to see any of the lights along the coast.

The clouds thickened and it began to rain. Dave shivered and his feelings were mixed. The rain blurred everything around them and meant that they would be harder to find if the police were looking for them. It also made it more difficult for them to find the trawler.

Dave had proved himself a fair sailor. He had known nothing about boats when Harry had first hired him as a deckhand, but he had some natural aptitude and he had learned quickly. He was smarter than Luis who had been brought up by the sea and he was automatically the leader of the pair. After two trips Harry had decided that they could be trusted to sail a boat alone, after he had done the initial killings. They were capable of almost anything else that was immoral and illegal but neither Dave nor Luis was capable of cold-blooded murder.

However, Dave's navigational skills were now being sorely tested. He had kept a mental note of his course and speed and every thirty minutes tried to pinpoint his location on the chart. He reckoned he was coming close to fifteen miles offshore somewhere opposite Porto Viejo, which was as close as he wanted to come to Spanish territorial waters, but he could not be sure. The bloody rain was driving hard into his face and he could see nothing except slowly heaving water. He ordered Luis to trim all the sail, letting the boat wallow as he searched and fretted.

Luis came to stand close beside him. Luis's face was pale and frightened, rain droplets dripped from his nose although they might have been tears.

'We cannot find her,' Luis said. 'We should leave now.' The anxiety of the moment was over-ruling his fear of Harry's wrath.

'Not yet,' Dave said stubbornly. He tried to tell himself that he was not just afraid of Harry. He wanted to complete this job because he needed his share of the money. He had promised himself maybe one or two more trips after this. Then he would cut and run. Now he was not so sure about any future trips, but at the very least he had to finish this trip in profit.

Just for a moment he allowed himself a memory. Before embarking on this voyage he had found the time to sober up and take advantage of Maria's offer to give her a call. She had met him on the harbour front and taken him back to a cheap apartment in the Old Town. There she had given him the traditional 'Good Time,' and even though it had cost him double as she had promised he felt that it had been worth it.

He knew that he was just another customer but somehow she had made him feel that she was giving him more than usual, that perhaps somehow he was special. One scornful part of his mind suggested that she was just good at her trade, she didn't keep grudges and she knew that it was in her own interest to keep her customers happy, to keep them coming back for more. However, the loner inside him wanted to believe that she had enjoyed it too, and that she was beginning to see him as someone special. She had told him that next time he need only pay the standard rate.

He could hardly believe his own totally reversed feelings about the girl but he wanted to see her again.

The wind gusted and the rain stung his face harder. *Wave Dancer* was now beginning to pitch and roll heavily enough to make him feel sea sick. Luis was looking positively nauseous. Dave squinted into the pouring darkness again, searching for a light.

Finally they saw them, two lights close together, close enough to be the mast and stern lights of a trawler. They had lost the wind so Dave started the auxiliary engine to bring the yacht closer. The vessel was definitely one of the fishing fleet, but through the curtain of rain streaked blackness neither Dave nor Luis could read the name on her bows. If it was the wrong trawler she might have her nets out and to go too close would risk the yacht getting snarled up.

Dave used his torch and made the signal. There was no response. Either the trawler was not the *Benissa* or the dozy Spaniards who formed her crew were keeping a poor lookout. Dave swore and allowed *Wave Dancer* to close the gap by another fifty yards before he signalled again.

This time there was an answer, two flashes from another torch, the correct pause, then three more flashes.

Dave heaved a sigh of relief and grinned at Luis. Luis grinned back, his face still weak and wet. Dave brought the yacht close alongside the trawler and nudged up to her hull. A rope was thrown from the trawler's deck. Luis caught it and made it fast.

'What the bloody hell is going on?' A barrel-chested deckhand snarled from the *Benissa*'s deck. He was crouching down, speaking in angry Spanish, his face close to Luis, 'Why the change? Why do we have come so far out?'

Luis answered in a gabble that Dave could not follow, at the same time hauling up the heavy sacks and throwing them over to the trawler's deck.

'Careful,' Dave hissed. 'Don't drop them in the bloody sea. We don't want to lose them now.'

More hands were grabbing at the jute sacks, cursing at the unexpected weight and then manhandling them over to the open hatchway where they were unceremoniously dumped inside. A few boxes of fish from a previous catch were quickly tipped over the incriminating cargo.

Luis was still shouting explanations and warnings as he slipped the rope to let the two vessels drift apart. Dave gunned the engine and sped them away, heading the yacht due east away from Spain. The storm was blowing full into his face now but he was prepared to use precious diesel rather than waste time trying to tack into the wind. The transaction was complete and Harry could sort out the rest. Now he just wanted to get lost again in the rain-filled darkness and the open sea.

* * *

It was two days later when Ron Harding finally called back. By then Judy knew that the Spanish police and coastguard had missed their chance to apprehend *Wave*

195

Dancer. The yacht had not put into any Spanish port and the next daylight air contact had spotted her more than a hundred miles out into the Mediterranean and still heading east under full sail. Judy felt frustrated and despondent but the sound of Harding's voice cheered her up a little.

She called Isabella to continue serving the customer for whom she had just pulled a pint of Stella, pretended not to notice Ben's raised eyebrows and took the phone into the yard.

'Right, I've got some peace and quiet,' she told Harding. 'What have you got for me?'

'On one Harry Avery, nothing,' Harding said. 'The name drew a complete blank with the computer and all other records. But a fat man with an East End background and fists full of flashy jewellery, now that was another story. I talked to Tom Hagen, an old pal in the Met, we were detective constables together when we both started in CID. Hagen's got a long history with the East End. He reckons your description could fit Harry Arnold. He's a really nasty villain, dominant around that part of London through the nineties, but then disappeared about three years ago when things got too hot for him. The rumour is that Harry Arnold is hiding out with a load of other criminal ex-pats down Marbella way. But the location could be only guesswork. He could be your man in Porto Viejo.'

'I see,' Judy said softly. 'How close are the descriptions?'

'A fat East End gangster with a taste for flashy clothes who fills his knuckles up with heavy gold rings, that sounds as though it fits your man and Harry Arnold. I'm told Harry Arnold had grey hair, going thin. You said your man was bald, but in three years he could have lost his hair, or gone in for the shaved-dome look.'

'It sounds a good match. What else did you dig up? Was Harry Arnold into drugs?'

'Harry Arnold was into everything, prostitution, illegal immigrant smuggling, porno movies, gambling, drugs, you name it — he had a finger in it somewhere. He did start out in the used car racket, turned it into a stolen car racket before he moved into other things. There were probably a couple of murders along the way, rivals disappearing, that sort of thing, but nothing was ever proved. Harry was clever, he never did time. He came close over the stolen cars back in his early days, but he learned and left that behind. It all sounds as though in the later years he kept his personal involvement to the minimum. He controlled things and let others get their hands dirty.'

'So what made him move to Spain?'

'A big crack-down by the Drug Squad, they netted a couple of Harry's chief lieutenants and a string of small fry. There was nothing they could pin on fat Harry. The two bigger fish went down for a ten year stretch each with mouths glued shut. They've probably got a choice of a Swiss bank account or a pair of concrete boots waiting when they come out. However, it seems the Met made it hot enough for Harry to decide to emigrate.'

'So he's definitely in Spain somewhere and he could have retired here?'

'From what I've heard I don't think he would be fully retired. His kind gets to need more than just the money. They need the prestige, the respect, and they need to be in control.'

Judy saw Ben come out into the yard with two cups of coffee, indicating that there was a lull in trade and Isabella had been left in charge. Antonio had been working over his hot *tapas* dishes in the kitchen but now he came to the doorway for some fresh air and gave her a grin as he wiped sweat from his brow. Judy felt a little crowded and moved away to the patio corner but Ben followed her and sat down where he could listen.

Harding was still talking.

'Jude, you said that all this is probably

mixed up with drugs and perhaps with a couple of yacht hi-jacks. Did you say that your man also owned a yacht?'

'Yes, he has a boat named *Seagull Two*.'

'That name didn't ring any bells, but Tom said that Harry Arnold was something of a sailor. Apparently he had a boat of some sort which he kept on the River Orwell.'

Judy frowned. The River Orwell was ringing bells in her mind. Then she remembered. Jane Shepherd had said that Peter had kept his boat on the River Orwell. Was that significant or was it a coincidence. She tried to remember if the Shepherds had ever been in the *Conquistador* at the same time as Harry Avery. If they had it was probably on the really busy nights when the place had been crowded. She couldn't remember them coming face to face.

'You've gone quiet, Jude,' Harding said.

'Just thinking,' she answered quietly.

'That means trouble for somebody.' She could picture Harding grinning. 'But be careful, Jude, if your Harry Avery is Harry Arnold then you could find yourself in deep trouble. Harry Arnold was an East End gang boss. He had respect, and that means the underworld was afraid of him, with good cause. Just watch yourself.'

'I will. Thanks, Ron. I'll get back to you

when I've had time to digest everything you've told me.'

They closed the conversation and she switched off the phone. Ben was watching her, sipping coffee and looking displeased. He put down his cup and pushed the second cup across the table toward her as she sat down opposite.

'What was all that about?' he demanded bluntly.

Judy knew he had picked up on her mention of *Seagull Two*. Normally they had no secrets and it was something of a relief to tell him. Ben's face hardened as she explained and she knew he was angry. It didn't happen often but he could be like a browsing bull which had suddenly had a red flag waved under its nose. It was happening now and it wasn't the reaction she had hoped for.

'So you've been checking up on Harry,' he accused her. 'Harry's a mate of mine and you've asked Ron Harding to pry into his background.'

'Harry isn't exactly a long term friend,' she protested. 'He's someone you've met only recently and we know nothing about him. The only thing you have in common is that he likes fire engines and you can't stay away from the fire station.'

'He's still a friend, we get on okay. I just

don't understand what you've got against him.'

'He's too evasive. He shies away whenever anyone asks him anything about his background. And he tries to question me. He's not happy with the fact that I was once a cop and he's been trying to dig information out of me. He wants to know what I know about Georgie, and about how far the police are getting with their investigation.'

'Hell,' Ben snorted. 'Everybody wants to know about that. It's all anybody ever talks about in Porto Viejo. A dead mystery woman fished out of the sea, the whole town is buzzing with speculation and gossip.'

'But he is still hiding his past. And just what is behind his relationship with Arturo and the *Bomberos?* Have you ever really stopped to think about that? There must be thousands of men and boys who are fascinated by fire engines but they don't all get the free run of a fire station.'

'So what are you getting at?'

'Think about the hours you worked as a fireman, when I first met you and you were a Sub-officer in charge of a fire-crew. It's a twenty-four hour, seven days a week job. So you worked a day shift for seven days and then you had seven days off. That was followed by a night shift for seven days and another seven days off. The work pattern gave you a lot of free time. Most of your crew mates did other jobs on the side, often driving jobs because you all had a full HGV license with the Fire Brigade.'

'I still don't see where this is going,' Ben objected.

She said patiently, 'If drugs are being shipped into Spain from North Africa they then have to be distributed into Europe, or to the French coast where they could then be shipped into England. Remember that Harry Arnold has big, well established drug connections in London. That's where Arturo and perhaps some of his *Bomberos* could come in, using all that free time to ferry the drugs north from Porto Viejo.'

'This is crazy,' Ben said.

'Maybe, but it's a possible scenario.'

'Have you told all this to your friend Miguel?'

'No, to be honest I've only just thought of it. Ron said that Harry Arnold once kept a boat on the River Orwell. From the Orwell it's just a short trip from England to France. If the drug supply route is from North Africa to Spain by sea and then from France to England by sea then there has to be an overland route to connect the sea links. That's where this relationship with Arturo could fit in.'

'You're letting your imagination run away with you,' Ben said scornfully. 'Harry is okay and so is Arturo. Harry likes fire engines, he's teaching Arturo English and he gives Arturo free trips on his boat, so Arturo makes him welcome at the fire station. That's about as sinister as it gets.'

He paused and saw a chance to get in his own barbed comment, 'If we're looking at new friendships that might be dodgy then what about your relationship with Inspector Garcia? You've said that maybe the Met Drug Squad isn't cooperating fully with the Spanish police because there's no trust there. Some of the high-up Spanish police officers could be in the pocket of the drugs gang. So maybe one of those corrupt Spanish cops is Miguel. That could be why London doesn't trust him and why his enquiries are getting nowhere.'

Judy bit her lower lip. She felt that was a blow under the belt but she couldn't afford to get as angry as Ben. She tried to keep calm and said quietly. 'A tit for tat argument isn't going to get us anywhere. Perhaps I was out of order in asking Ron Harding to dig up the dirt on your friend, but the fact remains that the enquiry has come up positive. Harry Avery does fit the description of an East End gangster named Harry Arnold. Arnold disappeared from London at about the same time that Harry Avery seems to have popped up here, and it is generally believed that Harry Arnold bolted to Spain.'

'Alright,' Ben said belligerently. 'So what exactly was this description that fits so neatly?'

'A fat man of fifty, or thereabout, with a bald head, who likes flashy shirts and wears a fist full of gold rings and jewellery,' Judy said, trying to keep the irritation out of her voice. 'He gives vague hints of an East End past but refuses to be drawn on anything specific.'

'And this matches up in every detail with someone called Harry Arnold?'

'Yes,' Judy snapped too quickly and then corrected herself. 'Well, almost, Harry Arnold had grey hair, but he could have shaved it off or lost it naturally.'

Ben laughed derisively. 'Basically just a fat ex-pat named Harry, and there must be hundreds of them floating around the Costas. Hell, I can see two of them from here.'

Judy twisted round in her chair to follow the direction of his pointing finger. The back door into the kitchen area was still open and in direct line with the doorway that looked into the bar. On the opposite side of the bar counter two of the tall bar stools were now occupied. Isabella was serving two new arrivals with a pint of draught Stella and a bottle of Budweiser from the cold shelf.

'Tweedledum and Tweedledee,' Ben recited, 'Harry A and Harry B. Your East End gangster's hair could just as easily have turned white and he could have grown a beard. And he could be smart enough to dump the flashy clothes and the rings.'

Judy stared at Harry Avery and Harry Barlow as they chatted amiably and toasted each other. She realized that Ben could be right. Her psychic antennae had picked up similar doubts with Harry Barlow. The American accent could be a fake and the baseball cap proclaiming the New York Yankees and the taste for Budweiser beer could be just props.

Suddenly she had a headache.

12

Their disagreement and Ben's sense of betrayal soured the next few days until Judy decided that something had to be done to settle their quarrel. She woke up with the issue on her mind and, with her brain fresh, the solution was suddenly obvious. She jumped up, showered and dressed and then began to hunt through the drawers of her dressing table. She quickly found the digital camera that Ben had given her as a Christmas present. On receiving the gift she had photographed just about every aspect of Porto Viejo, the church, the castle and the harbour. Then she had forgotten it as the first flush of happy snapping had passed and the on-going business of opening the bar had monopolized all her time.

By now Ben was also awake, sitting on the edge of the bed still in his sleeping shorts and watching her.

'What are you planning?' He asked.

'A photo board,' Judy showed him the camera. 'You know the sort of thing, a big cork notice-board full of happy snaps to show everyone who comes in what a marvellous fun time we have here at the *Conquistador*. It's going to have pictures of you and me and Isabella, all smiling and pulling pints of beer. Pictures of all our happy punters with arms round each other's necks and all grinning and holding up glasses. Tonight we've got the trio again so this is a good night to start it off.'

Ben nodded dubious approval but he knew her too well. 'There's something more,' he guessed. 'There's more to this than just pinning up pictures of happy drinkers.'

Judy nodded. She sat beside him and said seriously. 'It gives me an excuse to wave the camera around and take pictures of everyone, and that includes Harry A and Harry B. Once I've got their faces on film I can email them to Ron Harding and he can email them on to his friend in the Met. If either of them is Harry Arnold we should be able to get a positive identification.'

For a moment Ben was quiet, his face thoughtful. Judy felt a squirm of apprehension. She wasn't sure that he would not still be resentful of her continuing suspicion of his new found friend. Then slowly Ben smiled.

'Okay,' he said. 'It's a good idea. We need to settle this. And I'll bet you a wild night in bed that Harry A turns out to be innocent.'

'A wild night in bed,' Judy raised her

eyebrows. 'How does a bet like that work, exactly?'

'If I win you have to give me a wild night in bed,' Ben explained solemnly. 'If you win I swallow my manly pride and I have to give you a wild night in bed.'

'I think there's a flaw in there somewhere,' Judy said, 'but I'm not going to look for it.' Her idea was half working already and she kissed him to seal the bargain.

★ ★ ★

By ten o'clock that night the *Conquistador* was crowded and the music was in full swing. The trio were giving their best as always, with Perez and Jaime resplendent in frilled orange shirts, tight-fitting black and silver pants and Mexican sombreros. Dolores wore scarlet again as she twirled and sang, her dark eyes flashing and her dark tresses flying, and looking the perfect example of a lusty gypsy beauty.

The drink flowed faster than the food, keeping Antonio busy in the kitchen making endless jugs of sangria. Ben, Isabella and Judy manned the beer pumps. Judy began to think that she would never get away from the endless task of filling beer glasses but eventually there was a brief lull when nobody was trying to attract her attention. She grabbed the opportunity and her camera and quickly slipped away from behind the bar.

Harry Avery had come in half an hour ago and was sitting on one of the bar stools with a drink in his hand but she didn't want to snap him straight away. First she wanted to set the stage by taking pictures of the trio and some general shots around the tables. It gave her the chance to explain what she was doing and, hopefully, to allay his suspicions.

She photographed the trio first. She had already told them what she intended and they were happy to oblige, posing and waving for the camera. Then she began to shoot the couples and groups around the bar, coaxing them into raising their glasses, pulling faces and exchanging kisses.

'It's for a picture board,' she explained brightly as she circulated. 'We're going to pin all the photos up on a board.'

The response was positive from her regulars and visitors. No one objected. She came back to the bar and took pictures of Ben and Isabella at the pumps, together and separately. She was shooting over Harry Avery's shoulder but he did not turn around to look at her. Finally she went behind the bar again. She stopped opposite Harry and raised the camera.

'You too, Harry,' she said cheerfully.

'No thanks,' Harry half turned his face away and raised a large meaty hand so that only his palm filled the lens.

'Hey, come on, Harry, we can't leave you out.'

'No,' Harry repeated stubbornly. 'I don't particularly like having my picture taken. I don't make a good picture. I always manage to look crosseyed.'

'It doesn't matter. In here everyone looks cross-eyed.' Judy tried to move his hand away with her free hand, keeping the camera pointed. Harry swivelled on his stool and turned his back toward her.

'I said no,' he spoke over his shoulder, keeping his face away from her. 'Anyway, I need a leak.' He stood up suddenly and walked briskly towards the toilets in the far corner.

Judy lowered the camera and exchanged silent glances with Ben who stood close beside her. Ben looked uncomfortable but could only shrug his shoulders.

When Harry emerged from the door marked *Caballeros* he did not return to his bar stool. Instead he stopped in conversation with another group of yachtsmen who were drinking near the door. Finally he made his excuses and left, disappearing into the night.

Judy was kept busy at the bar and had only brief opportunities to use her camera anyway. She took a couple of snapshots as new faces came up to be served, and then suddenly it seemed that her luck had changed. Harry Barlow came in and sat at the only vacant bar stool. The white-bearded American was in an expansive mood, buying drinks for the men on either side of him, and had obviously already partaken of a few bottles of Budweiser elsewhere.

Judy changed her tactics. Instead of setting the scene by making it plain exactly what she was doing with the camera she waited until Harry B had settled into an unsuspecting joke-swapping session with his neighbours. Only then did she surreptitiously slip the camera out from under the counter, point it quickly and click the shutter. In a split second she had a perfect full face photograph of Harry Barlow.

'Hey,' Harry had been caught by surprise but had not failed to notice what was happening. 'What's going on here?'

'It's for a photo board,' Judy said sweetly. 'We're going to have a board displaying pictures of all our major events and all our favourite people.'

Harry looked briefly undecided but then came down on the positive side. 'That sounds a great idea. Can I take a look at what you've got?'

He reached for the camera. Judy couldn't think of a sufficiently polite reason to refuse him and allowed him to see the picture she had just taken. Harry took the camera from her, holding it up and changing the angle of the viewing frame as though to get the best light.

'It's not a good picture,' he said blandly, and before she could stop him his fingers played rapidly on the buttons and deleted the shot. He made a show of panning through some of the other pictures she had taken, making generally approving comments. 'Now this one is not bad. This one is good. This one of Dolores is fantastic. You could sell copies of this one.' He showed it to his friends and received nods of approval.

Judy could only fume inside. When she was at last able to retrieve her camera she tried again, although she knew it was a vain hope.

'I'll take another one,' she said. 'Smile this time.'

'Hell, you don't need a picture of my ugly mug, it's going to spoil the whole tone of your pretty picture board.' He pulled the peak of the old New York Yankees baseball cap down over his face and ruined her next shot.

'Please,' Judy begged. 'Just one little picture.'

'Never could refuse a lady who said pretty please.' Harry kept the peak pulled down to his chin, pushed his thumbs into his ears and waggled his fingers at her, 'How about this one?'

Judy clicked the camera. It was a great fun shot for the photo board but not what she wanted. All that showed of Harry's face was the wisp of white goatee beard. Before she could argue any further Harry Barlow had jumped up from his stool. 'Hey, that's Marco over there. I need to speak to that guy.'

And then he was gone, ostensibly to talk urgently to someone at the back of the bar.

★   ★   ★

Later, when the crowd had gone and they cleared the bar of the last of the empty glasses, two almost full drinks remained. One was Harry Avery's pint of Stella, the other was Harry Barlow's bottle of Budweiser.

Neither of the Harrys had come back.

'Well,' Judy said wryly, 'We've learned one thing. Both of them are camera-shy.'

Ben nodded. He had been thoughtful since Harry Avery had disappeared and Judy knew that at last she was getting the benefit of some doubt. Finally he said reluctantly. 'Well, I guess neither of us wins that bet.'

Judy looked suitably downcast and nodded agreement. Then she fluttered her eyebrows and said, 'I suppose we could call it a draw and award ourselves some sort of a consolation prize.'

★ ★ ★

The next morning Judy awoke with a feeling of gloom. She and Ben had enjoyed their consolation prize so at least she had repaired some of the rift in their marriage. However, she was frustrated because she had failed to get the pictures she wanted. Her elaborate and carefully staged performance of the previous night had all been for nothing.

She toyed with the idea of keeping the camera in the kitchen and then taking sneak snaps through the open doorway from the kitchen to the bar. The problem now was that both Harrys were forewarned and she didn't think she could do it without being seen. Both men were adamant they did not want to be photographed and her bland photo board excuse would no longer serve its purpose. She didn't think either of them would dare to pursue her into the kitchen to grab the camera but at the same time she didn't want a big argument or an unfriendly scene.

In the end her indecision was irrelevant as it all became an academic question. Over the next few days neither of the fat Harrys showed their faces inside the *Conquistador*. It seemed they were taking no chances and had both decided to drink elsewhere. All she had succeeded in doing was to lose two of her best customers.

The fact that both Harry Avery and Harry Barlow had refused to have their photographs taken fuelled her suspicions even more, but suspicion was still all she had and there seemed to be nothing she could do about it.

When Miguel Garcia strolled into the bar she was pleased to see him. She had begun to believe that his investigation must have ploughed into another dead end and his cheerful smile gave her hope. He ordered coffee and she joined him at one of the outside tables. It was mid morning and all of the other tables were empty allowing them to talk freely. However, Ben soon came over to sit with them.

Judy felt a stirring of irritation. Ben's move was pointed, as though he did not trust her. She sensed he was still jealous. She pushed the feeling away, telling herself that she had nothing to hide. She just needed to talk to Miguel.

'What's happening?' she asked. 'Is there any news on *Wave Dancer?*'

'This is what I have come to tell you,' Miguel said quietly. 'I have put out a request to the police forces of all the Mediterranean countries, asking to be informed if *Wave Dancer* should appear at any of their ports. Three days ago I received a report from the Italian coastguard to say that the yacht had been spotted sailing mid way between the Island of Sicily and the coast of Tunisia. I thought at first that she was aiming to lose herself somewhere in the maze of the Greek Islands. Then yesterday another report came in, this time from the police in Turkey. They tell me that *Wave Dancer* has stopped at the port of Bodrum. As far as I know she is still there.'

'Can you have her investigated and boarded?' Judy asked quickly.

Miguel shrugged. 'I have made that request. The answer is that the yacht's papers are all in order. The owner is a Mister David James Blondell and he has a legitimate bill of sale. Without some evidence of a crime or some infringement of the law, the Turkish authorities cannot act.'

'The bill of sale has to be a fraud,' Judy said.

Miguel nodded. 'They probably had it

drawn up with all the correct signatures and stamps before *Wave Dancer* left Porto Viejo.'

'Isn't there anything we can do?'

Miguel spread his hands in a helpless gesture. 'I fear not. My initial request for information was accepted as a matter of routine. But I fear that now someone higher up in the Bodrum police hierarchy has intervened to block any further cooperation on this matter. This criminal operation we are trying to uncover is very big. It has tentacles into many countries. And obviously it has the money to pay for the blind eye wherever it is needed.'

'Damn it,' Judy swore. 'They can't just get away with it. We're as sure as we can be that Peter and Jane Shepherd must have been murdered.'

'You are sure,' Miguel pointed out. 'But I have no evidence. There are no dead bodies.'

'You have Georgina's dead body.'

'Yes. But there is no evidence to link Sergeant Harrington's murder with the yacht hi-jacking or with *Wave Dancer*. We are only making guesses.'

'You can't just leave it at that.'

'I have made the strongest request to the Bodrum police, asking them to detain the yacht and her crew. They have refused and there is nothing I can do to force them to change that decision. I am sorry. I will, of course, continue to do everything I can here in Spain.'

'Thank you,' Judy said bitterly. It was little consolation when she knew that *Wave Dancer* would never return to Porto Viejo.

Miguel looked uncomfortable. 'I came to tell you because I know of your interest. You have been so much help to my investigation that I owe you this much. I regret I cannot do more. Both cases will remain open, of course, and I will continue to do what I can.'

'Thank you,' Judy said. Ignoring Ben she squeezed his hand. 'I know you will do your best.'

'I'll keep you informed.' Miguel rose to his feet. 'I am sorry but I have to go now. My work load is very heavy.'

They watched him walk away along the promenade, disappearing under the palm fronds. Judy was tight-lipped. She wanted to spit out her frustration. Instead she silently ground her teeth.

Ben reached across the table and touched her arm. 'You've done your best,' he consoled her. 'You can't win them all.'

'I haven't lost this one yet,' she snapped at him and then regretted it. The dead ends were not Ben's fault. 'I'm sorry,' she apologized. 'But I'm not letting this go.'

'What else can you do?'

The question stopped her for a few seconds. Then without thinking it through she said grimly, 'I can go to Bodrum. That's where *Wave Dancer* is now. If I can get on board maybe I can find out something.'

'That's crazy.'

'Oh no it isn't, it's only about an hour's flight from here to Madrid. From there I should be able to get an international flight to Turkey. I can be there and back in a couple of days.'

'Are you forgetting we've got a business to run?'

She turned to look at him fiercely. 'You can run the *Conquistador*. You've got Isabella and Antonio, and we can get Juanita in to help.'

Ben met her gaze and for a moment his stare was unreadable.

'You are serious about this aren't you?'

She nodded, her lips again set tight.

Ben sighed. 'Alright, we'll get Juanita in. Isabella probably knows a few more girls who do bar work so we'll ask her to find us another barmaid. We'll leave Isabella in charge because I'm coming with you.'

It was Judy's turn to be caught off balance. She hesitated and then objected. 'It's our bar, our business, we can't both go.'

Ben said firmly, 'We have to trust Isabella

219

and Antonio at some stage, unless you've decided that we're never going to take any more holidays together. So we might as well start now. One thing is certain. This trip could be dangerous, so you are damned well not going alone.'

13

Once Judy and Ben had made up their minds they moved quickly. *Wave Dancer's* stay in Bodrum could be limited to days or even a matter of hours so there was no time to waste. Isabella and Antonio were at first startled but then pleased to be asked to run the bar for a couple of days. It was a position of trust which they had not expected to receive quite so suddenly. Isabella made a flurry of excited phone calls and within half an hour had arranged for Juanita and another friend to come in and assist them.

The difficult aspect was in lying to Isabella about the reason for their sudden departure. Judy still had the mental picture of Antonio and Arturo conversing amiably by the harbour. She believed Isabella's explanation that they were old school friends, which meant that the link between the two men was probably innocent. However, her police training had given her a suspicious mind. She did not reveal what they had learned from Miguel and told Isabella that they had received a phone call to say that her mother was ill in England. Ben gave her a curious sideways look but made no comment until they were alone.

'You're getting paranoid,' he said when she explained. 'First Harry and now Arturo and Antonio. You'll be suspecting me of being up to something sinister next.'

'I'm just taking no chances,' Judy said defensively.

Ben shrugged. 'Okay, but if they are all in league with the villains and smart enough to fool us then they are probably on to us anyway. This sudden flight to England immediately after talking to Miguel must look suspicious.'

Judy knew he wasn't serious but the thought disturbed her.

★ ★ ★

Early the next morning they drove their car up to Alicante and took the first of the regular daily flights from Alicante to Madrid's Barajas Airport. Their best option with a scheduled international flight to Turkey was the 11-40 a.m. Iberia flight from Barajas to Attaturk Airport at Istanbul. Entry with UK passports was easy with a three month visa being granted and stamped into their passports on arrival. From Attaturk they were able to get a short internal flight with Turkish

Airlines to Bodrum's brand new Milas Airport. They hired a car at the airport to make the last 35 kilometre drive along the coast road to Bodrum.

Ben took the wheel. Their previous careers had turned them both into fast, safe drivers, capable of reaching any emergency at high speeds. Since moving to Spain they were also well accustomed to driving a right hand drive vehicle on the right side of the road. The hire car was a medium size Renault and Ben kept it carefully to the top of the speed limit. One delay they didn't need at this stage was to be pulled over by the Turkish traffic police looking to levy an on-the-spot fine.

Judy tried to enjoy the superb coastal views. The rugged landscape and headlands were reminiscent of parts of Spain, with glimpses of minarets and small mosques replacing the familiar blue-dome churches in the white cube villages. There was a similar blanket haze of dust and heat and the sun shone hot from the blazing blue sky. They were on the other side of the Mediterranean but some things were still the same. They needed sun glasses and sun cream. They still wore shorts, tee shirts and hats. Judy wore a wide-brimmed straw hat with a flowered hat band. Ben wore a baseball cap.

Finally they saw a glimpse of the

magnificent old Crusader Castle over a maze of square white roof-tops and turned off the highway and into the city sprawl of Bodrum. Ben was thinking of finding a cheap hotel where they could dump their back packs and wash up before going any further. Judy was impatient. They had moved as fast as possible but already more than thirty hours had elapsed since they had talked with Miguel. She won a short argument and Ben gave in gracefully and drove straight down to the harbour to find a car park.

They walked on to the harbour, a vast circle of promenade and harbour wall that was lined with a bristling armada of yachts and gulets packed hull to hull. The small harbour of Porto Viejo was dwarfed by comparison. The forest of masts and rails was liberally festooned with bright red lifebelts and every other ship was flying the crimson flag of Turkey with its white star and crescent. The traditional gulets built from the sturdy red pine that grew in profusion along Turkey's southern coast gave a timeless touch to the scene. The square brown walls and towers of the ancient castle which overlooked it all added the final mediaeval brushstroke.

'So where do we start?' Ben asked, looking at the daunting array of hundreds of different vessels.

'At the beginning,' Judy said. 'We'll go out to the harbour arm and then walk back and all the way round.'

She led the way up on to the walkway that ran above the promenade shops and out to the harbour wall. From here there were good views over the centre of the harbour where a variety of sailing vessels were moving constantly in and out. The volume of traffic worried her, reminding her that *Wave Dancer* could already be gone, or even at this moment be on the point of sailing away. She took a small pair of binoculars out of her bag and paused to try and read the names on the moving yachts.

There was nothing heading seaward that looked like *Wave Dancer* so she lowered the glasses and moved on. They walked to the far end of the harbour arm where it turned to stab out to sea. Here they were at the harbour mouth, a relatively narrow gap in the almost closed circle with a small white lighthouse on the end of the opposite arm. They watched a few boats sail in and out and then turned back to circle the whole length of the harbour.

They walked back with the castle ahead of them and then on their right, its tiers of bleached walls and towers rising up against the scorching blue of the sky. Judy knew that it had been built by the Knights of St John at the time of the Crusades and held until nearby Rhodes was conquered by Suleyman the Magnificent in 1523. Then the knights were forced to surrender it to the Turks and withdraw to Malta. The castle was a magnificent intact monument with much more history than the poor ruins at Porto Viejo and she would have been happy to explore it properly. On this visit there was no time and with a sigh she looked back to her left and focussed her attention on the boats in the harbour.

They soon came down on to the harbour front again, losing the high view but walking close to the seemingly endless wall of packed sterns. The boats were moored side by side with their bows pointed out to the centre of the harbour and with hardly a gap between them. Most of the gulets were charter boats and had their sales boards set up on the harbour, advertising island cruises, snorkelling and diving and beach barbecues on secluded coves. There were stalls selling fresh caught fish or shell souvenirs, and once a bored camel giving harbour front rides to tourist children.

It was now mid-afternoon and the sun burned from a cloudless sky. They bought bottles of water to slake their thirst and splashed more sun cream on their bare arms and faces. Then they continued walking. It took them an hour to circle the harbour and get round to the yacht marina on the far side. Here Judy used the glasses again to read the names of the yachts out on the central pontoons. This was where she had hoped to find *Wave Dancer*, moored up with others of its kind, but again they were out of luck.

She sat on a large iron bollard feeling hot and defeated. The anticlimax had suddenly sapped the last of her energy and she stared gloomily at the splendid scene before her. Ben took off his cap and used it to rub sweat from his forehead.

'There was a Custom House out on the harbour wall where we started,' he said calmly. 'Perhaps we should ask there.'

'I was hoping to avoid that,' Judy said. 'I didn't want to draw any official attention to us.'

'So what are our options?'

She thought about it and then said wryly, 'None, I guess, now that we've drawn a blank on our own.'

Ben reached out a hand to help her up and they began the long, weary walk back to the Custom House.

When they arrived the building was busy with visitors seeking information or going through the formalities of registering the arrival or departure of their craft. They had to wait for five minutes but at least the air conditioning was efficient and there was cool relief from the blistering sun. Finally they had the attention of a harassed young official who wore a white shirt and a small moustache.

'We are looking for an English yacht,' Judy explained. 'Her name is *Wave Dancer*. We think she arrived here about two days ago.'

A tired white smile showed beneath the wisp of black fuzz on his upper lip, and a small pad and a pencil was pushed toward her. 'Write it, please.' His English was adequate but he needed to see the name. 'There are so many different language boats,' he explained.

Judy wrote it down. The customs officer keyed it into his computer and pursed his lips as he studied the screen. 'She is gone,' he said at last. '*Wave Dancer* sailed from Bodrum early this morning.'

'Where did she go?'

He shrugged. 'Perhaps a cruise along the coast, perhaps out to the Greek Islands, perhaps another part of Turkey. The pleasure boats come and go as they please. They have to show passports and pay mooring fees, but they do not have to say where they go next. Often they do not know.'

Judy was frustrated. She wanted to argue with him but she knew it would do no good. In all probability he was being honest and had already given her all the information he had. She thanked him and moved away.

For a moment she and Ben just stood and looked helplessly at each other. Another couple in the short queue behind them had taken their place and already the young customs officer had forgotten them.

'Dead end,' Ben said and Judy nodded dumbly. Ben had no more ideas and nothing more to say. He didn't want to be negative and waited for her to make the next move. The silence dragged and Judy saw a tall Turk in the patient line who was watching her with interest.

The man wore old jeans that had been cut down to shorts, brown leather sandals and a faded blue shirt that was open to the navel with the sleeves rolled up above his elbows. On his head was a dirty blue sailor's cap with imitation gold edged around the peak. He made up his mind suddenly and stepped out of the line to approach them. His flashing smile was all for Judy but he spoke to Ben.

'Hello, you look for your brother, hey?'

'My brother?' Ben was baffled.

For a second Judy was also perplexed and then she had a flash of understanding. There was enough likeness between Ben and

Blondie Dave for them to be mistaken for brothers.

'Yes,' she said, smiling warmly. 'Ben's brother Dave was here with his yacht *Wave Dancer*. We were hoping to meet him but we've just been told that he has already left.'

'*Wave Dancer* leave Bodrum this morning. I hear you ask.' Their informant nodded and then introduced himself. 'My name is Nuray, Captain Nuray. I am captain of the *Dalyana*. She is a lovely boat, a real Turkish boat, one of the gulets. For two nights *Wave Dancer* was tied up beside my boat but now she is gone.'

'Did they say where she was going?' Judy asked.

Nuray shrugged. 'Your brother does not talk much,' he told Ben. 'He was not friendly. I ask him and his friend to come on board for a glass of wine, just being good neighbours, but they say they have no time.' He looked back to Judy, smiling again, and she knew that she was the only reason that he was giving them his time. He would not have bothered to talk to Ben alone.

She sweetened her own smile a little more. 'Did you hear them say anything that might give us a clue,' she coaxed him.

'This man's brother did not sail with the yacht.' Nuray avoided using the term husband or boy-friend, obviously hoping that this was not the case. 'I saw him and his friend get into a taxi with their bags. I heard them say Milas Airport to the taxi driver. They left their boat behind.'

'So who sailed out with *Wave Dancer?*' Judy almost held her breath, hoping desperately for a straight answer.

'They were two Turkish men,' Nuray frowned for a moment and tapped his cheek with a forefinger, as though somehow that would help him to remember. 'I know them. I have seen them before. They work for one of the boatyards further down the coast.'

He looked toward the young customs official behind the desk. The couple who had taken Ben and Judy's place had just completed their business and were moving away. Nuray interrupted the official before he could begin dealing with the next man in line and a swift flurry of Turkish questions and answers echoed back and forth.

'The name of the boatyard is Keskin Boatyard,' Nuray said at last. All his attention was on Judy now and he was beaming because he knew he had pleased her. 'It is along the coast, west from here. You follow the road through Gumbet and down to Kargi Bay. Ask for Keskin Boatyard, if the boat has been taken in for maintenance or repairs then the people there will know when your friend's brother will come back to pick her up.'

'Thank you,' Judy said. 'We'll do that. You've been very helpful.'

'It is my pleasure,' Nuray touched his cap in a smiling salute. He had glanced once at the wedding ring on her finger but chose to ignore it. 'If you wish to cruise perhaps you will come on my boat instead. *Dalyana* is a real Turkish gullet. I take you diving, cruising, anywhere you want to go, do anything you want to do. All meals cooked on board, lovely Turkish food, lovely Turkish wine.'

'We'd love to,' Judy said. 'But right now we just don't have the time.'

'But you are on holiday, you have plenty of time. One week cruising or just one day, you tell me what you want.'

'We need to speak to Dave,' Judy insisted gently. 'But we will come back. Next time we will look for your boat.'

'*Dalyana*,' Nuray reminded her, 'Captain Nuray and the *Dalyana*.' He fished into a shirt pocket and pulled out a leaflet and a business card which he pressed into her hand. 'Here is my card with my telephone number, and all the details of my trips. My boat is always moored in the centre of the harbour. Come and find me. Ask for me.'

'We will,' Judy promised him.

It took another five minutes before they could decently disentangle themselves and escape. Judy waved goodbye and Nuray blew her a kiss. Then at last he turned away to look for his lost place in the line.

'That was a stroke of luck,' Ben said as they walked back to the car.

Judy disagreed with a grin. 'We've worked damned hard for it, flying out here and looking at every boat in the harbour. But that's how every crime investigation gets its lucky break. You just keep at it until something shows up. It's all down to hard leg work and routine perseverance.'

'Okay.' Ben was thoughtful and after another minute he asked, 'But why did they come to Bodrum anyway? I mean if their job was just to hand the boat over in Turkey then why didn't Dave and Luis just sail her direct into this boatyard?'

'One reason is that Dave and Luis were not intended to know where the boat was going next. This was a hand-over on neutral ground, just another cut out.' Judy thought some more and then added, 'Another reason might be that they needed to enter Turkey legally. We had a visa stamped into our passports at the airport, remember. They must have had their passports stamped on arrival here at Bodrum. We all need a legal entry in order to make a legal exit. You can bet those entry visa dates will be checked when we leave.'

Ben acknowledged her reasoning with a nod and they said no more until they had returned to their car. The Renault was oven hot inside and they opened up the windows and doors and drank what was left in their water bottles before they hunted out the package of maps that had been supplied with the car. Ben made no more mention of finding a hotel, knowing that they were hot on the trail and there could be no letting up.

They opened up a map of the Bodrum peninsular and quickly found the road from Bodrum through Gumbet that led west to Kargi Bay. Ben started the car while Judy kept the map open on her lap. They closed the doors and windows, trapping the sticky heat inside but trusting the air conditioning to make it bearable once they were moving. Ben decided it was quicker to go back the way they had come and rejoin the main highway that by-passed most of Bodrum and continued west.

They drove in silence but Judy was happy. Ben was at last taking an interest and they were working together. It was like the old times when she had been a real police officer. Talking her cases over with Ben had often given her new perspectives and insights. Until now she had missed that with Ben feeling that she was neglecting their new lifestyle.

They drove through Gumbet, the first of a series of towns that were packed with waterfront restaurants and bars, with long crowded sand beaches heaving with sunbathers and sunshade umbrellas. Out in the bays yachts and small boats dotted the glittering waters and a variety of water-sports were taking place which Judy watched with envy. A cooling dip in those inviting blue seas would have been most welcome but she was fired with a sense of urgency that left them no time.

There were more beaches, bays and promenades, all fringed with citrus and olive groves, and inland the dusty grey hills of the peninsular. It was a beautiful coastline with endless indents and islets, enjoyable even though they had to rush through it. They reached Kargi Bay, again fronted by palm trees and a small promenade and Ben slowed down as they began to look for a boatyard. They passed several but none had the right name. They drove through the town and the road turned inland.

'Perhaps we've missed it,' Ben said as Judy turned her head to look back at the disappearing sea.

'Perhaps,' Judy echoed reluctantly. She consulted the map on her lap. 'The road goes inland to get round a couple of little streams and then doubles back to the coast again. Perhaps it's on the other side.'

'That's another bay,' Ben had a good memory for maps and didn't need to look again. 'Our helpful captain who fancied the pants off you definitely said Kargi Bay.'

'Yes he did,' Judy smiled. In this case it would do Ben no harm to be jealous. 'Perhaps we should turn back.'

Ben slowed the car, looking for somewhere to turn. The next road that came up on their left was a narrow white dirt track that led between two olive flanked hills. Beside it was a worn wooden sign with flaking white paint lettering that was still readable. They both recognized the word Keskin.

'Keskin boatyard,' Judy said. 'I think we've found it.'

Ben nodded and turned on to the dirt track. He drove slowly until a gap showed between the two low hills on their left. They were looking down into a shallow valley where a small inlet meandered to the sea. The stream and the mudflats on either side gleamed silver in the sun. The boatyard was visible through the screens of olive trees, a fenced enclosure with two score of boats

236

inside, some of them in the water and others high and dry on stilts and chocks. There were low stone buildings on one side that looked like workshops, and set back a little from the yard were two stone houses.

Ben stopped the car and they stared down the hill. Then Judy rooted in her handbag and found her binoculars. She raised the glasses and studied the boats below. Finally she handed the glasses over to Ben.

'There in the left hand corner of the yard, near to the stream. There's a white yacht jacked up out of the water. There's a man painting over the stern. My guess is that he's painting out the name. I think that's *Wave Dancer*.'

'I think you could be right,' Ben said at last. He handed the glasses back. 'Look around and you'll see that there are at least three more men working in other parts of the yard. It's a busy place. So what do we do now? There's no point in just driving down there and asking when my brother Dave is coming back, because we've already worked out that Blondie Dave won't be returning to collect her.'

'We have to get a closer look at that yacht,' Judy said, 'Without being seen.'

'So it's a night job,' Ben decided. 'We'll have to come back after dark when the

237

boatyard is shut up.'

Judy nodded.

Ben started the engine and began what eventually became a five point turn to reverse the car on the narrow road.

'We can't just sit here for the rest of the day without being noticed,' he explained. 'So in the meantime we might as well drive back to one of those promenade restaurants in Kargi and eat. We haven't had anything since the in-flight meal between Madrid and Istanbul this morning and I'm starving.'

14

They ate at one of the promenade restaurants overlooking the beach. The sun-bathers were beginning to withdraw and by the time they had finished their meal they were watching a glorious red and gold sunset framed in the darkening fronds of the overhanging palm trees. Judy had not realized how hungry she was and did as much justice as Ben to a plate of deliciously grilled swordfish with rice and salad. They were tempted to add a bottle of wine but it had been a long, tiring day and any alcohol would have made them sluggish. They had to remind themselves that they were not on holiday and the day's work was not yet over. Reluctantly they drank water and coffee.

They lingered to watch the last blaze of the sun etching a rim of fire around the deepening black of a roll of cumulus cloud and then paid their bill and left. Back in their car Ben retraced their route to the dusty side track that led down into the low river valley and the boatyard. He found the spot where they had parked before, although now it was too dark to see anything except a faint glimmer of a light through the intervening trees.

Deftly Ben executed another five point turn on the narrow road, bringing the Renault round so that it faced back toward the main highway. He edged it off the track to where it was partially concealed in the gloom beneath an ancient olive. There he switched off the lights and engine. They sat for a moment and looked at each other.

Judy could see that Ben was doubtful. 'We'll just have to hope that we haven't already been seen or heard,' she said at last. 'There's room for another car to get past, but this one is sure to be spotted, so we'll just have to hope that there's no more traffic tonight, or that no one takes any notice.'

'That's a whole lot of hoping,' Ben pointed out.

'So let's make it quick,' Judy said and got out of the car.

Ben got out and locked the car and then joined her on the white dust track that ran like a ribbon of dulled silver through the shadows of the olive trees. For a moment they looked toward the far twinkle of light which marked the location of the boatyard down in the valley.

'That's got to be one of the two houses we

saw,' Ben offered. 'Do we head down to it or stay on the track.'

'Stay on the track,' Judy decided. 'To start with anyway, we don't want to get lost in the dark.'

They began walking in silence, both of them listening for the first sound of a vehicle or another human voice. They wanted to be warned of anyone else approaching without giving their own presence away. A light breeze ruffled the olive leaves and somewhere distant a goat or a sheep bleated. Neither of them knew how to tell the difference. Above them a scattering of stars pricked the blackness, giving them a faint light. There was no moon.

After a hundred yards the track turned and began to loop down into the valley. A light began to flicker on their left, and then another and they knew they must be approaching the two small stone houses they had seen earlier in the day. Judy led the way into the olive trees on their right, giving the lights a wide berth but keeping the track in sight and following its general direction.

Judy was beginning to feel tense, her nerves were on edge and all her senses were heightened and alert. As a police officer she had been in more scary situations than this but there had always been the comfort of knowing that she was the law and the law was on her side. Here and now she was in a foreign country, committing an act of trespass and contemplating a forced entry into private property. Even if the people who owned the boatyard were innocent of any crime she could still be in trouble.

On this escapade she was not mob-handed with a squad of colleagues and she had no radio to call for back up. There was only Ben and suddenly she was glad that Ben had insisted on coming along.

The olive grove came to an end and their way was barred by a chain link fence that was six feet tall. Beyond it they could see the outlines of hulls and masts reaching up into the sky. The wind sighed and tinkled wire stays. The dusty air was tainted by the faint smells of paint, varnish and engine oil, and the mud of the river bank.

They had found the boatyard. Ben touched her shoulder and pointed to their left. Where the track entered there were double gates closed and barring the way. They could just make out a large padlock on a heavy chain and above the gates a sign in Turkish lettering that included the word Keskin.

'This is it,' Ben whispered softly.

Judy tried to remember all that she had seen through her binoculars earlier in the afternoon. 'I'm sure I saw another little track leading away on this side,' she murmured softly. 'It looked as though it was leading inland along the edge of the river.'

She began to move to the right, away from the main gateway and the window lights of the two small buildings, following the fence down to the creek. Ben made no comment but kept pace behind her.

They were walking through long grass and small bushes. The trees beside them changed shape and they smelled pines instead of olives. Judy stumbled against a small pile of rubble and they moved more slowly as they stepped over what looked like an abandoned building site. There was more rubble, a sand pile, stone building blocks and pieces of broken masonry. Some sort of structure had either fallen down here or been started and then left. It was all tangled with weeds and hard to discern in the darkness.

Suddenly water gleamed in the starlight ahead of them. They had reached the narrow stretch of river where more boats were moored. The steel mesh fence continued into the water for a few yards so there was no way round it without getting wet. However, here there was another single gate where a footpath appeared on the river bank. The gate was again padlocked, although this was a smaller lock.

Judy frowned and pulled at the padlock. Then she looked at the shelving bank of black mud and the black water. 'I guess we have to swim,' she muttered.

'Sod that,' Ben said. 'Hang on a minute.'

She waited and watched as he returned to kick at the piles of builder's rubble they had just traversed. He found what he was looking for and came back with two short pieces of rusty steel-fixer's iron rod, each one about a quarter of an inch in diameter. He grinned at her and then inserted both pieces into the hasp of the padlock. He jerked the two rods sharply in a scissor opening motion and the hasp snapped up with a loud click.

'An old fireman's trick,' Ben said calmly. 'If you haven't got a pair of bolt-croppers handy then a couple of screwdrivers are the next best thing, or any sort of narrow steel rod.'

'Interesting,' Judy smiled. 'We had several unsolved breaking and entering jobs when I left the force. Perhaps I should ask you for a statement of your whereabouts on those nights.'

Ben opened the gate and they passed through. They were inside the Keskin boatyard which was silent and deserted. The bows and sterns of various craft on chocks and trestles reared up over them, casting short shadows in the starlight. A bank of cloud had obscured half the sky, shutting out half the twinkling constellations but they could see enough to find their way through the maze and avoid falling into the open dry docks and fingers of water. Judy headed directly for the far corner and the yacht which she was sure was *Wave Dancer*.

The yacht was still there, its familiar silhouette raised out of the water and supported on a cradle of rough timber props. They approached it with caution, trying to keep the hull between themselves and the lights of the two buildings on the far side of the fence which were now dangerously close. Judy guessed that whoever owned the boatyard must live in one of the houses, and perhaps a worker family in the other. She had counted four men working here earlier in the day and perhaps there were more. They could all be relaxing over their evening meal now in those two houses.

They stopped under the yacht's bow. There was a smell of fresh paint and the smooth fibreglass gleamed pristine eggshell white. There was no name on this side of the bow. Judy poked her head under the bow and looked up. There was no name on the other side either. The yacht had been here two days, time enough for two coats of paint to obliterate her old identity.

Judy moved to the stern of the boat with Ben patiently following. Here there was a name but it was not *Wave Dancer*. A new name had been carefully drawn in flowing black script. She realized that she had watched the yacht being re-christened through her binoculars. The yacht was now the *Samisakali*.

'They haven't wasted much time,' Ben whispered in her ear.

'By this time tomorrow they'll have *Samisakali* painted on the bows,' Judy agreed softly. 'We've found her only just in time.' She looked back toward the bows, wondering what to do next, and then glanced up. Suddenly she smiled. 'Look,' she said, with barely suppressed excitement and pointed.

Ben looked up. The yacht had a small ship to shore rowing boat slung on low davits at the stern. On the stern of the rowing boat the name *Wave Dancer* still showed in wavy blue letters.

'I can get both names in one shot,' Judy said, still smiling. She unslung her small shoulder bag and took out the digital camera she had last used for her picture-taking charade in the *Conquistador*.

She risked moving out into the open for a few seconds to frame the picture, pulling out the zoom for a wide angle. She had to take another step backward to get both names,

Samisakali and *Wave Dancer* into the frame. She could barely read the smaller name now, but the picture could always be enhanced and enlarged. She pressed the shutter button. The camera flashed and Ben grabbed her suddenly and hauled her quickly back into the shadow behind the boat.

'That might not have been such a good idea,' he hissed. 'Someone could have seen the flash.'

Judy realized he was right and felt embarrassed and cross with herself. She should have foreseen the danger. They crouched together in the shadow for almost a minute, waiting for the alarm to be raised, but nothing happened. Judy relaxed. She had made a mistake but she had the evidence to show that the new *Samisakali* and the missing *Wave Dancer* were the same boat.

'I think we've got away with it,' she said.

'So let's get out of here.'

'Not yet, I still want to know what happened to Jane and Peter.'

'It doesn't take a lot of imagination to figure that one out. They must both be dead.'

'So let's get on board. There may be some clue as to exactly what happened.'

There was a crude wooden ladder propped against the side of the hull and she climbed up nimbly before he had a chance to protest.

The ladder creaked under her weight but seemed sturdy enough.

'Don't rock the bloody boat,' Ben said, but he climbed up after her. The ladder creaked even more but the propped yacht seemed stable enough. They crouched down in the cockpit behind the wheel and waited again for any sound or sign of alarm.

Again all was still and silent.

Judy looked all around the decks, fore and aft, and then turned her attention to the varnished wood door beside the wheel. The door was not locked and she pulled it open. With another cautious glance toward the lights of the two houses she made up her mind and went below. After a moment Ben followed her down the short stairway.

They were in the small galley and dining area. It took a few moments for their eyes to become accustomed to the deeper gloom. The only light was starlight coming down the stairway and through a single porthole on either side. Ben moved closer to one of the portholes where he could keep watch on the buildings beyond the fence. Judy fished in her bag and pulled out a small torch. She flicked it on and probed all around with the narrow beam.

'Keep it low,' Ben said. 'Don't shine any light through the portholes.'

Judy nodded and began to explore the interior of the boat. There were two small cabins aft and a larger cabin forward of the galley and dining area. There were toilets fore and aft and a small shower. Judy checked them all while Ben kept watch. She knew what she was looking for. She was searching for bloodstains or any signs of interior damage that would have indicated a struggle. She lifted all the mattresses and shone her torch under all the bunks. She looked into all the cupboards. She lifted rugs and carefully criss-crossed every inch of decking with her beam of light.

There was nothing suspicious in any of the cabins. Both toilets and the shower were clean. She came back into the galley and dining area and checked all the cupboards there. Finally she turned her torch-beam on the deck and began sweeping it slowly back and forth. She stopped at the corner of the table and knelt, holding the beam closer. There at last was a faint stain on the decking.

Ben saw what she was doing and knelt beside her.

'They've tried to clean it up,' Judy said softly. 'But they didn't bother too much because they knew they were handing the boat over. Blood is hellishly difficult to scrub out.'

'How can you be sure it's blood?'

'Call it an educated guess,' Judy answered.

There were even fainter marks within the large, misshapen blot of the ominous stain. Ben peered closer. 'It looks as though someone tried to write something.'

Judy stared hard. The marks could be finger marks and they could be letters. Judy remembered that Jane had been an avid reader, on the beach or lazing on the deck of the yacht she always had a book in her lap. They were usually crime novels, Judy recalled. Writing something in blood was an old crime mystery stock in trade. It was something Jane had probably read in a book. Something she might have tried for real.

'It looks like an H,' Ben said slowly.

'It looks like H A R,' Judy tried to interpret the scrubbed out scrawl but could get no further. 'Harry,' she guessed the rest. She turned to look at Ben, remembering his silly rhyme and repeating it back to him, 'Tweedledum and Tweedledee, Harry A or Harry B?'

Ben's mouth tightened. He swore softly but he didn't argue.

'Hold the torch.'

Judy gave it to him and took her camera out of her bag. She took two pictures to be sure, risking the sharp flashes of the camera.

Then she put the camera back in her bag and took out a small penknife. She snapped the blade open and dug it into the stained wood, prising out a few large splinters. She wrapped the splinters into a paper tissue and tucked it safely into her bag.

'A good forensic lab can get a DNA sample from that,' she said grimly. 'I think we've got enough.'

'Good,' Ben breathed a sigh of relief. 'Now can we get the hell out of here?'

They climbed back up into the cockpit and crouched there to stare at the two separate squares of pale yellow light that marked the locations of the two houses. The scene was unchanged. There were no more lights and no signs of movement. Ben stepped over the side of the yacht and used the rickety wooden ladder to return to the ground. He reached up unnecessarily to help and steady Judy as she followed.

'Always the gentleman,' she grinned at him as she turned away from the ladder.

They began to walk back across the boatyard and that was when they heard the clink and rattle of the chain on the main gates. They froze and stared at each other. Then the chain rattled again and there was a scraping sound as one of the gates was pushed open. A ferocious sound of loud barking suddenly erupted into the peaceful stillness of the night.

'Dogs,' Ben said and they both broke into a run.

They headed for the side gate where they had entered. The need for silence and caution was abandoned as they raced a zig-zag course through the maze of boats awaiting service or repair. The sound of frenzied barking was close on their heels and Judy risked a hasty glance over her shoulder. She saw the black and brown shapes of two large Rottweiller dogs streaking through the gaps behind them, the white slaver spilling from their jaws. They had a head start but the dogs were gaining rapidly.

Judy put on a spurt, realizing that a fall or a broken neck was probably the lesser of the two evils. She was drawing ahead of Ben who was trailing because of his limp. She looked back for him and saw one of the dogs attempt a short cut with a flying leap over one of the repair docks they had just avoided. The animal misjudged its jump and fell short, crashing into the edge of the pit with a howl and sliding with a loud splashing into the water.

The second dog swerved around the pit and kept coming, only yards from Ben's back and closing fast.

Judy reached the gate and ducked through, turning to hold the gate open for Ben. The massive rottweiller was already launching itself into a spring, its body hunched as it thrust forward with powerful hind legs.

Judy yelled a warning.

Ben swung to face the danger. The dog was within inches of landing on his chest and Ben allowed himself to fall backwards. He kicked up as he fell and kicked the dog square in the chest. The impact added to the animal's momentum, deflecting its leap and sending it onward at a tangent. With a howl of pain and anger the brute crashed into the steel fence, clawing wildly at the mesh as it slid down and rolled in the dust.

Judy stepped back into the boatyard. Ben was struggling to get up. She grabbed him by the shoulder and despite his size and weight she managed to half pull and half throw him through the gateway. The second dog had extricated itself from the water-filled pit and flew dripping into the pursuit. Its snapping jaws lunged for Ben's arm, drawing blood and ripping his shirtsleeve. Judy punched it in the face as it fell away.

They had both stumbled through the gateway. Judy grabbed the gate and slammed it into the face of the first dog which had recovered its balance and resumed its attack.

She could barely hold it and then both dogs were clawing and snarling at the gate, pushing her back and forcing the gate open. One of them had its face through the gap, its slaver spraying over her as it tried to snap at her, straining to get the bulk of its shoulders through the widening gap.

Ben kicked it in the muzzle, forcing it to howl and withdraw. Then he added his weight to Judy's and between them the pushed the gate shut. The two dogs continued to howl and claw at the mesh. Ben kept his shoulder to the gate as he stooped. He picked up one of the pieces of steel rod that he had used to break the padlock and then straightened up. Deftly he closed the latch and used the steel rod to slip through the hasp and secure it. With both hands he bent the steel into a tight U shape to stop it being rattled out.

They could hear voices now, the sounds of at least two men cautiously approaching across the boatyard. The beam of a flashlight jumped and weaved, trying to pick out the dogs which were drawing them to the spot.

'Let's go,' Ben said hoarsely.

They left the frustrated dogs still snarling and throwing themselves at the gate. With every impact the whole section of fence shuddered and bulged outward as though the whole thing could come down at any moment. Even if it held, the dog owners would soon see how the gate was fastened and let the animals out. The knowledge spurred Ben and Judy on and they raced back through the olive trees to find their car.

Judy pulled Ben out on to the dirt track as soon as they were past the two houses. Moving out into the open was a risk but the rough ground under the olive trees was causing them to trip and stumble as they floundered in the darkness. The track was a smoother surface and better lit and they could run faster. Ben was cursing and dragging his left leg more with every step.

The baying sound of the dogs faded, which was a relief. Judy had expected to hear them growing louder as they were released to continue the chase. She began to hope that having scared their intruders away the boatyard people were prepared to leave it at that. She slowed to keep pace with Ben and then heard faintly the sound of an engine starting behind her.

'Damn,' she said, and grabbed Ben's arm to hurry him along. The open track was not the best place to be but it still offered their best hope. They just had to win the race back to their car before the four wheel pursuit caught up with them.

They ran desperately, fearing that they were not fast enough. The engine sound gained in volume behind them and they could hear the sound of the vehicle's gears grating and scraping. Then suddenly they recognized the spot where they had left the car. The black paintwork of the Renault gleamed under the gloom of the olive trees. Ben stumbled toward the driver's side but his stiff leg was obviously hurting.

'I'll drive,' Judy gasped.

Ben didn't argue. He gave her the keys which were already in his hand and turned toward the passenger seat. Judy used the remote click on the ignition key to unlock the doors as they ran up and swung quickly inside. She started the engine while Ben was still getting in. A quick glance in the rear view mirror showed headlights coming up the track behind her. She spun the wheel, throwing up gravel and bounced the car back on to the track.

She heard the instinctive squeal of brakes from the vehicle behind and then angry shouts. Another look in the rear view mirror showed the square outline of an old Land Rover. The passenger door was opening and a man was getting out. Judy stamped on the accelerator and the Renault shot forward. Ben slammed their passenger door shut. The man who had emerged from the Land Rover scrambled back inside and the Land Rover accelerated in continued pursuit.

Judy led the way down the dirt track, ignoring what was happening behind her and concentrating now on simply driving as fast as the road allowed. There was no room for the Land Rover to get past her and she knew that once she turned on to the main highway she could use her high speed driving skills to get away.

Ben strapped himself in and then reached past Judy to pull her seat belt across her chest and click it into place. Moments later the main road appeared. There was a gap in the traffic and Judy spun out on to the tarmac without stopping. She moved smoothly into top gear and put her foot down. A lorry, two cars and a bus appeared in her headlights and she overtook them all in quick succession. The lights of the Land Rover had followed them out on to the main road but were quickly lost and indistinguishable as the other headlights intervened.

They sped through Kargi and were well on the way to Gumbet before Judy slowed down to the upper speed limit and allowed the car to cruise.

'Where to now?' Ben said at last.

'Back to the airport,' Judy said. She still had her shoulder bag tucked in her lap and she patted it with one hand. 'We've got everything we wanted right here.'

15

Miguel was horrified.

They met at the half way point on the bench beside the shaded Fishermen's Square at the corner of the harbour. As she approached Judy noted that *Apache* and *Seagull Two* were moored at their usual berths, although both had empty decks and looked unattended. She did not have time to look any closer because Miguel was already waiting in response to her telephone call. She showed him the prints of the pictures she had taken and the sample splinters she had dug out of the galley deck of *Wave Dancer*. While she talked and explained his expression gradually changed from one of polite curiosity to one of shock and disbelief.

'What do you expect me to do?' he demanded. 'You actually flew to Turkey and broke into this boatyard. How can I explain all of this to the Turkish police if I send them copies of these photographs?'

Judy shrugged. 'Just tell them the truth. There is not much they can do about it now that Ben and I are back in Spain. The picture that includes both names shows that the boat that is now the *Samisakali* is *Wave Dancer*.'

'But we already know that the sale papers are in order.'

'That can't stop an investigation once we prove that the previous owners were murdered. I dare bet that once we analyse these wood splinters we'll know the stains are bloodstains. I'm also as certain as I can be that DNA testing will show the blood must have belonged to Jane or Peter Shepherd. If you send a sample to London you can get the police over there to check. The Shepherds lived in Suffolk. The police there must be able to find their address and find some DNA to cross check. There are always hairs on a hairbrush, in a comb, or caught in the plug hole of a washbasin.'

'It is still all very irregular. And how can the police in Turkey know that the pictures are not fakes? How can they know that the splinters, even if they contain blood, were dug out of the deck of the yacht that was *Wave Dancer*?'

'They can go and look at the yacht,' Judy said impatiently. 'Tell them to look at the deck boards in the galley. They'll be able to see the stain for themselves, and see where the splinters came out.'

'The yacht may not be there. If these people are smart, and we know they are, then the yacht will have been moved by now. Or the damaged planks with the stain will have been replaced.'

'It's possible, but I don't think anyone actually saw us at the boatyard. I think we gave ourselves away with the flashes from my camera. The people there were nervous. They put the dogs into the yard and let them flush us out. We escaped without our faces being seen. They don't know who we were or what we were actually doing. We could have been just a couple of stray thieves, looking for something to steal.'

'Opportunist thieves do not carry a camera and photograph what they intend to steal,' Miguel said in exasperation. 'If you betrayed yourselves with your camera then they must know which boat interested you. I think they would be able to work it out.'

Judy felt suddenly frustrated. For a moment she wondered whether he was being deliberately obstructive but then she realized he was right. If someone had brought this kind of story to her in the course of a criminal investigation then she would probably have made the same sort of objections. Miguel was only looking at the whole thing in a professional light. Plus he not only had to accept her story, he also had to pass it on to another national police force where they had already guessed there was a level of deliberate obstruction. She knew she was asking a lot.

Her downcast face revealed some of what she was thinking and Miguel covered her hand with his where it rested on her knee. His touch was gentle, just a reassuring contact.

'I am sorry, Judy. I do not doubt that the evidence you have gained is genuine. It is just that the way it was obtained makes it awkward for me to use it. Even if I do pass it on and the police in Turkey can be persuaded to act upon it, the odds must be that the yacht will have vanished or be cleaned up by the time that they arrive.'

'But you will act on it?'

'Of course, I will have these wood splinters tested for DNA and pass the results on to London. Also I will make a formal request for the Turkish police to investigate the Keskin Boatyard. I only ask that you do not expect too much from this. We are still a long way from finding out who murdered your friend Georgina.'

Judy forced a smile. 'We must be getting nearer.'

He nodded seriously. 'The picture is a lot clearer. Now that we have been able to track *Wave Dancer*'s voyage all the way to Turkey we can surmise that this was the probable route followed by all the other yachts that have gone missing. We know that *Wave Dancer* sailed all the way to the North African coast, and then came back to within a few miles of Spain before turning again and sailing for Bodrum.'

'You said that she didn't put in to any Spanish port so she must have made a contact at sea. She must have been used to pick up and run a cargo of drugs.'

'Exactly, we have two major crimes being run in a tandem. Expensive yachts are being hijacked and then used to run one or two drug smuggling trips before being re-fitted, re-named and sold on. This must be a very lucrative business. What we have to find out is who is running this organization here in Spain and then prove it.'

'The name that was spelled out in blood began with an H. I'm sure it was Harry, and there are two prime suspects right here in Porto Viejo.'

'Who do you mean?'

She told him about Harry Avery and Harry Barlow. When she had finished he was frowning.

'Judy, I think I would trust your instincts. But as a police officer I must have some proof. The fact that Senor Avery and Senor Barlow refused to let you take their photographs is not proof of anything.'

Again Judy felt frustrated. She wanted to argue with him but again she knew he was right. She twisted her face away and glared tight-lipped at the boats in the harbour. After a moment she felt his fingers and thumb touching her chin. Gently but firmly he turned her face until she was looking back into his eyes. She realized that he had very deep, dark, almost luminous brown eyes that seemed capable of searching into her soul. They made her feel suddenly weak and vulnerable.

He moved his hands to hold her shoulders. Their faces were very close. 'Judy,' he said softly. 'I will do everything I can. But now I want you to promise me something.'

Her mouth felt dry. Her heart was suddenly fluttering in her breast. She had heard of people having butterflies in the stomach but this was the first time she had realized that the sensation could also be experienced in her loins. She said slowly. 'What do you want me to promise?'

'I want you to promise that you will never do anything so foolish again. This crazy adventure in Turkey could have gone so badly wrong. Breaking into the Keskin boatyard was a criminal act. You could have been arrested by the Turkish police for trespass at the very least. Right now you could have been in a Turkish jail. Or the people at the boatyard could have killed you. Your friend Georgina has already been murdered. Your friends Peter and Jane have probably been murdered. All the other owners of the yachts that have disappeared have probably been murdered. These people are ruthless. You must not give them another opportunity or another reason to kill you.'

Judy felt a tumult of emotions and the dominant one came from the fact that he cared. He was genuinely concerned about her safety. She nodded and said, 'I promise.'

Miguel smiled. 'If anything bad happened to you I would be devastated,' he said and then he leaned forward and kissed her.

Perhaps it was meant to be a polite, brotherly kiss on the cheek, but Judy turned her lips to meet his. The attraction between them was mutual and the moment was slipping out of control. They kissed hard and held each other close.

They had to remember that the Fishermen's Plaza was still a public space so they broke apart quickly before they were disturbed. Miguel smiled again and Judy felt her heat beating very fast.

★ ★ ★

Judy walked back to the *Conquistador* with her thoughts in a hopeless tangle. The sudden change of pace and excitement of the past few days had renewed and revitalized her relationship with Ben. They had become a team again, working together to solve a mystery just as they had in the old days. The stirring of new feelings for Miguel had been forgotten and she had felt that the strain in her marriage had eased. Now, by the simple act of kissing her, Miguel had turned her head and her heart upside down once more.

There would have been no problem if Miguel had not been such a handsome and attractive man. There would have been no problem if he had not shown his concern for her. The fact that he was good looking and that he did care had screwed her all up. She was happy with her marriage. She was happy with Ben. She was old enough and sensible enough to know that it couldn't be wine and roses for every single minute of every day. Even so she had enjoyed being kissed by Miguel and she wanted more.

She wondered if this was what they called the Seven Year Itch, the time when marriage and one partner became tame and the excitement of change and adventure beckoned. She didn't want to be unfaithful to Ben but she did fancy Miguel. She found herself thinking the unthinkable: if she did have an affair, would the thrill be worth the possible consequences?

She reached the *Conquistador* and tried to push the idea out of her mind. Ben was waiting for her and eager to hear what had happened. She told him an edited version and this time Ben seemed to suspect nothing untoward, which only increased her feeling of guilt.

'I guess he would be caught on the hop.' Ben showed some understanding of Miguel's dilemma. 'Our freelancing must be something he couldn't condone. He's still a policeman who has to obey the rules. But he did say he would use what we found?'

Judy nodded. 'It's not conclusive and it probably won't hold up in court, but we have helped to clarify the picture.'

Ben was still disappointed. He too had expected more. 'I've been talking to Isabella,' he said. 'While we've been gone the two Harrys have stayed away. Their yachts have not left the harbour so they are both around somewhere, but they're not drinking here.'

Judy understood. In helping her he had been hoping to clear away the suspicion surrounding his friend. Now he still didn't know what to think.

'Maybe Arturo will have seen Harry A.' She

suggested. 'He was a regular visitor at the fire station. Perhaps you could call in and ask discretely.'

Ben considered the idea. 'We've got a couple of letters to post. That will give me an excuse to walk past the fire station.'

'Do it,' Judy said. 'I can manage here with Isabella.'

Ben needed no more urging. He collected the mail and went out. Judy got on with the job of running the bar. She wanted to sort out her thoughts and feelings about Miguel but there was no time. There were customers to serve and Isabella had two days of gossip and stories to relate. The bar had done well while they were away, the takings had stayed steady at the till and there had been no problems. Isabella was pleased with herself. She chattered happily.

Judy was pleased too, but for once she wished Isabella would shut up. She was tired after the second night of flights that had brought them back to Spain from Turkey. It had been uneventful except for one uneasy moment at Milas Airport. A young emigration officer had checked the entry date on their passport and asked why they were leaving his beautiful country so soon. Judy had used the sick mother story again to explain their rapid turnaround and departure. The Turk had looked sympathetic and made them promise to come back. However, each subsequent passport check had tensed them up a bit. Now it was all beginning to catch up with her and she had too much to think about.

Half an hour passed and Ben came back, shrugging his shoulders and looking gloomy.

'The *Bomberos* are out,' he told her. 'The bay doors are wide open and the fire pumps are all gone. They must have a decent shout.'

He sounded both envious and frustrated.

★　★　★

Ben and Judy were not the only ones who had returned to Spain. Blondie Dave and Luis had made an earlier flight from Istanbul to Madrid and then taken the internal flight to Alicante. They were back in Porto Viejo but were carefully avoiding their previous haunts. Dave had not gone back to the old fishing boat that had been his home for the past six months, and Luis had reluctantly refrained from going home to his mother. They did not know for certain if they were under suspicion but Harry had decided to take no chances. They were lying low and Harry had put them up temporarily at his villa.

It was a short term measure while they

waited to perform one last job. They had one small room to share but there was plenty of room on the large private patio and it was only a short run across the beach to the sea. They could sunbathe and swim and there was plenty of food and bottled beer in the massive fridge. Luis was quite content to be idling away his time but Dave soon became bored.

Eventually he made a telephone call and left the villa. Both were in defiance of Harry's instructions and Luis's objections. Luis was afraid of Harry but Dave still considered himself his own man. He wasn't just a hired help, he had private business.

It was a long walk into Porto Viejo and then he took a roundabout route through the back streets to the Old Town. He was determined to do his own thing but he wasn't a fool. He was avoiding the tourist areas and the harbour where he might be recognized.

He managed to get lost in the maze of narrow streets that led up the hill to the back of the cathedral. Approaching from an unfamiliar direction meant that there were no landmarks he recognized. He began to swear as he turned the same corner for a third time. There was a bar there with two outside tables where three old men sat smoking and talking. They grinned at him and asked where he was going but he ignored them and pushed on.

He didn't want to tell anyone where he was going.

At last he saw a street name and an overhanging row of iron framed balconies which he remembered. The street was empty. He felt a sense of relief because there was no one here to watch him. The door he wanted stood open in silent invitation. He went inside quickly and hurried up an ancient wooden staircase with plaster peeling walls. There was a small landing at the top and he knocked gently on the door of her small apartment, hoping that neither of the other two doors would open before he could slip inside.

Maria opened the door and let him in. She was wearing a light-weight white silk dressing gown belted at the waist and she greeted him with a warm smile and a kiss. Dave hugged her tight.

'I've missed you,' he said. And it was true, during the two week voyage on *Wave Dancer* he had thought of very little else.

'I miss you too,' Maria said and giggled. Dave knew it could be a lie, just a stock in trade answer, but he didn't want to believe that. He wanted to believe she meant it. He kissed her again and squeezed her against his chest, feeling her small breasts flatten. At this hour of the afternoon her face was clean and it suddenly occurred to him that without the heavy late-night make-up she was not very old.

He broke away, fished in his pocket and gave her a wad of money. He wanted this bit over quickly as though it was no longer important. Maria smiled, kissed him lightly again and then turned and led the way into the bedroom. She opened the drawer of a bedside table and dropped the roll of notes inside. It pleased him that she hadn't bothered to count it.

She came into his arms again and they kissed some more. He fumbled with the belt at her waist and pulled the knot loose. The white silk fell open. She was naked underneath and he pushed the dressing gown back over her shoulders. Part of him wanted to prolong this, to do things gently and tease her slowly, to make real foreplay as though they were real lovers. At the same time he was impatient and horny. He wanted her badly.

Need won and they did it quickly. Afterwards they lay together on the large bed and she seemed content to stay. He began to wonder if they could do it again. He stroked the curve of her hip and kissed her nipple. She laughed and seemed pleased. She snuggled closer. He began to feel that this was for real. He wasn't just another customer.

'Why do you do this?' he asked. And then

he wished that he hadn't spoiled the moment. The question sounded so trite and corny.

Maria looked at him blankly.

'What about your family?' Suddenly he wanted to know. 'You must have a family.'

Maria pushed herself up on to one elbow to look at him. She was uncertain now. Some of her hard confidence was gone.

'What do you mean? My family are nothing.'

Dave felt uncomfortable, prepared to let it go.

Then she sighed, as though it was not an important secret.

'My father died when I was a little girl. My mother married again. My new father hit me a lot. I was always in the way. When I got older he began to look at me different. He stopped hitting me. He started to do other things to me. My mother she knew, but she didn't hate him, she hated me. So I ran away. I came to Porto Viejo. I meet Conchita, she is a little older than me. She showed me how to make a living.'

It was a simple story, quickly told. Maria shrugged her bare shoulders. 'Most men do not treat me as badly as my stepfather,' she finished.

Dave pulled her close to him once more. He wanted to hold her tenderly, to be the one who treated her best. He began to stroke her dark hair, then to caress the back of her neck and her shoulder, then to stroke her hair again. His big clumsy hands were not made for a gentle touch but he was trying to be gentle.

Without quite knowing how he had started he was telling her about his life. He had never talked to anyone like this before. He told her about the long succession of uncles that his mother had brought home. He hadn't been wanted either but at least he hadn't been sexually abused. He told her about the drab estate where he had been raised, about the gang warfare between the Rambos and the Diehards. He even told her about the way Big Jase had died and how he had run away. He was beginning to see Maria and himself as two of an unhappy kind.

At last it was all said and he laid back and closed his eyes. He felt emotionally drained. Maria had listened to him without making any interruptions. He believed she understood. After a while he felt the touch of her mouth on his lips, she was kissing him again. He opened his eyes and saw tears in hers.

They made love again and this time he was sure it was something special. Afterward they lay side by side and it felt wonderful. When he thought back to how they had started it seemed like a miracle. He remembered losing his temper and hitting her and bitterly regretted it. He promised himself silently that he would never hit her again, that he would never let anyone hit her again.

The shadows lengthened in the small dingy room and reluctantly he realized that he would have to go. He needed to get back to the villa before Harry returned. The harsh reality was that he couldn't really afford to enrage Harry if he could avoid it.

He sat up and dressed and then kissed her for the last time, a long, lingering kiss.

'I've got one more job to do,' he told her. 'It means I have to leave Porto Viejo again for another couple of weeks, but I will come back. Then we'll both leave Porto Viejo, together. And we'll never come back. I'll have plenty of money. You won't have to do this anymore. I won't have to work anymore. We'll go to South America, Rio de Janeiro maybe. We'll start a new life, just you and me.'

Maria stared at him. Maybe she didn't believe it, but she nodded her head and smiled.

16

After the Easter celebrations the biggest event in Porto Viejo was always the annual Moors and Christians festival. The Berber Arabs from Morocco had invaded Spain early in the eighth century and Islam had dominated the country for almost eight hundred years. Those years and especially the later years of re-conquest by the Christians were remembered with passion and vigour and two days of mock battles and parades. It brought flocks of extra tourists into the town and the locals turned out en masse in their Sunday best.

Judy heard the sounds of the first brass band starting up along the harbour front and moved to the door to see what was happening. Crowds packed the promenade and she stood beside the old wooden conquistador to watch them. After a moment Ben and Isabella came to stand beside her. Isabella could sense her frustration and said cheerfully.

'Go and watch them. I can manage here for a little while.'

'It doesn't seem fair to leave you with all the work,' Judy objected.

'I have seen it before,' Isabella shrugged and smiled. 'For you it is the first time. I can see you are eager to take some pictures.'

'Go for it,' Ben said. 'I'll stay and help Isabella.'

Judy hesitated for another moment, then thanked them and grabbed her camera. She headed for where the band was playing and the first parade was starting to form up. It seemed as though every able-bodied local male was dressed up as either a Christian knight or a Saracen soldier. Turbans and pantaloons mingled with white surplices emblazoned with the red cross of Christ and all of them were in some sort of chain mail and bearing shields and swords. The men were colourful and the women were gorgeous. It seemed that every senora and her daughter were dressed in a rainbow of flared gowns of silk brocade with white lace shawls thrown carelessly around their shoulders. All of them had their glistening black hair rolled and braided and held in place by elaborate gold and silver clips and pins.

Judy wandered along the edge of the crowd, clicking her camera and waving at the people she knew. She saw Pedro the fisherman dressed up as El Cid and carrying an elaborate banner trailing a stream of pennants, and recognized Arturo the *Bomb-ero* fire chief in the robes of an Arab sultan. She had learned from Isabella that the parades took place in the morning and the battles in the afternoon. Later today the Moors would defend the old castle ruins against an assault by the Christians. On the first day they would repulse the attack but tomorrow the Christians would be victorious. First they all had to march to the church for a service and a blessing.

Judy stopped to photograph a particularly attractive family. The smiling young woman wore a richly patterned gown of green and gold and the toddler daughter was a miniature of her mother in a matching dress. With them was a boy of about seven who wore smart black trousers, a green and gold shirt and a golden waist sash. They posed willingly and Judy thanked them for the picture. She turned away and saw Miguel Garcia watching with an uncertain look upon his face.

Judy grinned and said, 'Hello.'

She walked over to him and he managed a smile and said, '*Bueno Dias.*'

'What a fantastic show,' she waved her hand to indicate the parade. 'When does it all start?'

Miguel looked at his wristwatch. 'They

have to be at the cathedral for noon. It takes them time to organize themselves. Nobody is in a hurry.' He shrugged. 'After all, this is Spain, *mañana* country.'

Judy nodded. She watched the milling crowd for a moment and then looked back at his face. It was three days since they had last talked and although she could see he was off duty and probably didn't want to talk shop she couldn't stop herself from asking. 'Is there any news?'

Miguel hesitated. She sensed that he was impatient to get away but then he answered. 'The analysis of the splinters you gave me shows that they were stained with a mixture of human blood and sangria. We have notified London. Now we wait for them to make their investigation and reply.'

Judy felt cold although this was no more than she had expected. She said slowly. 'Did you have any luck with the police in Turkey?'

'They have been informed. They were very displeased but they have visited the Keskin boatyard. They found the *Samisakali* was back in the water, ready to sail, and she has all new deck boards in the galley.'

'Damn,' Judy said softly.

Miguel shrugged. 'I did warn you. The people we are up against are not fools. They act quickly.'

His behaviour was strangely defensive and Judy sensed that something was wrong. She was puzzled and for a moment she thought that there must be something that he did not want to tell her. She had forgotten the parade now and her mind was focussed again on the missing yachts and Georgina's murder. Then suddenly she realized that he was bothered by something else altogether.

She became aware that the lovely young woman in the green and gold dress had not moved away to rejoin the parade. The whole family were standing behind her, patiently waiting and watching. The little girl could finally wait no more. She ran forward to pull at Miguel's hand and ask for an ice cream. Slowly Miguel stooped and lifted the child up into his arms. She was grinning happily and leaned forward to whisper in his ear.

Miguel looked apologetically at Judy and said. 'This is my daughter, her name is Felicia.' The boy came up and Miguel ruffled his neat black curls. He said simply, 'This is my son, Juan.'

Judy stared at him and all her emotions began to perform sickening cartwheels. She turned slowly to face the lovely young woman in the green and gold festival dress.

'This is my wife, Elena,' Miguel continued. 'Elena, this is Judy Kane, the English woman who now runs the *Conquistador*. She was a police officer in England. She has been helping my investigation into the death of the poor woman who was dragged up in the nets of the *Serrano*.'

Judy found herself shaking hands and smiling. Her smile felt as though it had been painted on and could crack at any moment.

★   ★   ★

The harbour was packed to capacity and most of the boat owners were ashore or standing at their yacht rails watching the events along the edge of the harbour. The fishing fleet had the day off and all of the trawlers stayed tied up at their dockside while the crews enjoyed the holiday. Only one boat was putting out to sea, a sleek white-hulled yacht that chugged slowly out through the gap between the breakwater walls of grey rock. With so much excitement on land nobody took any notice of her departure.

She was the *Apache* and Blondie Dave stood in her stern, legs splayed to maintain his balance as he coiled a mooring rope into loops on his arm. He was glad to be sailing, happy to be leaving Porto Viejo for the last time. This was definitely the last job and he had no intention of coming back. When it was over he would telephone Maria and tell her where to come and join him.

Luis was standing beside him, looking sad and downcast. This was his home and he had not had any chance to visit his mother. He probably would come back eventually. Dave knew that their friendship was coming to an end. They would soon be parting. It didn't matter because he would have Maria.

Apache cleared the harbour and Dave hung the coil of rope on its cleat. He stepped down into the cockpit and grinned at the fat man perspiring at the wheel. 'Okay, Harry?'

Harry Barlow nodded cheerfully. 'Okay, Davey. Let's hoist some sail and let this baby fly.'

Dave and Luis busied themselves with setting the mainsail. The canvas caught the slight breeze and *Apache* gathered speed. Harry cut the engine and allowed the wind to do the work. The wind was free and there was more enjoyment in sailing. This was what the sleek craft was designed to do, to lean with the breeze and race over the waves.

They cruised south along the coast, passing beaches and coves and outcrops of pine covered rocks. Inland there were villas and vast *urbanisations* covering the hills in a sprawl of red and yellow tiled roofs, broken up here and there by the larger apartment blocks and the green ovals and circles of the golf courses. Dave didn't like it too much. He preferred the more natural stretches where the hills were too rugged to permit easy building. He was a city boy who had learned to hate housing estates and city streets. He fancied wild open spaces.

He began to wonder if he really did want to go to Rio de Janeiro. The travel brochure pictures always looked nice, Sugar Loaf Mountain and all those gorgeous nearly naked girls on Copacabana Beach. But one trip on the cable car would be enough, and he would have Maria. The rest of Rio would be another city full of slums. Maybe he would move on and find a quiet little coastal town in Brazil.

Harry called him out of his reverie by asking him to take the wheel.

'Get the feel of her,' Harry said. 'She handles like a dream.'

They changed places. Harry sat down on a small deckchair in the stern of the boat, pulled his cap down to shade his eyes and folded his hands comfortably over his ample stomach. Luis was still sitting in the stern lost in thought. All three of them were mostly silent, as though it was too hot for conversation and a natural camaraderie had already been established. Dave now had to handle the yacht, but for the moment that job amounted to no more than standing with one hand on the wheel.

They cruised for just over an hour and then Dave said casually, 'The cove is coming up.'

Harry Barlow opened his eyes, pushed back his baseball cap, stretched and yawned. 'Okay,' he said. 'Take her in. I'm ready for a swim.'

Luis got up and lowered the sail as Dave started the engine and switched power. The mouth of the cove was on their starboard bow and Dave turned the boat in toward the small enclosed beach as she slowed. He was familiar with this spot now. This was the fourth yacht he had brought to anchor in this quiet and secluded place. He tried not to think too much about the things that had happened here. He was not a highly imaginative man and he could push anything he didn't want to remember into the back of his mind. He found it helped him to sleep at nights. He eased *Apache* to within fifty feet of the shore and then stopped the engine. Luis dropped the small anchor.

Harry stood up and dropped his cap and sunglasses on the chair. He shrugged out of his shirt and dropped his shorts. Underneath he wore bathing trunks.

'You guys coming in?' he asked.

'Sure thing,' Dave answered.

Dave and Luis pulled off their shirts. They didn't mind swimming in the shorts they were wearing. They would soon dry out again in the sun. All three of them lined up on the stern of the yacht and dived into the sparkling blue water of the cove. They swam and dived and splashed for ten minutes before Harry climbed out. Dave and Luis followed him. Harry found a towel and began to rub himself dry. Dave and Luis were happy to just sprawl on the deck and let their bodies steam dry in the sun.

'Beers are in the fridge,' Harry said.

Luis took the hint and went down to the galley. He came back with three ice cold bottles of Budweiser which he handed round. All three of them relaxed and drank deeply.

Their idyllic moments of peace were finally interrupted when another sail appeared. They watched as the second sail grew larger and then she too turned her bows into the cove. It was another yacht, as large and similar in design to *Apache*. The lone sailor at the wheel moved forward to lower his sail and then despite his fat bulk dropped nimbly back into the cockpit. Harry Barlow shaded his eyes with one hand under the peak of his cap and then recognized the yacht and the man at the wheel.

The yacht was *Seagull Two*.

'Hey, Harry,' Harry Barlow yelled at the fat man in the gaudily flowered shirt who could have been his twin. 'What brings you here?'

'Just cruising,' Harry Avery shouted back. 'I thought I recognized that white beard and your boat. Where are you headed?'

'Anywhere and everywhere, it just seemed like time to explore a bit more of Spain. Are you looking for that race we never got round to?'

Harry Avery grinned. 'I'm still looking forward to it, but it's a bit calm today. We need a lot more wind for a really good race.'

'Too right, but stop and have a beer anyway.'

Seagull Two was now within a few feet of *Apache* and as she drifted alongside Harry Avery threw a rope to Blondie Dave. Dave caught it and tied the two boats together.

Harry Barlow tilted his Budweiser bottle to his lips and drained the last swallow. He tossed the empty bottle into the sea and wiped his moustache and beard appreciatively with the back of his hand.

'I'll get another couple of bottles,' he said. He turned and went down into the galley as Harry Avery stepped on board.

★　★　★

286

Judy spent a few minutes forcing herself to indulge in polite small talk with Elena. Mercifully Felicia was insistent upon her need for an immediate ice cream and Miguel led his children over to the nearest vendor. Judy saw that the parade was now taking definite shape and with it her opportunity to get away.

'I think they will soon be moving,' she said. The band was starting up with another tune and she had to almost shout.

Elena said happily, 'Yes, I must go. We must speak another time.'

Elena hurried to collect her son and daughter and take her place in the fluid line up of swirling colour and white lace. Judy slipped away while Miguel was still paying the ice cream vendor. She made the move casually but as soon as she was out of their sight she let the crowds swallow her up and walked more briskly. Initially she moved without any conscious direction and it was not until she passed the Fishermen's Square that she realized that she was walking away from the *Conquistador*.

The square was another rallying point, complete with a second brass band and a large group from one of the churches who were struggling to lift a large shrine of Christ crucified on to their shoulders. The shrine was almost buried under flowers and most of the women and girls here were carrying a large bouquet. It made a splendid picture but Judy was no longer interested in pictures. Her camera trailed forgotten from its loop around her wrist.

She remembered when the square had been empty, when they had sat together on the stone bench and Miguel had tenderly kissed her. Now she wanted to kick herself for being such a fool.

She wondered how on earth he could behave like that when he had a lovely wife and two beautiful children. They had all looked such a perfect family with their happy smiles and all dressed in their best parade clothes. She was furious with Miguel and she was furious with herself. She remembered that she had been equally responsible for that kiss and she had actually considered being unfaithful to Ben. Perhaps Miguel was no more contemptible than she was.

Suddenly she wanted to hit something, or someone. The festive scene in the square was unbearable in her present mood and she hurried on her way again. She was still heading in the opposite direction to the *Conquistador*. She felt that she just couldn't go back to the bar yet. There was no way that she could face Ben and Isabella and pretend that nothing had happened.

She walked past the Fishermen's wharf and down on to the beach. With everyone watching or participating in the parade the sands were almost empty. She walked down to the edge of the sea and watched the white swirl of the waves as they rolled in towards her. Her angry thoughts chased round and round in her head.

What she remembered of her silly fantasies now seemed like all stupid schoolgirl stuff. She should have known better. Just one simple kiss and she had let her head and her heart get into a spin. He had not even led her on. He had just shown some concern for her safety. The kiss was probably only intended as a friendly gesture. She was the one who had responded to it and blown the whole thing out of proportion.

The anger she felt toward Miguel began to evaporate but she still felt angry with herself. How could she have been so foolish?

She still wanted to do something. The frustration inside her was a mass of seething energy which she somehow had to burn off. The desire to lash out had faded, there was no one here to lash out at anyway, but still she had to do something. On impulse she kicked off her sandals. She dropped her camera into the sand beside them, then pulled off her tee shirt and discarded that too. In shorts and a halter top she began to run along the beach, heading blindly south, away from the harbour, away from the *Conquistador,* and away from Miguel Garcia and his lovely, happy family.

It was a long time since she had given herself a good work-out. Too much work had got in the way and because Ben could no longer run so well she had got out of the habit. She too was getting out of condition. She got into her usual stride but soon she was panting. However, she wanted to punish herself. She increased the pace and ran harder.

Her bare feet flew over the soft sand or splashed through the rivulets of expiring waves. The sea sparkled blue and silver on her left, the yellow beach blurred past on her right. She hardly saw any of it. She just ran until her calf and thigh muscles began to ache and the pain started to push her rage and disgust into the background of her mind.

She reached the far end of the beach and without pause pushed up a continuing footpath which snaked up between the rocks and pine trees of a small headland. She plunged down the other side and found another beach. She kept running until she came to another headland. She was gasping now and the sweat was trickling into her eyes. She had no headband. She hadn't prepared for this run. She had done no easy exercises to tone up her muscles before pushing them to the limit. She was suffering for that now and everything was beginning to hurt. She ignored it all and scrambled over the next headland.

There was a third beach. She guessed that this pattern of beaches and rocky headlands probably continued all the way south to where the Mediterranean met the mouth into the Atlantic. She no longer cared. She just kept on running.

Her chest was heaving. Her heart was hammering. She stumbled over a piece of bone-white driftwood that was half buried in the soft sand. She swore, regained her balance and staggered on. She was slowing down. She just couldn't keep up her speed. This was ridiculous anyway. She reduced her pace to a trot. Her head ached. There was a sharp stitch pain in her side. Her heart was going too fast. She was going to give herself a heart attack if she didn't stop.

She came to a stop, leaning forward with her hands braced on her knees. The sweat trickled down her face, down the sides of her neck, over her chest and between her breasts. She felt drained, exhausted. She blinked. Her eyes stung and she tried to wipe them with the back of her hand.

Eventually she sat down, almost collapsing in the sand. She folded her arms on her knees and sat with her head bowed. She was gasping for breath but somehow she felt better. She had purged all that stupid emotion. Now she was ready to see sense.

She raised her head and looked around to see where she was. On her right the sea still sparkled empty and blue. She looked around the beach. She was in another small bay. On the landward side there was just one large villa with white walls and heavy red roof tiles. The villa had a large patio facing the sea, enclosed with a low wall of white balustrades and an arched gateway. Bougainvillea spilled over the wall in a wave of red and purple flowers. Beyond were grape vines and palm trees. The house had shuttered windows painted yellow and yellow-railed balconies.

Judy stared at it and forgot all the complaints of her tortured body.

She had seen this villa before, in the photograph that Sally Russell had emailed to her computer. In that picture Georgina Harrington had been sitting cross-legged in the sand, not far from where she was sitting now. Georgie had been alive, smiling happily for someone's camera.

Here.

Georgie had been here.

Judy was certain. This was the villa in the photograph.

17

Dave felt the familiar deep churning in his guts as he extended a hand to help Harry Avery step on board. It was always the same. His mouth felt dry and his stomach felt as though it was going to let everything go loose, exactly as in those eternal seconds when he had watched King William and his Rambo mates start kicking the life out of Big Jase, just before he had run away.

What always got to him and made his skin crawl was that Harry was so calm. They both knew what was going to happen next and yet Harry had the same happy grin on his fat face that he always presented to the world. Harry with his flashy rings and shirts and his endless capacity for beer and laughs was emotionally empty and ice cold inside. And no one who had not seen him at work would ever guess. Dave just couldn't understand Harry. It seemed as though he had some sort of alien internal switch that could simply disconnect all human feeling below the cheery surface.

Luis had moved to the stern of the yacht and was staring down into the water, not wanting to be part of what was coming. Dave wanted to do the same but somehow he couldn't disassociate himself completely. It would be a bit like running away again. He had always felt guilty about leaving Big Jase, even though he knew that there had been no other choice, none that would have let him stay alive anyway. Even so he didn't want to be a complete chicken.

So Dave stayed in the cockpit by the wheel after Harry Avery had stepped down to join him. Through the open doorway that led down into the galley they could see Harry Barlow taking four bottles of Budweiser out of the refrigerator. The fat, white-bearded American seemed unsuspecting as he lined the bottles up on the stainless steel worktop. He pulled open the cutlery drawer, selected a bottle opener and began snapping the caps off the bottles.

'Permission to come aboard, Skipper,' Harry Avery shouted as he put his head through the open door and placed one foot on the top step of the short companionway.

'Sure thing,' Harry Barlow looked round and grinned. 'You can help me carry these beers up on deck.'

Harry Avery eased his fat bulk through the narrow doorway. With his right hand he reached back for the automatic handgun that was jammed into the waistband of his shorts close against his spine.

Dave wanted to look away. After the first time he had always looked away. Harry Avery wasted no time. He never gave his victims a chance. Harry Avery just stepped aboard, all bright and breezy, the eternal jolly fat man, and before anyone could blink, 'Bang, Bang,' it was all over.

Somehow, this time, Dave had a premonition that it was not going to be so easy. There was something he had sensed in fat Harry Barlow. Perhaps he had been around Harry Avery for too long, but it seemed to him that these two happy fat men were two of a kind. It was not just because they were both obese, or that they both loved their beer and the same free and easy, laughing lifestyle. What Dave sensed was that there was a similar streak underneath. It was as though both men were living an act, taking part in a perpetual game that had no intervals and no end.

Over Harry Avery's shoulder Dave saw Harry Barlow flip the last cap off the last bottle of Budweiser and drop the opener back into the open galley drawer. He saw something else. He saw the reflection of Harry Avery as he descended the gangway, blurred but definable enough on the bright steel surface of the galley worktop. The reflection showed Harry Avery's right hand coming round from behind his back and holding the gun.

Harry Barlow saw it too. He had his back to Harry Avery but the reflection showed him what was happening behind him. Dave could partly see the hardened change of expression on the American's face and knew that he had been warned. He wanted to shout a warning to Harry Avery but his mouth was too dry and nothing came out.

Harry Barlow moved with speed that seemed incredible for such a large man in such a tightly confined space. With both hands he grabbed the half open cutlery drawer, pulled it free, turned and threw it at Harry Avery.

The sharp edge of the drawer hit Harry Avery hard in the stomach, knocking him back against the companionway. Knives, forks and spoons showered out of the drawer as it spun, a cascade of stabbing and bruising steel that poured over Harry's gun hand. The gun went off with a loud cracking sound but the first bullet missed.

Harry Barlow plunged his right hand into the cavity left by the kitchen drawer and came out holding an almost identical weapon. The two fat Harrys traded shots but Harry Avery had recovered his aim a split second before Harry Barlow could get his gun clear.

Harry Barlow was blasted back against the galley worktop. A flower of red blood, like the slowly expanding petals of a rose appeared on his fat belly, just a little left of centre. Harry Barlow fired and missed. Harry Avery shot him a second time, putting a second rose just above and to the left of the first. Harry Barlow sagged and began to slide down toward the deck. His face was contorted and his mouth worked but nothing but a strangled coughing sound came out. He tried to lift his gun again but it wouldn't lift far enough. He squeezed the trigger anyway and fired another shot that missed and punched a splintered hole through the bulkhead.

The galley was filled with harsh echoes and acrid smoke. Harry Avery backed up, coughing but unharmed and rejoined Dave in the cockpit. They both moved to where Luis stood ashen-faced in the stern and drew deep breaths of the clean, fresh sea air.

'Jesus,' Harry said at last. 'I had a weird feeling about that guy, but I wasn't expecting a second shoot-out at the OK Corral.'

Dave just nodded. He didn't know what to say. All three of them stood silent for another minute. Dave and Harry were both shocked. Luis looked as though he wanted to cry.

Finally Harry went back to look down into the galley. Dave looked all around the cove, worried that the sound of the shooting might have been heard. The beach and the overlooking hills were all deserted. A bird warbled somewhere among the pine trees but there was nothing else. It was as though the peace had never been disturbed. Dave moved to join Harry. They both stared down at Harry Barlow who sprawled motionless on his back on the deck of the galley below. The red flowers on his bulging stomach were large, glistening and wet.

'The crafty bugger,' Harry said, almost in admiration. 'Who would have thought that he'd have a gun hidden away like that?'

'Who was he?' Dave asked. 'I mean, he wasn't just another ordinary yachtsman was he?'

'I guess not,' Harry said. 'Perhaps he was another one sent to spy us out.'

'So what do we do?' Dave felt blind panic. 'Perhaps we should just sink this boat and him with it. It's time to get out of here.'

'Just hold on.' Harry infuriated him by staying calm. 'This doesn't change anything. We wanted him dead and he is dead. We've got a job for this boat and it's too late to set you two up to hi-jack another. We've got a time schedule to meet and another consignment to pick up from the Algerians. Besides, *Apache* is worth another small fortune. We're not going to just scuttle her when we can still sell her on to the Turks.'

'But if he was on to us then somebody must have sent him. We can't just carry on. We're asking to get caught.'

'Just stop and think,' Harry ordered harshly. 'Even if he was another cop, nobody knows what just happened here. Even if his people know that he took you and Luis on as deckhands, and even if they know that I recommended you and set it up, it doesn't matter. You were going to disappear after this run anyway. I might even have to disappear too. But in the meantime nobody knows yet that he's dead.'

'You think he was a cop?' Luis almost blubbered.

'He had a gun hidden away,' Harry snarled. 'So he must have been something.'

'That's two cops we've killed.' Dave was sweating. 'We're not going to get away with this.'

Harry grabbed each of them by the arm just above the elbow. His big hands gripped hard enough to hurt, his fingers digging into their flesh.

'Now you listen to me. If you cut and run now you'll probably be picked up at the nearest airport. Show your stupid faces on shore and somebody is going to want to know right away what happened to *Apache* and Harry B. The best way is to just carry on. That way nobody can be sure that anything has happened. Take her down to the Algerian coast, bring back the consignment and then run her over to Turkey. You can both disappear there. You don't want to ever come back to Spain.'

'If we bring a consignment back we'll get caught.' Dave wasn't totally stupid. 'A coastguard plane found us last time.'

'So you change the return route. Sail up towards France, make a wide circle and then drop down from the north. The Mediterranean is a big sea, you can get lost in it. I'll put back the rendezvous date with the *Benissa*. Or I could arrange another hand-over off the French coast. While you're sailing south I'll have time to think. I can work something out.'

'It's too risky,' Dave said. 'It's crazy.'

Luis nodded dumb agreement.

'Look, we've got a lot invested in this. And I'm going to need time to move out. We can either scuttle *Apache* with the body, or dump the body and carry on as planned. The risks now are probably even whichever way we go.'

Dave hesitated. He still wanted to argue but some of what Harry said was making sense. To run in panic could attract more attention than to just carry on. What galled him was that he and Luis would be taking the biggest risk if they stayed with *Apache* while Harry returned to Porto Viejo with *Seagull Two*.

However, Dave was also aware that Harry still had the gun. He had tucked it back into the waistband of his shorts. Only three bullets had been fired which meant that the magazine was still more than half full, and Harry was not a man who could be crossed or defied. Harry killed too easily, and Dave could see from the cold, hard look in his eyes that he was getting impatient.

Dave was suddenly afraid. He decided that it was best to appease Harry and do what he wanted, at least until the two yachts had parted.

'Okay,' he said, ignoring the appalled look on Luis's face and trying to sound as though he had been convinced. 'We'll do it your way.'

Harry Avery grinned. 'Good man. Trust me and let me do the thinking and we'll still retire rich. Now let's get this boat started and get out of here.'

Dave nodded and still avoiding any direct eye contact with Luis he went back to the wheel. He turned the ignition key to fire the engine and get them under way. The engine roared into life.

'Cast away,' Dave ordered Luis.

The Spanish youth stared at him. His lip trembled. He wanted to argue but he didn't dare. Reluctantly he bent to slacken off the mooring rope that held the two yachts together.

Harry Avery stepped back on board *Seagull Two* and *Apache's* engine spluttered and died.

All three of them froze and looked at each other. Dave tried the ignition key again. The engine kicked in and then stopped again. He tried twice more with the same result.

Harry came back on to *Apache's* deck. 'Check the engine,' he growled.

It was a job for Luis. He was the smallest of the three and could work more easily in the confined space of the engine hatch. As a boy he had often watched his father work on the diesel engine of the old fishing boat and he had no objection to getting his hands dirty. Working on an engine was one of the few kinds of work he didn't mind doing. It took him three minutes to find the problem and then he wiped his forehead with the back of an oil-smeared hand and looked up with a hopeless expression on his face.

'The engine cannot start because the fuel pump is smashed.'

Harry Avery swore. Dave twisted his neck

to look over Luis's shoulder and saw that the fuel pump was just a mess of mangled metal. Looking round he saw a splintered hole in the wooden bulkhead that separated the engine hatch from the galley. He realized that one of the stray shots from Harry Barlow's gun must have caused the damage.

'It's been hit by a bullet,' he said bitterly. 'The daft bastard sabotaged his own boat.' He knew there was no way that Harry Barlow could have deliberately aimed the shot. It was just a stupid accident. He still felt like kicking the fat American anyway.

They returned to the deck for some fresh air. Luis looked from Dave to Harry, searching for a lead. 'What can we do now?' he asked.

Harry scratched his head and scowled. 'Only one thing to do, I'll have to give *Apache* a tow with *Seagull Two*.'

'Out to sea,' Luis said hopefully. 'We will have to sink her now.'

'No,' Harry contradicted him. This time there was an iron hard determination in his tone that didn't allow for any more arguments. 'We'll tow her back to Porto Viejo and you can fit another fuel pump. It shouldn't take long and then you two can sail again and carry on as planned.'

Judy sat on the warm sand with her ankles crossed and her hands resting on her knees as she waited for her racing heart beats to slow and for her heaving chest movements to subside. Everything she had felt about Miguel was purged and forgotten. All her reasons for punishing herself with a blind, gruelling run had simply evaporated as she had lifted her head, opened her eyes and recognized the villa.

She had behaved like an idiot but that was behind her now. In an instant everything had changed. This was the place. This was where the last photograph of Georgie had been taken, with Georgie smiling as though she owned the place, or was at least a welcome guest.

This was the lucky break that every crime investigator waited for, the moment when all the long, grinding hours of routine work suddenly paid off. Ben might say that it was pure luck, but it wasn't luck that had phoned Sally Russell and brought the photograph to Judy in the first place. Without the photo-graph she would not have been able to recognize the villa or know its importance when she saw it. As always it was the routine work that brought the result.

As she recovered from the run she began to think about what to do next. It was pretty stupid just sitting here in full view of the villa but she had collapsed and sat here gasping for several minutes before its significance had clicked in her dopey brain. Now it was too late but the villa looked deserted. There was no sign of life or movement.

She could just get up as though she had rested and resume her run or just walk away, but she didn't think that was necessary. She had the gut feeling that the villa was empty.

She could call the police but inevitably her call would be routed through to Miguel and she was not ready yet to talk to Miguel. She could call Ben but for the moment she didn't want to talk to Ben either. She didn't particularly want to talk to anyone. She did want to take a closer look at the villa.

She stood up slowly. She had been here on this beach for almost ten minutes and nobody had appeared to show any interest. She was ready to gamble that the villa was empty. If it wasn't then she needed a good excuse to knock on the door. The obvious answer came to her and she smiled. She began to walk across the soft sand to the villa, affecting a deliberate limp. If there was anyone there then her story would be that she had sprained her ankle and she needed help.

There was a low stone wall surrounding the property and a stone archway over the gate. The gate was open which was promising. It was not likely that there would be a dog. She remembered the Keskin boatyard with a shiver of apprehension. She went through the archway and walked across the patio beside the small swimming pool to the French windows that were the rear entrance to the villa.

She knocked loudly, just like any ordinary, innocent visitor, on the glass door.

The villa was still and silent. There was no response from inside. Judy rapped again with her knuckles. Finally she tried the door. The handle turned and it opened.

Judy hesitated. A door that was not locked seemed too good to be true. She wondered if she was walking in to a trap but this was a chance discovery and there was no way that she could be expected. She put her head inside and called out cheerfully, 'Hello, is anybody there?'

Her voice echoed around an empty room and there was no answer.

Judy went inside.

She was in a large living room with amber floor tiles and white rugs. The walls and curtains were shades of cream. There was a large black leather suite, a massive wide screen television set and a stereo music system. The racks beside the television were full of videos and she read some of the titles, *Backdraft, The Towering Inferno, Ladder49*, and a whole collection of *London's Burning*.

'Harry A,' she murmured softly.

She checked out the rest of the ground floor. There was a large double bedroom and a large open-plan, Spanish-tiled dining room and kitchen. She spared each of them a quick glance, not wanting to be caught snooping. There were no feminine touches and her feeling was that this was a purely masculine environment. She opened the refrigerator in the kitchen to check and found it well stocked with beer. There were at least two dozen bottles of Budweiser.

'Or perhaps Harry B,' she frowned and amended her first guess.

She went back into the living room. There was a stairway leading to the upper floor. More bedrooms she guessed but she was reluctant to go up there. She had come looking for help and found the French doors open, which might explain her presence in the living room, but it would not justify her prowling through the upper rooms.

She called out again, 'Hello, is anyone at home?' just to keep up the act. Again there was nothing but she was still reluctant to go up the stairs.

She went into the dining area again. The large window here overlooked the front patio and a gravel driveway. Beyond she saw a car drive past on the main road. There was no vehicle parked on the drive or anywhere on the premises, reassuring her that she must be alone.

She returned to the living room. There was one more door she had not tried. She opened it and peered into a small bedroom or study room that had been fitted as an office. There was a desk with a computer, more bookshelves and a polished wooden filing cabinet.

Judy stood listening. There was still no sound. She looked at the filing cabinet but the computer seemed more promising. She went inside and sat at the computer desk. She was at the point of no return but the temptation was too great. She switched the computer on and waited for the screen to warm up.

The screensaver image that slowly appeared was of a large red American fire truck. Again she thought Harry A. Then a menu screen appeared demanding that she enter a password.

Judy swore under her breath although she knew she couldn't expect everything to be easy. She typed in Harry. The screen flickered and then repeated its demand. She typed Avery. Again the demand was repeated. She typed in Arnold, and then fireman, fire-fighter, fire engine, and none of them gave her access. She tried Seagull and Seagull Two.

She sat back frowning, wondering what else he might have chosen. She had no way of guessing his mother's name, or knowing if he had ever had a wife or children. She should have asked Ron Harding to dig out more background information.

She looked around for inspiration. There were files and folders and books on the shelves around her. The books had titles like *Fire-fighting and Fire Engines, Fire Departments of the USA, A history of the British Fire Service.* She remembered how Ian Fleming had chosen the name for his immortal James Bond. He had simply borrowed it from the nearest book jacket. She began to try the author names on the books in front of her. With the third name she hit the jackpot. The screen flickered again and then said, 'Welcome Harry.'

She was in and brought up a list of documents. She opened up an excel spread-sheet and saw a mass of dates and figures, pound signs and transactions. She didn't dare study them all here but she felt certain she had found what she was looking for. She closed the file and hunted through the desk drawer beside her. She found a box of blank CD rewritable discs. Quickly she slipped one into the tower slot beside the computer screen. As fast as she could she began to copy all the files on to the CD, starting with the spreadsheet.

Somewhere in amongst all this information there had to be enough to nail fat Harry and close down his entire operation. All she had to do now was to get away with it and hand it over to Miguel.

18

An hour had passed and Ben was beginning to wonder what had happened to Judy. He had expected her to be back within ten or fifteen minutes, which was all she should have needed to take a few pictures. The *Conquistador* was quiet, still almost empty. Only two of the tables were occupied.

He wandered over to the door and looked out. The crowds had moved off. The parade had formed up and started. He had heard the sounds of the brass bands fading as they marched along the promenade. They had turned in to the town at the far end of the harbour through the Fishermen's Square. From there they had circled through the main avenues of the new town and he could still hear them faintly as they now headed up into the old town and the cathedral. He wondered if Judy had followed them.

Isabella came to stand beside him. She tilted her head to listen to the distant fanfare of trumpets. 'They walk slowly,' she said. 'And they go the long way round so that everyone gets a chance to see them. In the old town all the people will be at their window balconies to watch.'

'I didn't think Judy was going to follow them all the way,' Ben said.

Isabella smiled at him. 'Go and find her if you want. I will be okay here. Antonio will come out and help me if I need him.'

Antonio had arrived shortly after Judy had left, bringing in his usual baskets of fresh meat and fish, salad and vegetables which he had picked up on his way from the market. He was busy now chopping and preparing it all in the kitchen but he was a willing helper, always ready to pitch in with anything.

'Okay,' Ben decided. 'I'll go and fetch her back.'

He went out on to the promenade. He noticed that there was a gap in the boats that lined the harbour front. *Apache* was no longer moored at what had become her regular berth. Perhaps she had sailed in the night, or earlier in the morning when the crowds and the parade had blocked the view from the *Conquistador*. He didn't think about it too much because his thoughts were concentrated on Judy.

He walked the length of the harbour, passing between the Fishermen's Wharf and the Fishermen's Square. Here was where Judy would have turned into the town if she had followed the parade. Somehow he was sure she would not have done that. Her intention was just to take a few snaps and then come back to the bar. The bar had stayed quiet but she would not have known and would not have left all the potential work to him and Isabella. Judy was always fair and never selfish. It was one of the reasons why he loved her.

He walked on slowly, past the start of the long beach and paused where the road branched up to the castle. There were plenty of people up there, grabbing the best places well in advance to watch the mock battles the Moors and Christians would pretend to fight later in the afternoon. Judy could be instinctively drawn to that sort of spectacle but again he did not think she would abandon the bar to just sit out in the sunshine and wait for the fun to start. He was beginning to think that something else must have drawn her away.

He stood thoughtful and uncertain and for a moment he stared out to sea. He saw two yachts sailing close enough to collide and watched them. Distance was deceptive when looking out to sea. Vessels always looked as though they were going to crash when actually there was plenty of sea room for them to pass. Even so, the natural thing was always to watch and see. The two yachts stayed together and after a moment Ben realized that one was trailing the other. As they sailed along the coast towards him he realized that the first boat had the second on tow.

There was something familiar about the shape and rig of both yachts and as they neared the harbour mouth it clicked. The first yacht was *Seagull Two*. The yacht being towed was *Apache*.

'Tweedledum and Tweedledee,' Ben mused softly, 'Harry A and Harry B.'

For the moment his search for Judy was forgotten. The two yachts sailing together posed much more interesting questions.

There was another bar at the corner here and Ben walked over and sat down at one of the outside tables to watch. A large white sunshade put him in shadow and he was a lot less conspicuous than if he had remained standing at the edge of the beach.

A waiter came over and he ordered a coffee. When it was served he sipped it once. It wasn't quite as good as the coffee they served at the *Conquistador* and he pushed it to one side and forgot about it. He watched the two yachts sail slowly up to the harbour mouth.

Both yachts hove to about fifty yards from the breakwater wall and about fifty yards from the beach. He recognized the fat bulk of Harry Avery at the wheel of *Seagull Two*. There were two figures in the cockpit of *Apache* and he recognized them just as easily. Blondie Dave was wearing the old yellow tee shirt and the yellow baseball cap that he always seemed to wear. The slim dark haired figure beside him could only be Luis.

Ben's eyes narrowed and he frowned as he stared at the two white yachts. This was the first indication that Dave and Luis had returned to Porto Viejo, but what were they doing on board *Apache* and where was Harry B. And why was Harry A towing Harry B?

Ben recalled the two Harrys discussing their plans for a race. Perhaps that was the answer. They had taken both yachts out for a race and *Apache* had broken down. Blondie Dave and Luis had made up the crews. That much was obvious, and it proved that one of the two fat men had a direct link with the two casual deckhands who had sailed with *Wave Dancer*, but which one?

While he watched, *Seagull Two* began to move again. Harry Avery had cast off the tow line and was continuing in to the harbour. Ben watched the first yacht disappear behind the long arm of the breakwater wall and the warehouses along the fishermen's wharf. Ben guessed Harry was taking *Seagull Two* back to her mooring. *Apache* stayed put and he realized Blondie Dave had dropped her anchor. He watched as Dave and Luis launched the small rowing boat that was stowed at the stern of the yacht. Both men climbed into the rowboat with Dave at the oars. Briskly he began to pull for the beach.

Ben sank lower into his seat, trying to disguise his height and build. He watched as Dave and Luis jumped out of the rowboat and hauled it up on to the sand. They left it there and hurried up the beach. They reached the promenade almost opposite the spot where Ben was sitting but did not even glance in his direction. Luis was carrying what looked like a small engine part in one hand. They turned towards the harbour and walked away.

Ben saw Harry Avery come out on to the harbour promenade. He waved an acknowledgement to Dave and Luis but did not wait for them. Instead he walked a few yards in the opposite direction and disappeared down the entrance to one of the underground car parks. Dave and Luis turned on to the Fishermen's Wharf. Ben remembered that there were some machine repair shops and a marine chandler's stores just before the fish sheds.

Ben's curiosity was fully aroused now. The

fact that Harry Avery, Blondie Dave and Luis all seemed such good pals made him think maybe Judy had been right about Harry. He still didn't want to admit that. He liked to think that he was a good judge of a man and he didn't like the idea that maybe he had made a mistake about Harry. However, it was beginning to look that way.

And the other question remained, where was Harry B?

Ben got up and left a couple of euros on the table to pay for the coffee. He crossed the promenade and followed the concrete road that ran along the top of the breakwater behind the Fishermen's Wharf. He stopped above the shoreline and looked down at the rowing boat that Dave and Luis had left unguarded on the sand.

He was tempted to borrow the rowboat but decided against it. He walked out to the far end of the jetty and stared across at *Apache* only fifty yards away. There was no sign of movement on the yacht's decks, no sign that anyone had been left on board.

Ben climbed down the large black rocks until he was level with the sea. Small waves broke and splashed at his feet. On impulse he took off his tee shirt and left it with his sandals on one of the rocks. He slid his body into the sea, kicked out against a buttress of smooth worn stone and began to swim out to *Apache*. He swam with a slow, careful breast stroke that didn't disturb too much water. He didn't want to be noticeable from the shore.

The water was blue and cooling and not too deep. He could see the white sand seabed if he looked down. Any closer and *Apache* would probably have run aground. Ben swam gently until the yacht was between him and the shore. There he stopped, treading water and thinking about what he was doing.

This far he could claim that was enjoying an innocent swim. He could explain his presence as just a refreshing dip on a hot day. He could swim back to the rocks, pull on his shirt and go back to the bar without causing any offence to anyone. However, that would not give him any answers to any of the questions that frustrated him. Ideally he wanted to show Judy that Harry A was innocent and that Harry B was the villain. This was beginning to seem less likely now that he had seen Harry working with Dave and Luis but Ben still wanted to know the truth. A quick look on the boat might just tell him more about what was happening.

There was still no sign of movement on the yacht and finally Ben made up his mind. Three more firm strokes pulled him up to the stern of the yacht. He reached up to get a grip on the short boarding ladder and hauled himself dripping out of the sea. He climbed on to the stern deck of Apache and moved quickly forward to the cockpit where he could crouch down out of sight from the shore. On the way he shot a quick glance toward the beach where Apache's rowing boat still lay unattended on the sand. There was no sign of Dave and Luis returning.

Ben turned his full attention to the boat. The low door beside the wheel that led down into the interior of the yacht swung half open. Ben decided upon a quick search below decks, hoping that he would find something to answer some of his questions. He stepped on to the short companionway and squeezed himself inside. The first thing he saw was Harry Barlow lying on the deck below him. The big American's fat belly was smothered in blood but his eyes were painfully open and staring upward.

★　★　★

As she waited for the files to copy Judy wondered about the quick flickers of information she had seen. There had been what looked like a list of monetary payments to someone called Hassan, an Arab name which could mean the supplier in Algeria.

There was also a list of larger payments to someone called Mr Bean. The only Mr Bean she could think of was the bumbling comedy character played by Rowan Atkinson on television but the link made no sense. Mr Bean had to mean someone else and there was something in the back of her mind that was trying to emerge. It was like some slippery mental fish which she could not quite get on to a mental hook. She wished that she had spared a few more moments to study the details of the files but she knew they would have to wait until later.

The computer screen finally flashed a blue panel to show six files copied. There had been six files in the My Documents folder and she had copied the lot. She thumbed the button to eject the loaded CD from the tower and then shut down the computer. She stood up from the desk and with nowhere else to put the CD she tucked it down the front of her shorts.

She went back into the living room. The villa was still silent but now her mouth was dry. She had invaded the owner's privacy and if it was found the incriminating CD would prove that this was no innocent visit. She wanted to get out.

She retreated on to the back patio and closed the door behind her. Now she only had to run away along the beach. She hesitated. It was a long slog over soft sand and a lot of clambering over rocky headlands. She guessed that the main road would be the shortest and quickest way back to Porto Viejo.

It was mid-day and the sun was high above her head in an unbroken sky of blue. She could feel the heat blazing down, burning the back of her neck and shoulders. She had no hat, sunscreen or sunglasses. Running blindly along the beach with no protection in the hottest part of the day had been stupid and going back the same way was not such a good idea either. She decided to take a chance and circled round the side of the villa.

She stood for a moment and watched a couple of lorries lumber past on the main road. She waited for a lull in the traffic, not wanting to be seen emerging from the villa. A car went past and then there were no more engine sounds. She started to walk up the drive to the main gates which stood wide open but now all her senses were alert and wary. She heard a car coming up fast from the direction of Porto Viejo and her heart jumped. She held back and heard the engine note change as the approaching car slowed its speed.

She remembered her fall back plan for when she had first walked up to the back of the villa. She realized that she was going to need it now and turned quickly and made two fast steps on to the front porch. She heard the on-coming car swinging into the open gateway behind her, its wheels throwing up a spray of gravel as the driver braked. She had her hand raised and let it knock on the door before she turned her head.

She saw Harry Avery staring at her from behind the windscreen of a smart blue Jaguar saloon.

Judy was inwardly cursing her sudden bad luck but she forced herself to outwardly smile. She turned away from the door and remembered to favour her left ankle as she limped towards the car. Harry got out of the driving seat and came to meet her. He wore shorts and the usual flowery shirt. His expression was puzzled and suspicious. There was no immediate smile of welcome.

'Harry,' Judy said brightly, as though she was pleased to see him. 'Is this your place?'

'It is,' Harry said briefly, the words barely escaping through his tight lips.

'What a coincidence, I was just knocking on your door.'

'I can see that. How did you get here?'

'I was running along the beach.' Judy rested her hand on the long bonnet of the Jaguar, letting the car take her weight as though she needed its support. 'I tripped over a piece of driftwood and managed to sprain my ankle, a silly thing to do. I saw the villa so I came over looking for help. If I can just make a telephone call to Ben I can get him to come out in the car and pick me up. It hurts too much to walk back.'

Harry looked down dubiously at her left ankle. Judy rested one buttock on the car bonnet and held the supposedly injured foot off the ground to prove her point.

'It's no problem.' Harry suddenly decided to resume his jolly fat man role and grinned at her. 'You can phone Ben or I can give you a lift home. First though, I need a cold drink'. He squinted up at the sun and made a show of wiping some sweat from his forehead. 'I guess you could too if you've been running. Come inside and relax a minute.'

He took hold of her arm, a firm but solicitous grip that she would not have been able to easily escape. Judy leaned her weight against him a little and allowed him to help her back to the villa. Harry fished a key from his pocket and let them in. He guided her through the kitchen and dining room and back into the living room she had so recently vacated. He smiled into her eyes as he lowered her down into one of the black leather armchairs but behind his eyes the smile was unreadable.

Judy knew she was in deep trouble.

'I'll get us that drink,' Harry said. He went back into the kitchen and called over his shoulder, 'Beer or a coke?'

'A coke please,' Judy answered.

Harry took a bottle of Budweiser and a can of Diet Coke from the fridge. He snapped the cap off the bottle with an opener fixed to the edge of his worktop, raised the bottle to his lips and took a deep drink. He came back into the living room and gave Judy the can of coke. He watched while she pulled the tab and then raised it to her lips to drink. He raised his beer bottle to her in a vague toast and then drank from it again. His gaze stayed fixed on her face.

'That's good,' Judy said as she lowered the can. 'I didn't realize how much I needed a drink. Thanks, Harry.'

'My pleasure,' Harry said absently.

His gaze moved away from her and he frowned as he looked all around the room. Judy knew he was searching for any signs of intrusion and felt deep flickers of apprehension. She was sure she had covered her tracks. She had disturbed nothing. But Harry was not fooled. He just hadn't figured out yet the exact how and why she had come to be here. She sipped again and the ice cold coke struck a deep chill in her stomach.

She glanced sideways at the telephone on a side table. 'If I could just phone Ben?' she suggested casually.

'There's no need,' Harry said. 'I can give you a lift home. Ben's probably busy with the bar.'

'Well thank you,' Judy said. She put the coke can down on the floor beside her chair. 'I'm ready when you are.'

Harry was staring at the closed door to his computer room. He knew where he was vulnerable.

'Just give me another minute,' he said slowly. 'I need to check my emails before I go out again. There's something important I've been waiting for. It won't take a moment.'

He opened the door to his office and took a long look around, checking that everything was in its place. Judy tried to stay calm and unperturbed. Finally Harry went inside and sat down in front of the computer. He pressed the buttons to switch it on.

Judy stood up and limped to the doorway. She stood just behind Harry, leaning on the door frame. She pretended indifference but she was checking his desk, worrying that she might have moved something. Harry was checking too but failed to find anything.

The fire engine picture came up on the

screen. Harry keyed in his password. Judy realized that he was not bothered about hiding it from her. He knew she was behind him and he must be guessing that his password was no longer a secret. It was time to run but she didn't think that she would get very far. She stayed with the act of innocence.

Harry brought up his documents file, not his email inbox. He stared at it for a few seconds and then opened the top drawer where he kept his blank CDs. Judy was still prepared to deny that she had been anywhere near his desk but Harry wasn't wasting any more time with doubts or questions. He opened up the lower drawer and swivelled on his seat to face her. Suddenly there was a gun in his right hand.

'You're a clever little bitch,' he said conversationally, 'Just like the other one, clever but not clever enough.'

'I don't understand.' Judy knew it was a waste of time but she couldn't think of anything else to say.

'My files were last accessed eighteen minutes ago,' Harry said harshly. 'Computers tell you these things. That helps me to understand.'

He stood up and hit her with a back-handed blow across the face with the squat, black steel muzzle of the gun. Judy fell back against the door post, shocked and stunned by the brute force and the blinding pain. Harry shoved his left hand down the front of her shorts and inside her knickers. The gold and diamond rings on his fat fingers scratched at her belly and then he had found the CD disc and jerked it free.

'Right first guess,' he said grimly, 'You don't have many hiding places at the moment do you?'

He flipped the disc and spun it neatly into the waste paper basket beside his desk. Then he slapped her thighs as she still sagged helplessly against the doorpost. He found what he was looking for, dug his hand into her shorts pocket and pulled out her mobile phone.

'I guess the sprained ankle and needing to call Ben was just a pack of lies.' He threw the cell-phone after the CD but it hit the edge of the basket and bounced off onto the tiled floor. 'Damn,' he said, as though his missed aim was the only thing that really irritated him.

Judy regained some of her senses and tentatively wiped the trickles of blood away from her mouth and cheek.

Harry watched her as he pulled his own mobile phone from his pocket and keyed open a number with his left hand. His right hand, still holding the gun, was pointing the blunt nose at her navel.

'Keep still,' he warned her. 'I don't want any blood messing up my house and carpets. I'm calling up the boys who take care of my rubbish disposal. They can take you away.'

19

All Ben had hoped for was an opportunity to search the yacht, to find some clue to what had been happening or something to incriminate Harry Barlow as the villain. He still wanted to prove himself right and Judy wrong about Harry Avery. Finding Harry B covered in blood was a shock but he recovered quickly. As a fire officer he had frequently attended road accidents and other incidents with messy casualties and his natural instinct was to take control of any given situation and give what help was possible. He moved quickly down the companionway and crouched beside Harry Barlow.

'What happened here?' he asked directly.

Harry Barlow's eyes were glazed and his breathing was shallow as though every intake was causing him pain. He coughed but there was no blood on his lips which was a good sign. 'I guess I lost the shoot-out,' he said weakly.

Ben was peeling back the blood-soaked shirt and easing down the perforated waistband of the worn grey shorts. 'These are bullet holes,' he said and he wasn't sure if it was a statement or a question. Bullet wounds were outside his experience but the dark red circles still welling blood were fairly obvious.

'Two of them,' Harry Barlow said. 'Hurts like hell but I don't think they hit anything vital. There's a lot of beer blubber down there to take up the impact.' He grimaced and his face was almost as white as his moustache. 'There's a first aid box in the centre cupboard above the work top. You'd best patch me up.'

Ben found the first aid kit and began working to clean and pad the wounds. 'We need to get the bleeding stopped,' he explained his priorities. 'Then we have to get you to a hospital. The bullets have to come out, and they've probably carried shreds of your shirt and shorts inside which could turn nasty if they're not removed.' He paused for a second and asked his first question again. 'What happened?'

'I hired a couple of deckhands to take a little cruise,' Harry said slowly. 'You know the guys, Blondie Dave and his Spanish pal Luis. They came highly recommended by our mutual friend Harry Avery.' He winced as Ben worked and then went on. 'I knew I was being set up but that was the name of the game. I was baiting my trap with *Apache* as the prize. I had to draw the bastards out somehow.'

He clenched his teeth tight and closed his eyes as another wave of pain passed. For a moment Ben thought he had passed out but then his eyes opened again. Harry went on with an effort: 'A couple of hours sail down the coast there's a cove, inaccessible by road, I guess, nice and secluded. Dave suggested we stop there for a swim. I went along with it. Sure enough, good old Harry A turns up ten minutes later in *Seagull Two*.

'I wasn't unprepared. I had a handgun hidden away in the galley behind the kitchen drawer. I made sure I was close to it when Harry A came on board but that bastard is pretty ruthless. He doesn't mess around with any small talk. He practically came on board shooting. I got a couple of shots off but I missed. He didn't. After that I played dead. There wasn't much else I could do.'

'So who the hell are you?' Ben demanded.

'The name is Harry Barlow, genuine American, all the way from Chicago.' Harry found a weak grin. 'Although I'm pretty damned sure Harry A isn't flying his true colours. I'm with the United States Drug Enforcement Agency.'

Ben had finished taping two large wound pads in place and Harry Barlow made an effort to sit up. Ben pushed him down gently. 'Just lay there. Keep your movement to the minimum and you won't bleed so much.' He wanted to hear more and asked, 'Why is the United States involved in all this?'

'Two reasons,' Harry Barlow said. 'One of the hi-jacked yachts that disappeared from Porto Viejo, the *Vagabond*, was owned by US citizens. But mainly my job is to help stamp out the drugs trade. The heroin that passes through Porto Viejo ends up in Europe and the UK. The United States Air Force has a couple of major airbases in your country, at Lakenheath and Mildenhall, plus we've got big bases in Germany. All those young US servicemen make up a massive drugs market and that's where a good proportion of good old Harry A's shipments are ending up. We want it stopped.'

'So you were another undercover operation.'

'That's right. My department has worked with Scotland Yard and the Metropolitan Police Drug Squad. They put in one of their best officers under cover here in Porto Viejo, a Detective Sergeant named Georgina Harrington. You've heard of her. Your Judy identified her body. After Georgina turned up dead we knew the honey trap wasn't going to work anymore. We had to think of something else. Offering *Apache* as a hi-jack target with just one fat old guy who needed help to sail her seemed the best option.'

While Harry talked Ben had been keeping watch on the beach through the galley porthole. Now he interrupted the American with a curse.

'What is it?' Harry struggled to sit up but again Ben pinned him down with a firm hand.

'Stay put,' he said. 'It's Blondie Dave and Luis. They're coming back to the boat. And there's nothing you can do about it.'

★ ★ ★

Dave hadn't wasted any time. He knew they were taking a risk in coming back to Porto Viejo but there just hadn't been any other option. He had wanted to leave Luis with the yacht but Luis had refused to stay on board with only a dead man for company, although neither of them had gone down into the galley to make sure. Harry Avery had brought up Harry Barlow's gun and tossed it over the side and after that they had all stayed on deck.

When they had reached the beach Dave had tried again to make Luis stay with the rowing boat, to keep watch on the boat and the yacht. Again Luis had been reluctant to be left on his own. He was clinging to Dave as though Dave was now his substitute mother. Dave was getting irritated but there was no time for arguments. He allowed Luis to stay with him.

They found most of the shops and workshops along the working wharf to be closed. Most people were taking the day off to watch the Moors and Christians playing out their mock heroics. Only one marine store was open and the proprietor there was just about to shut early for lunch. Dave pushed the door open before the man could shoot the bolts and insisted on being served.

Luis had dumped the bullet-mangled fuel pump on the trade counter. The shop owner stared at it and asked questions in rapid Spanish with a puzzled look on his face. They had brought the damaged pump to show exactly what they needed but suddenly Dave realized that this could be a mistake.

'He asks what has happened to it,' Luis translated.

'Tell him you dropped it.' Dave tried to keep the impatience out of his voice. 'Tell him to mind his bloody business. Think of something.'

Luis frowned. The shop owner jabbered. Luis answered. Dave couldn't follow it all but the shop owner shrugged and grinned. He was a small man with a lop-sided grin that only creased one side of his face. Luis laughed weakly. The little man wandered off into a back store room.

'I told him a spanner fell into the engine,' Luis said.

They waited until the man with the crooked smile came back with a new boxed component. He unpacked the box to show them that the new pump was identical to the old one. His movements were slow and methodical. Dave wanted to yell at him to hurry up but he bit back his frustration. He also didn't want to antagonize the man or do anything to make this transaction stand out in his memory.

At last the box was packed again and a carrier bag was found for both the old pump and the new. Dave paid with the cash Harry had given him. He knew that traceable credit cards were always best avoided. They hurried away and returned to the beach.

Dave saw with relief that the rowing boat was still there, exactly as they had left it on the sand near the breakwater wall. He had been half afraid that kids might have played with it or let it float away on the sea but today the beach was only sparsely populated. Most of the kids were with their parents up in the

Old Town or up at the castle, watching the festival.

They pushed the small boat out and climbed back in. There was barely room for the two of them as they sat facing each other. Dave took the oars and used the left hand oar to pull the boat round so that the stern was to the yacht. Then he began to pull at both oars, propelling the boat swiftly backwards. In less than a minute they were bumping against the hull of *Apache*.

That was when the mobile phone in his pocket began to ring, sending out the *Crazy Frog* tune that had recently become popular.

Dave rested the oars and took out his phone. Luis pulled them hand over hand along the hull until he could get an anchoring grip on the access ladder at the stern. There he waited.

The call was from Harry Avery. It scared the hell out of Dave when he heard what Harry wanted and he started to argue. Harry cut him short.

'Just do it,' Harry snarled. 'Have you got that bloody fuel pump fixed?'

'We've got the new one,' Dave told him. 'It won't take long to put it on.'

'So do it, then bring *Apache* round to the villa. You can dump the woman when you dump the Yank.'

'Harry,' Dave felt the dry desperation of fear in his throat, 'this will make a dozen corpses we've dropped over the side, and three of them are coppers. We're filling the bloody Mediterranean up with bodies. This is crazy.'

'Okay, so after this we're all definitely getting out. But right here and now the same arguments still apply. We've got no other option. So get the engine fixed and get round here, the sooner the better.'

Harry rang off and Dave sat staring at his silent phone. He began to swear, fluently and violently.

Luis waited for him to finish. His normally dark face was now white and pale. 'What is wrong?' he finally plucked up the courage to ask when Dave subsided.

'That bloody ex-policewoman who runs the *Conquistador* has turned up snooping at the villa,' Dave snarled. 'Harry caught her at it but he needs us to get rid of her.'

★ ★ ★

Ben had no intention of being trapped below decks where there was no room to manoeuvre. He left Harry Barlow with a warning to stay silent and then moved back up into the cockpit. He crouched there out of sight, listening to Dave and Luis on the other side of the yacht's hull and deck rails, weighing his options.

There was still time to slip over the seaward side of the yacht and drop back into the water. He could be half way back to the rocks before he was spotted and if he was lucky and Dave and Luis got busy straight away on the engine he might not be seen at all. Either way he could get back on shore and use his own mobile phone to call up the police and an ambulance before they could do anything about it.

It was the easy option and a tempting one. He had pulled Harry Barlow's bloody clothing back over his first aid work, hiding the taped padding so Harry could still play dead. However, the phone call he was overhearing kicked that option out of his mind. He understood that Judy was in trouble and even though he could get the police here quickly enough to deal with Dave and Luis it would only take one more call from Dave to Harry to put Judy in even greater danger. He didn't know where Harry's villa was, so if he was seen swimming away and Dave made the call, then there was no way he could help Judy.

With retreat and flight untenable there was only one other option.

Ben closed his fists and waited.

Luis was the first to climb on board. He stepped off the ladder and moved forward to the cockpit as Ben suddenly straightened up to meet him. Luis jumped as though stung, terror showing in his eyes as his jaw dropped open. Ben hit him with no more warning, a savage right punch and then a left punch to the stomach. Luis doubled over forwards with a strangled yelp and Ben hit him a third time with a right uppercut between the eyes. There was nothing sporting about the unexpected attack but this was not a sporting event. Ben wanted the first of his opponents down and out quickly and showed no mercy. Luis was knocked back into the stern corner of the cockpit and slid down senseless to the deck.

It had only taken seconds but Blondie Dave had already followed Luis up the short ladder. He reached the stern of the yacht and stood dumb for a moment as he saw Luis fall.

Ben stepped back panting to face him.

'You bastard,' Dave said. Until now he had not realized how fond he had become of his smaller Spanish friend. Luis had befriended him, found him a place to stay and introduced him to Harry. Until he had met Maria no one had ever given a damn about Dave. Now Luis was hurt and bleeding, knocked out, his sprawled body demanding vengeance. Dave forgot his earlier irritation with the clinging little Spaniard. He balled his own big fists and felt rage surge through him.

'We've got some unfinished business,' Dave reminded Ben. He was piling all the former humiliation on top of his anger over Luis. 'And this time you haven't got a pub full of your mates to get in the way. This time it's just you and me.' He leered wolfishly, 'Harry's got that ex-cop bitch of a wife of yours so she can't help you either.'

They were evenly matched for height and weight and with that final taunt Dave charged at Ben with a ferocious swing of his right fist.

★ ★ ★

Harry finished his call and put his mobile phone in his pocket. With his left hand he took a firm grip on Judy's shoulder and pushed her back into the living room. She was still too stunned to resist and he thrust her down into one of the black leather armchairs. She slumped there weakly, trying to rally her senses.

Harry sat on the arm of the opposite armchair. He was sitting high, almost upright, where he could quickly and easily move if it became necessary. Judy's position in the deep armchair meant that it would take her more time and effort to get up. And Harry had the gun. He let the hand holding the automatic rest on his knee, relaxing a little as he watched her.

The flower-bedecked holiday shirt was a lie. He wasn't the happy, laughing fat man anymore. His eyes were cold as ice.

'I guess we've got an hour or so,' he said. 'The time it's going to take for Dave to fit a new fuel pump and bring *Apache* down the coast. So you might as well tell me what you know, or what you think you know.'

'I know your name is not Harry Avery,' Judy said slowly. 'I think your real name is Harry Arnold.'

Harry nodded as though he might be conceding a point, but his facial expression did not change and his eyes and body language were giving nothing away. He stayed silent.

Judy realized that she had nothing to lose in trying to tie up a few loose ends. She drew a deep breath. 'I think you killed Georgina Harrington.'

Harry grinned. 'Good old Georgie, she was a lot of fun while it lasted. I think she really enjoyed it. She thought she was making a fool out of me and that spiced up the sex for her. She was one hell of an erotic woman. It was a pity it had to end. She made the same obvious mistake as you, trying to hack into my computer. Document files always keep a record of when they were last accessed.' He scowled at her. 'I guess you were sent in to replace Georgie.'

'No,' Judy said. 'I am retired from the police. Ben and I only came out here to run the bar.'

'So why did Ben come snooping down the fire station?'

'He's an ex-fireman. He just couldn't stay away from fire engines.'

'But it was you and Good Old Ben who turned up in Bodrum asking questions. It was the two of you who broke into the boatyard.' When Judy didn't answer he went on flatly, 'It had to be you and Ben. I figured that one out. The descriptions fitted and it wasn't any coincidence that you both took a couple of days off from the *Conquistador*. Coppers aren't the only ones who can solve mysteries.'

Judy said softly, 'If word got back to you from Turkey then that links you to the whole operation, running drugs from Algeria into Spain and hijacking the yachts needed to do the job. That was a stroke of genius, Harry, tying two big money-making operations together like that.'

The flattery worked. Harry smiled and said, 'Any one boat making repeated trips to

343

North Africa would have aroused suspicion. This way I made sure we never used the same boat more than twice. I doubled my profit margins by selling the boats on the other side of the Mediterranean, and I kept *Seagull* clean. She's never been used for anything other than holiday cruising.'

'So what turned you into a pirate as well as a drug smuggler?'

Harry shrugged. 'The French couple who owned the *Celeste* were my original partners for the Algerian connection. They got greedy. They wanted a bigger cut. I had to get rid of them and it seemed a shame to just sink a perfectly good boat.'

'So you looked for a boat dealer who would buy and sell without asking too many questions and you found the Keskin Boat-yard.'

'Right, but then I needed another boat to make the Algerian drug run. That's when the two operations came together. I picked up Blondie Dave and Luis around that time, taught them to sail on *Seagull* and then used them to sail the hi-jacked boats as they came along. It was all running pretty sweetly until Georgie showed up. I had to kill her and then you appeared.'

'So where do Arturo and his *Bomberos* fit into all of this?' Judy tried to sound as though it didn't really matter anymore. 'I'm guessing you used some of them to ferry the drug consignments up into France on their way to the UK. They would have had the time in the breaks between their weekly shift changes.'

Harry looked surprised. 'No, Blondie and Luis did those trips as well. Why would I want to bring in anyone else? Why would I want to use firemen?'

'So why hang around the fire station?'

Harry laughed. 'A man's got to have a hobby. I like being around fire engines. Arturo humoured me. He liked the free trips on my yacht. He liked the extra girls I was able to attract. And I like to keep pleasure separate from business.'

Judy thought about it and decided that now there was no obvious reason for Harry to lie. He was being carelessly frank about everything else.

Harry smiled at her. 'You think you know it all now but you're still missing a piece.'

Judy stared at him. Harry was enjoying the fact that he could still tease her with his last secret. But he was angry too. There was a suppressed anger coming to the surface and Judy realized that this time it was not directed at her. She was puzzled. Then Harry looked away from her, shifting his gaze toward the open plan staircase that led to the upper floor.

'Peter,' he bellowed. 'It's about bloody time you came down here and showed your ugly face.'

Judy turned her head and looked up. There was movement at the top of the staircase and a man came into view. His face was familiar and had an uncomfortable twitch. Behind him a young woman in a light green summer dress was anxiously holding his arm.

'You must have seen her arrive,' Harry accused savagely, jerking his gun to indicate Judy. 'You must have heard her sneaking about down here. So why the hell didn't you come down and stop her?'

'Because I didn't want her to see me,' Peter Shepherd spoke as though it were the question and not his own actions that were incomprehensible, 'because I'm supposed to be dead.'

20

Peter Shepherd came slowly down the stairs and the woman in the green dress followed him, still holding nervously on to his arm. She had shoulder length blonde hair that was exquisitely groomed with a glossy shine, her face was beautiful and she had the poise of a catwalk model. She was in her early thirties and her face was vaguely familiar. She was not Jane Shepherd and Judy knew now that it was Jane's blood that had stained the galley deck of *Wave Dancer*.

'You let her come into my house, prowl around and break into my computer,' Harry was talking about Judy, continuing his harsh accusation. 'If I hadn't come home before she could leave she would have gone straight to the police. And you just stayed in hiding, you bloody fool.'

'We saw her come up from the beach,' Peter said. 'It looked as though she had genuinely collapsed after a run. I thought it best to stay out of sight so we kept quiet. We didn't think she'd find anything just by looking around. I didn't realize that she had broken into your computer. I didn't know she was taking anything away with her.'

Judy stared at him and suddenly it all fitted into place. He was the advertising man who had dreamed up the Beanie Gang. He had wanted to name his yacht the *Beanie*. So he had to be Mr Bean. Once she had made that connection she recognized the woman.

'Suzy Champion,' she said. 'You were the yummy mummy actress in the Beanie Gang adverts.'

Suzy Champion met her gaze and at least had the decency to look a little shame-faced and embarrassed. Her throat worked as though she wanted to say something but then she just nodded.

There was contempt in Judy's eyes as she turned her attention to Peter. 'You never did sprain your shoulder. It was just an act to justify getting Dave and Luis on board *Wave Dancer* to do your dirty work. I should have guessed when I saw you swimming.'

Peter scowled at her but did not bother to deny it.

'Let me guess the rest of it.' Judy recalled what Harry had said about the missing piece. 'You kept your yacht on the River Orwell in England. You made regular trips over to France. You picked up the drug consignments from Dave and Luis to take them into the UK.'

'Ten out of ten,' Harry said cheerfully. 'Now you've got the whole picture.'

'Damn you,' Peter said, and it wasn't clear whether he was talking to Judy or Harry.

Harry shrugged. 'She knows all about me so why shouldn't she know all about you.' His tone implied that it didn't really matter. He was just annoyed with his partner and enjoying his discomfiture.

'What about the latest consignment?' Judy asked.

'Scheduled for distribution in Germany,' Harry said casually. 'We had more than one outlet. It wasn't all destined for the UK.'

'But you're closing it all down,' Judy guessed. 'Peter's got scared. He wanted to get out and swap Jane for Yummy Mummy.'

'Jane was a liability,' Peter said. 'I had to keep everything secret from her. She was too bloody honest. With Suzy at least I can relax, be open about who and what I am and where most of the money really comes from.'

'So why are you still here?' Judy asked. Then she guessed the answer. 'You're waiting for your share of the money. It takes time for all the payments to come through.'

Peter nodded. 'That's one reason. The other was that I had to wait for Suzy to come out and join me. In a couple of day's time we'll be flying out of here. And I'm not going to tell you where we're going.'

'New Zealand,' Harry said, and laughed at the look of shock and horror that came over Peter's face. 'They're flying to Auckland. There's plenty of fine weather boating down there. The Kiwis call it their City of Sails. They're going to buy a new yacht and have a honeymoon sail down to Milford Sound.'

'Harry, shut up,' Peter shouted, looking at Judy.

Harry shrugged. 'Keep your hair on. She's never going to talk to anyone.'

Suzy Champion was frightened. She too looked at Judy.

'What's going to happen to her?'

Judy answered the question. 'They're going to murder me,' she said, surprised at how calm she sounded even though her heart was suddenly beating faster. 'Do you think you can live with that?'

Suzy's lip trembled. Her eyes were shallow blue pools without any depth. After a moment she looked away without speaking. Judy realized she must know that Harry and Peter had already murdered Jane, and that they were responsible for the murders of god only knew how many others. There was no hope for any help or interference there.

'We're waiting for Dave and Luis,' Harry

350

said, as though there was nothing else to say on the matter.

★ ★ ★

They waited until at last the yacht appeared, cruising down from the north a few hundred yards off the coast. She had no sails hoisted but was moving under the auxiliary power from the engine. Soon they could recognize the sleek hull shape of *Apache*. The yacht slowed opposite the villa and turned in to the shore. They had a brief glimpse of the one man in the cockpit, a big man in yellow shorts and a yellow tee shirt, with the peak of the old yellow baseball cap baseball cap pulled down over his eyes.

'Good old Dave,' Harry said. 'His liver is nearly as yellow as that bloody hat but he usually does as he's told.'

Harry continued to sit on the arm of the chair, watching Judy with the automatic still pointed at her chest. His gaze only flickered occasionally out to sea and the yacht. Peter and Suzy moved closer to the French windows and stood watching as the yacht dropped anchor. They watched as the small rowing boat was launched from the stern of the yacht and the man in the familiar yellow shirt and cap began to row towards them.

'Where's the other one,' Peter said suddenly. 'Where's Luis?'

Harry glanced through the window. 'Probably stayed on the yacht,' he guessed. 'He's even more squeamish than Blondie Dave. Besides when I get in the boat with Judy there's hardly going to be room for Dave to pull the oars. There'd be no room for the Spanish runt.'

Peter nodded and said no more but he stayed by the window watching. Suzy leaned close against him as though she did not dare to move from his side.

Harry was watching Judy again. He seemed to be expecting some last ditch movement from her. Judy kept still, matching his gaze. Finally she looked over his shoulder again.

The rowing boat had beached. The big man in yellow got out and dragged the boat a yard up the beach just far enough to be sure it would not drift away within the next few minutes. Casually he picked up one of the short oars and balanced it on his shoulder, like a boy playing soldiers with a wooden rifle.

The schoolboy flourish gave Judy her first clue. She stared and although his face was hidden she saw that the blonde hair under the baseball cap was not long and shaggy. It was short cut and neat. He began to walk up the beach toward the villa and although he tried to hide it she could see the slight, dragging limp of his left leg.

Harry turned his head for another look. Peter and Suzy were also watching as the man in yellow approached.

Judy knew she had to distract their attention and said suddenly. 'Ben knows where I am, you do realize that?'

All three of her captors turned to look at her.

'You surely didn't think I would be stupid enough to come here without telling Ben where I was going?'

'You're a bit late thinking up that old chestnut,' Harry said scornfully but there was some doubt in his voice. He glanced at Peter. 'What do you think?'

Peter had turned away from the French windows. He was staring at Judy, pursing his lips uncertainly. Suzy turned with him, still clinging to his arm.

'She came running down the hill and collapsed on the sand,' Peter remembered. 'We watched her from the window. She sat there for a few minutes without even looking up. She looked buggered. She definitely didn't sneak up here. I think she just found us by chance.'

'So old Ben doesn't know where you are,' Harry said flatly.

The man with the oar had walked up the beach and was coming through the arch of stone that framed the gateway to the villa's patio and gardens.

'How do you think I recognized this place?' Judy held their attention with more questions. 'How did I know that this was your villa?'

Harry leaned forward, suddenly interested. 'How did you know?'

'Georgina sent some pictures to a mutual friend. You probably took them. She was sitting on the sand with the villa behind her.'

Harry nodded thoughtfully. 'My mistake,' he admitted. 'But it sounds as though you still didn't know where the villa was until you saw it.'

'The man they all thought was Blondie Dave was walking across the patio, passing the swimming pool.'

'True,' Judy said. 'But I used my mobile and called Ben as soon as I recognized the place.'

'A lie,' Peter said. 'We were watching. You didn't make any call from the beach. And if you had made one from inside the house we would have heard you speaking.'

Harry chuckled. 'Ben doesn't know where you are,' he repeated with conviction. 'Good Old Ben is just a dumb fool who still thinks that I'm Good Old Harry.'

Ben stepped in through the French windows and pushed the yellow baseball cap up and away from his eyes. His face was a mess of bruises. He had one black eye and a cut lip and there was more blood at his nostrils. The fight with Dave had been a brutal slugging match in the close confines of the yacht's cockpit. He had won that fight and now he was spoiling for another.

'The trouble with Good Old Ben is that you can fool him some of the time,' he said grimly, 'but you can't fool him all of the time.'

Harry twisted round sharply, the gun in his hand swinging to point at Ben. Ben changed his grip upon the handle of the oar that rested on his shoulder. Instead of a wooden rifle it became a wooden sword as Ben slashed it forward and down. Harry jerked the gun back and only just escaped a broken wrist. The oar blade knocked the gun from his fist and it went off with a bang as it tumbled to the floor. The bullet chewed out splinters from a smashed floor tile before it ricocheted off and buried itself in the black leather sofa.

Harry let out an echoing roar of pain and rage. He clutched his bruised fingers for a moment as tears spurted in his eyes. Then he launched himself from the arm of the chair and rushed at Ben. Ben tossed the oar to one side and met Harry with his fists. He had been fooled by the man he had believed was his friend, Judy had been threatened and he was on a high after his victory over Blondie Dave. He was ready for another fight. He had barely noticed Peter Shepherd and Suzy Champion standing just inside the French windows.

Judy saw Peter stoop to pick up the fallen automatic. She pushed up, flung herself to one side and rolled over the arm of her chair. She shoulder charged Peter and knocked him away from the gun. She couldn't reach it as she used her hands to grab at Peter and stop herself from falling, but she managed to give the weapon a kick that sent it spinning out of sight beneath the curtains.

Suzy put her hands to her mouth and shrieked as Judy wrestled with her lover and Ben and Harry traded savage punches. Judy brought her knee up into Peter's groin and had the satisfaction of hearing him cry out with pain. She kneed him again but then saw Ben reeling back from a punch in the face from Harry. Harry had recovered fast and he was a gutter fighter with a lot of hard practise. Harry charged Ben and Judy lashed out her left foot and kicked Harry's ankles from beneath him. Harry fell on to Ben and they both crashed on to the floor in a rolling bear hug.

Judy turned her attention back to trying to restrain Peter. As he turned away from her and tried to escape she almost succeeded in getting an arm lock on his left arm. She had him by the wrist and elbow and was forcing his hand up between his shoulder blades. Suzy saw what was happening and suddenly decided that she could no longer stand aside squealing. She jumped on to Judy's back, wrapping her legs around Judy's thighs and pulling hard on Judy's pony tail.

Judy felt her head being yanked backward, her hair felt as though it was being torn out at the roots and Suzy was screaming obscenities in her ear. Desperately Judy slammed back with her right elbow. Suzy was unseated and tumbled off. Judy turned and slapped her hard across the face. Suzy backed off and began crying.

Peter had picked up the oar which Ben had carelessly discarded. He swung a blow that hit Judy in the stomach but then she hung on gasping to the oar to prevent him using it again.

Judy was aware of Ben and Harry still fighting on the other side of the room. Ben had rolled on top and was smashing punches down into Harry's face. Harry's struggles were becoming weaker, as with every punch the back of his head was being hammered down on to the hard floor tiles.

From somewhere outside she faintly heard the whine of a police siren.

Peter heard it too. He gave an almighty heave to win the struggle for ownership of the oar and stepped back. Judy stumbled forward. Peter hit her across the side of the head with the oar but it was not a full powered blow. However, it was enough to topple her over and send her half stunned to the floor.

Peter looked round desperately for the gun but couldn't see it. The approaching police siren wailed louder from the main road. Peter panicked but he kept his grip on the oar. With his other hand he grabbed hold of Suzy by the arm. Dragging Suzy behind him Peter began to run, fleeing through the French windows and heading for the beach.

Judy got to her knees. Ben had battered Harry Avery until he was unconscious, and came to help her. His face was black and blue and bloodied but he wore a crazy grin. The police siren was one of two or three and they were getting nearer.

'I phoned your friend Miguel,' Ben said through split lips. 'I didn't want him charging in before I found you so I made the call just before I rowed the boat ashore.'

'But how did you know where to find this place?' Judy was still delighted but bewildered.

'Harry B,' Ben said simply. 'Tweedledee has been tracking Tweedledum. Plus he gave me a short talk on how to sail a yacht.'

Judy wanted to kiss him and ask a hundred questions but there was no time. Through the open French windows she could see that Peter and Suzy were already through the patio and gardens and on to the beach.

'If they reach the yacht they could still get away,' she gasped.

She pushed herself to her feet and began to run after the fugitives. Ben glanced over to Harry to make sure that he was still inert and then ran after her.

They skirted the pool and Judy was first through the archway of the gate. The soft sand slowed the first impetus of her run and now she heard Ben puffing as he fell away behind her. His limp made her the fastest runner but she could still do nothing to close the gap as Peter and Suzy flew like frightened quail down the beach.

The two fugitives reached the rowing boat and without stopping Peter threw himself at the bows with one violent push to send it skidding back into the water. The boat bobbed in the low waves and they both waded out beside it. Suzy climbed in and Peter pushed the boat out until he was thigh deep. He scrambled aboard, still clutching the oar which he had instinctively carried down from the villa. He found the second oar under the thwart and fumbled to get them both into the rowlocks.

Judy reached the sea's edge and ran straight into the waves. The water pressure against her knees and then her thighs slowed her down. She plunged forward and managed to get one hand on to the bows of the rowing boat. It was a slipping grip and Suzy Champion turned in her seat and clawed at Judy's fingers to break her hold. Judy floundered and fell face down in the water. She could taste salt and spray in her mouth as Suzy pummelled a fist on top of her head to push her under.

Peter at last succeeded in getting the oars fitted to the rowlocks and began to row. The boat shot backwards. Peter pulled hard and fast to take her out to *Apache*.

Judy recovered her balance, drew a deep breath and then dived forward again. She began swimming in the wake of the rowing boat, but the gap steadily widened. Behind her she heard the splash as Ben dived in and knew that he was still with her. She was the fastest runner but he was the strongest swimmer and gradually he caught up with her. They were neck and neck when the rowing boat reached *Apache* but they were still twenty yards behind.

Peter steadied the rowing boat and pushed Suzy up on to the yacht. Quickly he hauled himself up after her and allowed the rowing boat to simply slip away. Judy and Ben had to swim around it, one on either side. Peter looked back and saw them coming. This time he had let go of the oars and now he looked for another weapon. He found a boathook neatly stowed close to the access ladder and grabbed it with both hands. With frantic stabbing motions he fended them off.

Judy and Ben were forced to back up out of his reach. They were at a disadvantage now with the sharp steel point of the boathook stabbing at their faces. For a moment the situation was stalemate but then Peter called Suzy back to join him and shoved the boathook into her hands.

'Keep them off,' he shouted at her. 'I'll start the engine.'

He disappeared forward into the cockpit while Suzy stood frightened but formidable to guard the stern. Her hands were white and trembling but the boathook she held was still sharp enough to gouge out an eye. She thrust it aggressively forward each time either Ben or Judy got too near.

'I'll swim round to the bows,' Ben said.

He pulled himself round the side of the yacht with firm strong strokes and vanished from Suzy's line of sight. Suzy started to move backwards, looking over her shoulder. Judy edged forward. Suzy saw the danger and stabbed ineffectually at Judy's face.

'Peter,' Suzy screamed hysterically, 'I can't watch both ends of this bloody ship at the same time.'

Peter was at the wheel, grinning as he discovered that the key still hung in the ignition. He ignored Blondie Dave and Luis who sat on one side of the cockpit watching him. They were both securely tied up with mooring ropes and Dave wore only his underpants. They too had bruised and bloody faces but now they too were both grinning. Peter turned the ignition key and the engine fired.

The propeller spun into life just below the access ladder at the stern. It churned up the sea in Judy's face. Judy recoiled. Suzy looked round anxiously to try and see what Ben might be doing. Judy kicked forward again. Suzy turned her head back and lunged with the boat hook but this time she thrust too far. Judy twisted her head to one side and as Suzy overreached she grabbed the wooden shaft of